About the Author

Award-winning author Heather Peck has enjoyed a varied life. She has been both farmer and agricultural policy adviser, volunteer covid vaccinator and NHS Trust Chair. She bred sheep and alpacas, reared calves, broke ploughs, represented the UK in international negotiations, specialised in emergency response from Chernobyl to bird flu, managed controls over pesticides and GM crops, saw legislation through Parliament and got paid to eat Kit Kats while on secondment to Nestle Rowntree.

She lives in Norfolk with her partner Gary, two dogs, two cats, two hens and a female rabbit named Hero.

See more and sign up for Heather's free monthly newsletter at
www.heatherpeckauthor.com

Also by Heather Peck

THE DCI GELDARD NORFOLK MYSTERIES

Secret Places
Glass Arrows
Fires of Hate
The Temenos Remains
Dig Two Graves
Beyond Closed Doors
Buried in the Past
Death on the Rhine (novella)**
Death on the Norwich Express (novella)
Expedition to Death (novella)

Milestones (PageTurner Book Awards 2024: winner Best Crime novel)

BOOKS FOR CHILDREN

Tails of Two Spaniels
The Animals of White Cows Farm
The Pixie and the Bear

Spinning into the Dark

not all roads lead home...
DCI GREG GELDARD BOOK 8

Heather Peck

Ormesby Publishing

Published in 2025 by Ormesby Publishing

Ormesby St Margaret

Norfolk

www.ormesbypublishing.co.uk

Text copyright © Heather Peck 2025

Author photograph by John Thompson 2021

The right of Heather Peck to be identified as the author of this work has been asserted in accordance with the Copyright, Designs and Patents Act 1988 Sections 77 and 78.

All rights reserved. No part of this publication may be reproduced, stored in a retrieval system, or transmitted in any form or by any means, electronic, mechanical, photocopying, recording or otherwise, without prior permission of the copyright holder.

This is a work of fiction. Names, characters, places and incidents either are products of the author's imagination. Or are used fictitiously. Any resemblance to actual events or persons, living or dead, is entirely coincidental.

British Library Cataloguing in Publication Data

A CIP catalogue record for this book is available from the British Library.

Page design and typesetting by Ormesby Publishing

Acknowledgments

My thanks to Gary for everything

and many thanks yet again to my beta readers Geoff Dodgson, Alison Tayler and Gary Westlake for their constructive criticism and comments.
This book is all the better for your help.

Readers may notice a new authenticity in the chapters involving police dogs. This is entirely due to the advice and guidance of Clive Myhill and Neil Mace. Huge thanks to both of you for sharing your expertise. Any mistakes are mine!

Thanks also to Sharon Gray at CluedUpEditing for her meticulous and knowledgeable proof editing.

Contents

Key Characters	X
Glossary	XII
1. Norfolk: 31 August 2020	1
2. Addenbrooke's Hospital, Cambridge: 1 September 2020	3
3. 2 September 2020	13
4. Cycle 2	23
5. Thursday 3 September 2020	26
6. Friday 4 September 2020	31
7. Monday 7 September 2020 – back to work	42
8. Tuesday 8 September 2020	50
9. Cycle 3	56
10. Later on September 10	59
11. Evening: 10 September	69

12.	11 September	77
13.	Postmortems	86
14.	Next day: 12 September 2020	94
15.	Out and about	102
16.	Getting started – Wymondham: 12 September	110
17.	Aftermath	122
18.	Slow progress	131
19.	Evening: journeys home	142
20.	13 September 2020	151
21.	Further investigations	159
22.	14 September 2020	172
23.	Kain Smith	177
24.	Alpacas and neighbours	184
25.	The search	193
26.	Research and leads	202
27.	More digging	210
28.	Taking stock	219
29.	Checking up	224
30.	Checking out	232

31.	Checking around	238
32.	Man down	248
33.	The reckoning – part one	254
34.	The reckoning – part two	266
35.	Following up	275
36.	Winding up	279
37.	Five months later	287
38.	Action here	296
Hungry for more?		301

Key Characters

Norfolk police
Chief Superintendent Margaret Tayler
Main investigative team:
DCI Greg Geldard
DI Jim Henning
DI Chris Mathews
DS Jill Hayes
DCs Bill Street, Jenny Warren and Steve Hall
PCs Brian Foxton, Vicky Allen, George White , Jack Reed
Ned George   Lead crime scene investigator
Yvonne Berry   Deputy crime scene investigator
PCs Philips and Scouller   Dog handlers
PDs Meg and Pat   Springer spaniel search dogs

Legal services
Frank Parker   Crown Prosecution Service
Kenneth Wood and Mr Gregson   Solicitors

Medical experts
Dr Paisley   Police pathologist
Harper Vaughn   Forensic anthropologist

SPINNING INTO THE DARK

Toby Blackwood   Forensic anthropologist
Dr Lancaster   Director and Caldicott Guardian at the Mental Health Trust

Other participants
Mr Geldard senior   Greg's father
Bobby   Greg's cat
Tally   Chris's foul-mouthed parrot
Diana Grain   Teacher partner of DS Jill Hayes
Joanne Hamilton   Wife of Fred Hamilton
Joanne Hamilton/Chalmers   Their daughter
Roy Thurlow and Irwin Lloyd   Retired vicars
Phil Saunders   Carpenter
Jessy   Phil's Jack Russell
Tina Booth   Phil's neighbour
Carol Hodds   Care worker
Kain Smith   Young and enthusiastic cyclist
Tristan Smith   Alpaca farmer and weaver – no relation!
Lucas Willis   Mate of Kain's
Ann Cooper   Retired lady
Shirley Crabtree   Not the wrestler
Ben Lyell   Chef
Frank Gillan   Boat engineer
Fran Rix   Dog walker
Esther Meadowcroft   Proprietor of Meadowcroft Eggs
Moon River   Off-grid dweller and forager
Warren Thorne   Tree surgeon

Glossary

a 'living' in the Church of England, the term applied to an appointment such as parish priest (vicar).

ANPR Automatic Number Plate Recognition

Caldicott Guardian the Director on the Board of an NHS Health Trust, with the responsibility for ensuring patient confidentiality

CCTV Closed Circuit Television

Dyke a deep ditch

On the huh Norfolk colloquialism for 'messed up'

Shirley Crabtree the real name of the heavy-weight wrestler known as Big Daddy

RTA road traffic accident

1

Norfolk: 31 August 2020

After the light traffic of the past few months, the roads were, unfortunately for the cyclist wobbling a little at the edge of the quiet lane, getting back to normal. She'd already had to abandon the centre ground to get out of the way of an oncoming tractor. That had necessitated a hurried foot down, to save herself from flatlining on the grass verge. She'd acknowledged the cheery wave from the driver and pushed herself back into the saddle with another alarming wobble, reflecting that the old saying – you never forgot how to ride a bike – was some distance short of accurate – in her case at least. It had taken several days' swerving and teetering up and down her drive before she'd felt competent to emerge onto the quiet roads of lockdown. Even then, she'd fallen off twice – once onto the middle of a, luckily empty, road when her arthritic knee had failed to bend swiftly enough to reach the pedal. Once into a wild rose, from which she had extricated herself with much caution and considerable difficulty.

She was startled by the blast of a horn behind her, as the driver of a battered pickup lost patience with her slow progress.

She pulled as close to the verge as she dared, and he roared past, much too close, with another toot of the horn, then disappeared round the bend ahead. She shook her head and pedalled on, reflecting that if she'd held him up at all, it must have been for all of thirty seconds. *If the traffic is going to get much worse, then I'd better go back to my exercise bike*, she thought. *But I'll miss the fresh air, the scents and the sights.*

The sound of an engine approaching round the bend drew her attention back to the road, and she was surprised to see what looked like the same pickup coming back. That was her last thought. The four-by-four, coming much too fast and on the wrong side of the road, hit her right leg a glancing blow before scraping along her rear wheel. She flew sideways across the verge and went spinning into the ditch, landing face up with all the wind knocked out of her.

After the hot summer, the ditch was dry, but that was where the good news ended. Her cycling helmet had come off, and something was wrong with her leg. She tried to move, but agony shot through her right side. She was trapped, head and torso in the ditch, legs up on the higher ground. A shadow moved between her and the sun, and a pang of relief went through her. Help was on the way. Then her bicycle dropped on top of her and the shadow moved away. She tried to call out, to beg for help, but she had no breath to spare.

The pickup driver moved away, dusting their hands, and got back into the vehicle. Looking back, they noted that, from the road, all that was visible above the edge of the ditch was a foot and the slowly turning rear bicycle wheel. Then the truck drove off.

2

Addenbrooke's Hospital, Cambridge: 1 September 2020

Greg pushed the wheelchair, with its furiously protesting passenger, out through the main reception and on towards the car park.

'I keep telling you, I'm absolutely fine to walk,' Chris insisted. 'Don't treat me like an invalid.' Her mother had had enough. She stepped in front of the wheelchair, and Greg had no choice but to stop abruptly or run her over. Indeed, he stopped so sharply that Chris shot forwards in the chair and was only saved from an impromptu decanting onto the pavement by her mother's hand on her chest.

'Give the man a break,' Jane Mathews ordered. 'It's a half mile yomp to where the car is parked, and you're behaving like a toddler. You're a bit old for the terrible twos! And if you keep on like this, I wouldn't blame him for leaving you here.'

Greg realised it was relief from terrible anxiety that was making Chris's mother so harsh, and hoped Chris realised it too.

'When you two scary women have quite finished,' he said in as mild a voice as he could manage, 'we're nearly there anyway. Let's save the fighting for when we get home.'

Jane Mathews stepped back, Chris managed a slightly lop-sided grin, and Greg resumed his pushing.

Leaving Jane to assist Chris into the car, if allowed, he returned the borrowed chair to reception. By the time he got back, Jane was in her own car and driving off, waving as she went by, while Chris waited in the passenger seat of his red BMW, her fuchsia pink jeans clashing horribly with the paintwork of the car. She was flicking through something on her phone.

'Mum said she was in a hurry to get back, so she's gone on ahead,' said Chris, looking up. 'Sorry,' she added. 'This is going to take a bit of getting used to.'

'Which, this?' asked Greg, fastening his seat belt.

'All of it. The missing couple of weeks, the tiredness, the baby.' Chris was referring to the triple whammy of the induced coma that had followed her being attacked during a domestic abuse case, the remains of the traumatic brain injury that had been inflicted, and the overwhelming news, on being brought back to consciousness, that she was pregnant.

'I hate to admit it, but you're right. I do tire quickly. And whether that's my battered brain or the baby, I can't tell. And I know I'm being an unreasonable, stroppy cow...'

'But you're my unreasonable, stroppy cow,' said Greg. 'And it's an improvement on being comatose. If a rather small improvement,' he added with a wicked grin.

'Swine!' she said, and the smile seemed more genuine this time. 'Look, I'll do you a deal. I'll try to rein in the temper, if you stop treating me with kid gloves. I can't stand all this walking round me on eggshells. I'd rather you just told me when I'm being an old grouch bucket. Or better still, just walk away and give me some space.'

'I'll try both solutions,' promised Greg. 'But you'll have to let me spoil you a bit, oh mother of my child.'

'Once a week, no more,' said Chris.

'OK. It's a deal.' Greg put the car into gear and headed for the exit and the road north, to Norfolk and home.

***

At his desk in Norfolk Police HQ, Wymondham, DI Jim Henning was praying for Greg's prompt return. There was so much paper on his desk, largely due to Greg's absence on compassionate leave, he couldn't even find space to put down his bacon butty. Perching it on top of a – very boring – financial report, he took a swig of his coffee and flipped through the morning's intelligence summary. Unwrapping a deliciously fragrant pile of back bacon, just on the right side of crispy and barely contained within two crusty slices of supremely fresh bread, he took an enormous bite. As he caught the dribble of fat trickling down his chin on what remained of the top slice of bread he noted, with resignation, that within the miniscule space of time the sandwich had sat in its wrappings on the paperwork, a substantial quantity of grease had transferred itself to the report he was due to pass on to the Chief Superintendent. He was dabbing it to no avail with his clean hankie, when a cough attracted his attention to the woman in the doorway.

'I hope that's not for me,' she said, nodding at the now translucent top pages of the report while taking the seat in front of the desk. Jim stared at Chief Superintendent Margaret Tayler with faint horror and gulped down the last of his bacon so hurriedly he choked on it and had to tip some coffee after it to persuade it to move on down his gullet.

'No! Well, yes,' he admitted. 'Everything's for you ultimately, isn't it?'

'Glad you've noticed,' she replied briskly. 'Now, how're you getting on without Greg?'

'Struggling,' he admitted. 'I had no idea how much of this crap he got through. Sorry, I meant...'

'I know what you meant,' said Margaret with a dry smile as she ran her hand through her fluffy brown hair. If the gesture was meant to tidy it, it didn't. 'Just bring me up to date, will you?'

'OK. Let's deal with the issues that've been put to bed. The Waters brothers, Ade and Nick, have at last seen sense and put their hands up for the car thefts and arson attacks on farms. The last bit of evidence that placed Nick's fingerprints in the Range Rover found at Felixstowe docks clinched it. It'll be a while before the cases make it to court, but the hearings should be short.

'Similarly, Joanne Hamilton has admitted the unlawful burial of her son and the manslaughter of her mother, along with multiple counts of fraud arising from her masquerading as her mother for several years. That accounts for two of the bodies found in the garden in Ormesby, leaving us with the problem of the unidentified third body.'

'I thought that was Joanne Hamilton's father.'

'So did we. And it still looks like it's the body of the Mr Hamilton who'd been living in Great Yarmouth. But the preliminary DNA results have bowled us a googly. They say it's not Joanne Hamilton's father. No relation.'

'Really!' Margaret picked up a pencil from among the mess of papers on the desk, apparently for the sole purpose of tapping it irritatingly on her teeth.

'Either way, we don't have a suspect for the murder, if it *was* a murder. Joanne Hamilton claims to know nothing about the body, and unless she's a superlative actress, I'd say that's genuine. She certainly seemed surprised when Greg and I asked her about it.'

'You said "if it was a murder"?'

'We're treating it as a murder, not least because of how the body was buried in the garden, but the doc says she can't be definitive about the cause of death. Not from what she has to work with. The prime suspect was Joanne Hamilton's mother, until we got the DNA back. She must still be a front runner, but as she's dead...' Jim shrugged. 'Anyway, we're waiting on more results, but at the moment it seems likely to end up as a cold case.'

'What else have you got on?' asked Margaret, nodding her understanding.

'The usual drink, sex, drugs, and rock and roll,' said Jim. 'To be honest, I don't feel I have a proper grip on what else is out there. I just haven't had time to give it the thought it needs, not with Greg missing and us still short-handed without Sarah.' He looked at Margaret reproachfully. His colleague DI Sarah Laurence had never been replaced after her sudden departure following a death in custody. [1]

'The good news is, I believe Greg's back at work tomorrow,' said Margaret.

'So soon!' exclaimed Jim. 'But what about Chris? I thought she was going to need some support for a good while.'

'I gather he's got something organised – family or something. I've also got an idea that might help make up for losing Sarah.'

'A replacement?' asked Jim hopefully.

'Not exactly. Not full-time anyway. Leave it with me for now.'

She stood up and jerked her jacket straight before heading for the door, taking the mistreated, greasy, finance report with her. 'Thanks for all you're doing, Jim,' she said, just before the door slammed behind her.

Back in her own office, she scribbled some notes on a pad before checking the figures in the report, then scribbled again before reaching for the phone.

After speaking to her senior management, her opposite number in Suffolk, the HR lead, and then her bosses again, she

---

1. *See 'Dig Two Graves'*

rubbed the ear which had become hot and sweaty from lengthy phone use, made herself a cup of coffee, and rang Greg.

He answered the phone on the third ring. She could hear voices in the background, and some laughter.

'Sounds like things are looking up,' she said. 'How's Chris?'

There was a short delay and the rap of footsteps on a wooden floor before Greg replied.

'Better than I could have imagined, if not as good as she thinks,' he said. 'Sorry for the delay, I was moving into the conservatory. Ben Asheton has called in. That's the voices you can probably hear.

'Chris has healed amazingly well from the surgery to remove her spleen, and even from the blow to the head. But, as ever, she overestimates what she can do. She gets tired quickly and gets frustrated even quicker. She's already talking about when can she go back to work, but that's just not realistic, not just yet. And then, there's the baby to consider too.'

'I've got an idea and a suggestion,' said Margaret, 'which might help with several difficulties, yours and mine. Let me outline both. You don't have to decide yet, but I'd like an initial reaction before I go any further.'

Intrigued, Greg sat down on the sofa facing the River Bure, flowing powerfully past the end of his garden after the recent rain, and prepared to listen.

'First, it's plain that Chris can't go back to the job she was doing in Suffolk anytime soon, and then she'll need to be on maternity leave. That seems to me to make a return to Suffolk problematic.

'Second, knowing Chris as well as I do, I know she won't take well to idleness.

'Third, I've not had the budget to replace Sarah Laurence, which has left a hole in your team here and especially around the intelligence function.

'So, my idea and suggestion is that, when Chris is well enough, rather than returning to Suffolk, she comes back here and takes up a part-time DI role responsible for intelligence. It would play to her strengths of local knowledge and organisation. I know it might not be as active as she'd like but, for the time being, you and I might well regard that as a benefit.'

Greg was silent for but a moment. 'Thank you,' he said simply. 'I think it's brilliant, Boss. The only issue will be persuading Chris she can't start tomorrow.'

'Tell her to ring me,' advised Margaret. 'I'll leave it to you to decide when. Then I'll make her the proposition. I'll make it clear she can't start until the doctors say she can. And that I'm open to her working from home if that's advisable.'

When Greg rejoined the pair in the kitchen, it was obvious both that Chris was starting to tire, and that Ben had spotted the signs. Ex police officer, ex district nurse, and now first responder, Ben Asheton had more than his fair share of contact with the victims of traumatic brain injury. A slim, wiry man with dark hair greying at the temples, Ben somehow exuded an air of both competence and compassion. He was also a favourite of both Bobby, Greg's cat, and Tally, Chris's parrot, which was why his lap was currently occupied by a purring moggy and he was wearing a jealous parrot on his shoulder.

'I think I need to be off, Greg,' he said. 'And Chris, whatever her arguments, needs a rest.' He handed Bobby to Greg, the cat dangling in his hands like a fur stole, then put Tally, wings flapping, on the back of the sofa near Chris.

'Listen, young woman,' he said, wagging a finger in her face so that she blinked. 'It's only because you have a skull made of concrete that the damage was as mild as it was. That, and the prompt treatment from Addenbrooke's. But don't make the mistake of risking your recovery by being stupid. Rest when you need to, and you'll soon be back to normal.'

She pulled a face at him, nodded her agreement, then winced.

'You've got a headache now?' he asked. Taking silence for his answer he went on, 'Then listen to what your body is telling you.'

'But how long?' asked Chris plaintively. 'I'm bored. How long before I'm properly better?'

'No one can answer that for you,' said Ben. 'But I can tell you two things. First, you were incredibly lucky the damage was no worse. You got away with little more than a concussion, and it could have been a lot more serious if Addenbrooke's hadn't put you in that induced coma to give your brain time to recover.

'Second, the more care you take now, the quicker you heal. Think of it like a muscle strain. Yes, you need to keep moving, but you don't want to overdo it or you're back to square one or worse. So, by all means do as much normal stuff as you can but stop and take a rest when you need to.' He dropped a kiss on her cheek, ducking Tally's efforts to get in on the act, and made his farewells with a wave.

Greg followed him to his car. 'What do you really think?' he asked.

'Exactly what I said to her,' said Ben, looking up at him from his driving seat. 'She really has been incredibly lucky. Your main problem is going to be stopping her rushing back to Suffolk.'

'The boss has an idea on that front,' said Greg. 'I think we've got that covered.' And waved him off before going back to rejoin Chris and their small menagerie.

3

2 September 2020

Never had a Wednesday morning looked so promising. Greg had left Chris, made more cheerful by the news of a possible new role in Norfolk Police, sitting in the conservatory with Bobby, Tally and her mobile phone. His father was due to spend the day there. Greg had sold it to Chris as a break for his father from his isolated existence in supported housing, and to his father as support for Chris while she convalesced. He knew them well enough to know that both would have seen through his little ploy, but also that both would enjoy a relaxed day looking after each other. The perfect solution from his perspective.

Now he was on his way into work and looking forward to it with renewed enthusiasm. His phone rang just as he approached the Thickthorn roundabout.

'Jim,' he said cheerily on his hands-free. 'I'm on my way in.'

'So I guessed,' said Jim. 'Can you meet me in Ormesby? Ned's lot have turned up some new evidence I think we'd benefit from seeing in situ.'

'Can do,' said Greg, checking his rear-view mirror, then changing lane so that, instead of joining the A11, he went all the way round the roundabout and rejoined the A47 heading east. A car driver in a hurry alongside him gave him the finger, then powered away in considerable excess of the speed limit. Greg's hand hovered over the switch for the blue lights hidden behind his radiator grill, then returned to the steering wheel. Tempting as it was to pull the idiot over, it would be too great a waste of time.

'I'll meet you there in about half an hour,' he said to Jim, then rang off.

When he pulled up beside the bungalow in Ormesby where he had found two missing children held captive,[1] he found it still had crime scene tape across the driveway and blowing, tattered, by the front and back doors. Jim's car was already parked across the street, and a forensic services van was blocking the drive. He parked behind Jim's car, and walked over the road, ducking under the tape.

'Anyone home?' he called as he went round the side of the garage to the back garden.

Jim popped out of the garage, closely followed by Ned George, lead crime scene investigator. The latter was still clad in his paper overalls but had pushed the hood back from his shaved head.

'Hi, Greg,' said Jim. 'Welcome back. How's Chris? I gather congratulations are in order!'

---

1. *See 'Buried in the Past'*

'That got round quickly,' remarked Greg. 'Chris is being Chris, by which I mean she's recovering well but impatient to get back to work. Good to see you, Ned. Have you taken over this site from Yvonne?' Even as he spoke, the elegantly styled dark head of Ned's deputy also popped round the door jamb.

'I'm still here,' she said. 'But not for much longer, I hope. With luck I can hand over and get off on leave very soon.' She gave Ned a mock glare and led the way back into the garage.

'It's OK, you can go in now,' said Ned. 'We've pretty much finished in here. I just wanted you to see where the latest evidence came from, so you understand the implications.'

He stood to one side to let Greg and Jim, both pulling covers over their shoes, have a clear view of the space inside. What had been a wide expanse of smooth concrete was now broken up into shards by power tools, and two excavations lay dark and hollow. One was in the centre of the floor, the second, a smaller and shallower space, lay near the step leading from the garage into the porch.

'These are the two voids found by the ground penetrating radar,' said Yvonne.

'No more bodies, I hope,' said Greg.

'No, but some interesting material all the same.' She led the way to the larger, central void. 'This one contained the most interesting collection. There's a bundle of fabric that looks like it might be a shirt and trousers, together with this.' She held up two evidence bags as she spoke. One contained the fabric, well preserved but apparently stained, still tightly rolled inside the remnants of a tattered supermarket bag. As far as he could see in the sharp light from the floods that lit the void, some of the material seemed to be black cotton and the remainder a dark chino-like fabric. The second evidence bag contained what looked like a paper knife. Blunt-edged but narrow-bladed and very pointed.

'Are those bloodstains?' asked Greg.

'Think so. But it's impossible to be sure until we can unroll the bundle and take a closer look back at the lab. We're hoping for some DNA. And the doc is panting for a closer look at the knife. She thinks it could be a match for a chip on one of the ribs of the third body we found here.'

'As I recall, there were no signs of stab marks on the other two bodies,' said Greg. 'The doc was happy with the explanation that Joanne Hamilton's son had died of anaphylactic shock, and that her mother died of a blow to the back of the head when Joanne lost her temper and pushed her onto the stairs.'

'That's right, said Ned. 'But this body has been here a lot longer—'

'And I thought the doc couldn't come up with a cause of death,' remarked Jim.

'No more she can,' replied Ned. 'She has said that one possibility is a stabbing. But with only skeletal remains, it's hard for her to be definitive. On the other hand, if that is blood on the fabric and the DNA is a match for the skeleton, it strengthens the presumption in favour of a stabbing. What she still wouldn't be able to say is whether it was the cause of death.

'And the second void?' asked Greg.

'Now, that is very interesting. I don't think it was created at the same time as the bigger one. This' – he pointed at the larger hole in the centre of the garage – 'shows every sign of being created during the laying of the concrete floor. The surface is undisturbed, which is why the void was only evident on the GPR. But the lower layers of hardcore did show some disturbance. In my opinion, the fabric and knife were hidden in the hardcore after it was laid but before the concrete was poured.

'This, however...' He pointed to the smaller hole near the door. 'This was also under undisturbed concrete, but I think it was accessed from the side, by removing and then replacing the bricks that form the step into the porch.'

'And what was in it?' asked Greg, as it seemed Ned was never going to get to the point.

'Well, that's where it gets interesting,' he said, and held up a third evidence bag. 'Just this.'

Greg peered through the plastic at what appeared to be a small leather-bound book. 'A book,' he said.

'A Bible,' said Ned.

On his way to Wymondham, Greg succumbed to the temptation to call in on Chris as he was passing. He found her and his father deep in a game of Scrabble, mugs of tea to hand and a plate of biscuits between them – the latter being eyed up in a predatory fashion by Tally.

Greg snaffled one from under the bird's beak and headed back to the door as both Scrabblers glared at him.

'We're fine,' said Chris. 'Bugger off and get some work done.'

'Language!' said his father automatically. 'See you later, Greg.' Greg took the hint, and buggered off.

Back in his office for the first time in a week, he was pleasantly surprised by how much of his routine paperwork had magically vanished.

'Brilliant job, Jim. I must take more time off. You're better at this than I am.'

'It was easy once I took Margaret's advice,' said Jim.

'Which was?' Greg was intrigued. The Chief Super had never offered him any advice on time management.

'She said to chuck it down the stairs. Deal with the stuff that stuck on the first landing as a priority. Delegate anything that fell on the next flight of stairs to Jill, and bin anything that made it to the bottom.'

'She never!' Greg was open-mouthed.

'No, not really,' said Jim. 'At least, she did say divide into those three priorities, but the sorting system is mine.'

Greg opened his mouth to ask another question, then looked again at his empty desk and decided he didn't want to know the answer. *Better to quit while I'm ahead.*

'OK,' he said. 'So what's on the top landing now?'

'First, chase up the bank data and see if we can find Mr Hamilton's dentist. Then we can check whether body number three is him or not, even if it's not Joanne Hamilton's biological father.

'Second, see if we can accelerate the testing of the materials we saw today. And check back with the doc about her views on cause of death.'

'Anything on other cases?' asked Greg.

'Loads,' said Jim. 'But nothing standing out as major yet. On the other hand, no one's taking a very close look at it either.

The sooner we have Chris focussing on intelligence, the better. There may be stuff we're missing.'

It took until late afternoon before a shout of 'Eureka!' went up from where DC Bill Street was reluctantly spending his day scrutinising paper.

'Got it,' he declaimed, waving a pile of printouts. 'At least, I think I've got it. A lead on Hamilton's dentist. And the reason our local searches weren't successful. I've got a bill being paid to Havelock Dental Hub, in Chesterton, Cambridge.'

'Why on earth would he go all the way to Cambridge for a dentist?' wondered Jim. 'Worth a phone call, Bill. See what you can find out.'

Bill glanced at the clock above his desk, reckoned that if he was quick, he could just catch them at work before they knocked off for the day, and picked up his phone. It seemed to ring for a long time before there was a reply, and Jim turned back to the whiteboards at the end of the room, assuming that Bill was about to spend the next few minutes listening to options and tapping numbers for choices, none of which would exactly match his requirements. In reality, it wasn't long before Bill appeared at his elbow, with a note to add to the whiteboard under the name 'Frederick James Hamilton'.

'It *is* Fred Hamilton,' he said with triumph, sticking the large yellow Post-it in his hand onto the board with a flourish. 'At least, a man by that name has been on the Havelock Dental Hub books for the past twelve years and of their precursor before that, from a time when he apparently lived in Cambridge. They said they hadn't seen him since February 2010, but they still have all his records on file. I sent them the data we have from the postmortem and their preliminary reaction is that it looks like their patient. And all the dates fit, sir, so I'm betting our third body is definitely Fred Hamilton – Joanne Hamilton senior's ex-husband, even if he wasn't Joanne Hamilton junior's biological father.'

'Good work, Bill,' Greg said, having entered the room unnoticed. 'Let's go through what we know, before I get lost in the complexities of this case. Between suspects sharing the same name and multiple bodies, I'm getting confused.' He joined Jim and Bill at the whiteboards, and pointed to the first, headed 'Body No 1, Joanne Hamilton senior'.

'When we rescued the two Mirren children, Karen and Jake, from imprisonment by Joanne Hamilton/Chalmers, we also found a body concealed in a concrete garden ornament. This was identified as Joanne Hamilton's mother, also named Joanne Hamilton. After some argument, our Joanne has pleaded guilty to the manslaughter of her mother following an altercation, plus the false imprisonment of the Mirren kids, fraud arising from her impersonating her dead mother and drawing her pension, and finally preventing the decent and lawful burial of her son, Frankie Chalmers, body number two. OK so far?' Greg looked round and Jim nodded.

'Joanne Hamilton/Chalmers is due to be sentenced next month,' he said. 'And we're not looking for anyone else in connection to the second body. Not at present anyway. Both the doc and CPS are reasonably happy with the explanation that the poor tyke died from anaphylaxis, caused by his grandmother feeding him crab salad.' Greg moved past the board headed 'Body No 2, Frankie Chalmers'.

'Just to confirm, this body was found in the garden, exactly where and how his mother said she'd buried him,' he said. 'In stark contrast to body number three, which was found by the ground penetrating radar and seemed to come as a surprise to everyone.' He came to a halt by the final whiteboard.

'Correct,' said Jim. 'And unidentified until now, although the working assumption was that he was Joanne Hamilton/Chalmer's father. However, the latest evidence is contradictory. DNA data shows the body is not related to Joanne Hamilton/Chalmers, but it seems dental records indicate they *are* the remains of Fred Hamilton, husband of Joanne Hamilton senior.'

'Was this a messed-up family, or what?' Greg demanded rhetorically. 'Incidentally, remind me, wasn't there something about the older couple being divorced?'

'I suppose messed-up families are the only sort we come into contact with,' said Jim. 'Except our own,' he added hurriedly. 'I mean, her indoors would have my guts for garters if I described her as messed up! As for the question of divorce, according to the neighbours the senior Mrs Hamilton said she was divorced, but we can find no evidence of it. No paperwork and nothing in the official records.'

Greg stepped back to survey the three whiteboards again. 'To sum up, body number one is sorted: the perp is about to be sentenced. Body number two is parked, with no evidence of a crime having been committed, other than the concealment of a death, unlawful burial, etc, which is also dealt with. That leaves us with body number three, Fred Hamilton. How did he die? And who did it? Was it murder? And is the murderer still out there, or was she buried in the concrete pillar?

'What we really need to know now, is what the stuff from the voids has to tell us. It would be useful to know if it's contemporaneous with body three,' he added. 'I don't know about you, but I've tended to assume it is, partly or even mainly because of the knife and the bloodstains. But we don't know that for sure. For example, when was the concrete floor laid? Were the two voids created at the same time? And if so, why? Why wasn't the Bible hidden along with the bundle of fabric? And have we got anything from the third void the GPR found? The one in the basement. Questions for tomorrow, I think.'

4

Cycle 2

Phil was headed home. It had already been a long day for an ageing carpenter with plenty of experience but little hair and less energy.

'I'm getting too old for days that don't finish until after dark,' he muttered under his breath as he pedalled along in the shadows, towards the brighter lights near the road bridge. As he reached the junction with the side road to the old bridge, he had a change of heart and decided that a fish supper would be just the thing to revive him from the hours of wrestling with a finicky lady customer and her oddly shaped doorways.

'Just a couple of doors that need hanging,' she'd said. 'Won't take you long. I need it done in the evening, because I'm working during the day.'

The couple of doors had morphed into five. The doorways turned out to be in an old cottage with not a single right angle anywhere in its entire construction. Every door had had to be cut to size and shape. Every hinge had required adjusting, not once or twice, but multiple times, as the owner dithered, changed her mind, and then changed it back again. Phil had hung on to his patience with difficulty and a grim determination. When he came to its bitter end, he'd sighed heavily, turned to face his tormentor while holding the final door propped against its jamb with his left hand, and pronounced in weary tones, 'If I move 'er back to weer you said, it'll be all on the huh and I'll be 'avin to start again. To be blunt, missis, you're gettin' on me wick now, and best you can do is mash some tea, before I hull the 'ole job at yer.'

She'd retired from the fray in high dudgeon, and he finished hanging the final door in peace, if not silence. The sound of banging pots and pans had risen from the kitchen, but no tea had materialised, and Phil had hung his tool bag on his bike knowing that he'd probably wait a good while before he was paid.

He realised, as a glow of lights overtook him, that a vehicle had followed him down the side road and was coming up fast. The old bridge was too narrow for a car and bike to surmount it side by side, so he slowed his pedalling on the approach to allow the vehicle to pass. The sidelong blow from its wing came as a total surprise and he fell sideways.

Bugger me, he thought, assuming he'd land in the hedge on the approach to the bridge. But the collision had more momentum behind it than he realised, and he landed half on, half over the low stone parapet. He felt the ribs on his left side crack, and the arm he'd instinctively stuck out to break his fall snapped at wrist level. He opened his mouth to cry out, but the rib damage severely limited his capacity to even breathe, and he managed little more than a low groan. The car had stopped, and he heard a door slam. Footsteps came towards him, and he felt a surge of relief, which rapidly changed to incomprehension as a blow to his head was followed by hard hands pushing him from his precarious balance, forwards and over the parapet, into the fast-flowing river below. His last thought as the cold water closed over his face and the tide swept him upriver towards Martham and Hickling, was to hope someone would feed his dog, Jessy.

On the road above, the bike was pushed into the back of the pickup and driven away.

5

Thursday 3 September 2020

'Forgot to say,' Chris announced airily when Greg brought her morning coffee in bed. 'Do you know, I could get used to this. Can we adopt it as a regular thing? Even when I'm better?'

Greg stuck his head back round the bedroom door. 'Was that what you forgot to say?' he asked.

'No. Sorry. What I meant to say was that I spoke to Margaret yesterday, and I'm going to start the new job next week.'

'You what?' Greg shot back into the bedroom. 'It's too soon, surely.'

'Don't get your knickers in a knot,' she recommended. 'Only on a part-time basis and only working from home to start with. Basically, it amounts to me being given access to the database online and starting to review things. All quite low-key. And the hours I do are to be up to me, to start with. I'll log my time and I'll be paid accordingly, while I work up to a sixty per cent full-time equivalent as I get back to normal.'

'I suppose that sounds OK,' admitted Greg, aware that Scrabble wouldn't content Chris for long. 'We could certainly do with the help. At the moment, the only cases I feel on top of are the Ormesby multiple bodies. Just don't overdo it, eh? You know what Ben said.'

'I know,' said Chris. 'And I will be good, I promise. I'll work an hour or so at a time, and I promise I'll take a break when I feel tired.'

Greg kissed her then headed for the door again. 'I'll be off in a moment, so I'll say goodbye now. Bobby and Tally have been fed, so don't let them con you in to feeding them again.'

A thought occurred to him, and he paused in the doorway. 'If you're going back to work, I think that qualifies you as better,' he said. 'So you can get your own coffee tomorrow.' He ducked a flying pillow, and left, laughing.

Greg arrived in the Wymondham car park at the same time as Margaret Tayler and hurried over as she clicked the locks on her car.

'Just wanted to say thank you,' he said, but she stopped him in mid-sentence.

'No need,' she said. 'It's a win-win. We need the work done, and Chris will be an asset. But I just wanted to make plain that while Chris will obviously make a contribution to your team, she will report direct to me. In light of your relationship,' she added.

'Of course,' said Greg, and would have thanked her again, but she held a hand up and he took the hint.

In the incident room, he was pleased to see Jill back in her usual place in front of a curve of three screens.

'How's it going with the children?' he asked, remembering just in time that Jill and her partner, Diana, were being considered as foster parents for the, recently rescued, Mirren children. 'I'm sorry, I should have asked before but, with everything going on at home, it slipped my mind.'

Jill looked up with a smile. 'Fully understand that, Boss,' she said. 'And so far, so good, I think. Karen is adjusting to Diana as parent rather than just teacher. Jake is still a bit nervous about exposure to Covid, but as things open up more generally, he's getting more relaxed. We just need to make sure he sees us wearing masks when we go out and washing hands all the time. I've never had such clean hands,' she added, holding hers in front of her and surveying them.

'Pretty much like that for all of us,' agreed Greg. 'Roll on a vaccine, that's what I say. What about the court case? Presumably, as Joanne Hamilton is pleading guilty to false imprisonment, they won't need to appear.'

'I don't think so, no,' agreed Jill. 'The last thing I heard, they can record their victim impact statement; hopefully that will be done in the next week or so, by social services. Then we can all move on.

'I've got some news on those voids,' she added. 'The third one, the one in the basement, was empty. Nothing new there. Bill's currently doing some digging around to see if he can find out who laid the concrete floor in the garage, and when, to give us a timeline for the deposit of the clothes and knife. And I've had a thought about the house in Great Yarmouth. We know it's been empty for the past eighteen months – the neighbour told us. But we also know that someone must have been in and out before that. Otherwise, there'd have been huge piles of post and other stuff. Assuming the dental records confirm that body number three is Fred Hamilton, then Mrs Hamilton senior *must* have known about his burial in the garden, even if she didn't kill him. Maybe, from 2010 to 2018 when she died, she was visiting the Yarmouth house and tidying up, or whatever. And if so, then there should be some traces of her, even after a lapse of two years. What do you think, Boss?'

'I think you're on to something,' said Greg. 'Get Forensics back to that house and have them take it apart, looking for DNA, fingerprints, whatever they can find that might link the first Mrs H to that property.'

Jill hesitated, pleased but still worried. 'Will they' – she nodded in a direction intended to indicate their bosses – 'be happy with that, given it's a cold case?'

'We'll run with it until we're told to stop,' said Greg. 'It may be a bit on the chilly side, but for all we know there may still be a killer out there. Ten years isn't such a very long time.'

Back home in the cottage near the Bure, Chris was sitting on the sofa, her feet up and her laptop, somewhat appropriately, balanced on her lap. She was trying, and failing, to ignore the sounds of unnecessarily vigorous cleaning being undertaken by her mother.

Tally was sitting on her mother's shoulder, wings outstretched to preserve her balance as her perch moved around the sitting room, pushing the Hoover in front of her in an exasperated fashion. Bobby had left in a huff, tail raised and fluffed out to indicate her displeasure at the racket.

'I don't know what Greg is going to say,' complained Jane Mathews. 'Well, I do actually. He's going to say you promised to take it easy for at least another week, and he's going to blame me.'

Chris looked up from her screen. 'I have no idea what you're saying, Mother,' she said. 'Not with all that racket you're making.'

Jane turned the Hoover off and into the resulting silence announced, 'I said Greg isn't going to be happy about this,' nodding at the laptop.

'He doesn't need to know, not just yet,' said Chris. 'And I didn't promise anything about not working for another week...'

'So you could hear what I said,' replied Jane in triumph.

'I just guessed. And look, I know you all try to do your best for me, but weeks of sheer, unadulterated monotony don't make me feel better, they make me feel worse. Wall-to-wall Australian soaps and so-called reality shows stuffed full of the most unrealistic, unbelievable, self-obsessed, plastic-faced show-offs you could ever imagine just make me lose the will to live. And this...' She gestured at the laptop. 'This isn't real work, not yet. I'm just getting a feel for the challenge. What data is available, what isn't, and how best I can start to analyse it when I do start working properly.

'You know me, Mum, just let me do what I do best, and I'll be fine.'

'Just wait till you get morning sickness,' said Jane in gloomy prognostication.

6

Friday 4 September 2020

Tina was vaguely worried. She usually saw her neighbour coming and going on his bike or walking his little Jack Russell, Jessy. She was surprised she hadn't seen him either Thursday evening or that morning. Perhaps he wasn't well. As she went for the bus into Yarmouth and her job in the community cafe, she peered over the fence to see if she could spot the bike. It wasn't in its usual place, under the lean-to by the back door, so she assumed he'd had an early start that morning and she'd missed him.

The bus was held up by roadworks in Caister, making Tina late. Even though she was only volunteering, or perhaps *because* she was volunteering and she knew how busy they'd be, Tina was flustered and feeling guilty when she rushed from Market Gates to the old church hall used as a community centre.

'Sorry! Sorry,' she panted as she galloped in, her short hair dishevelled, and tore her coat off to reveal the voluminous apron underneath. 'What needs doing?'

'Calm down, dear,' said the volunteer chef, Max, in mock imitation of Michael Winner. Also in his sixties, Max had worked in chip shops, greasy spoons and – highlight of his career – for one memorable season on a cruise ship specialising in elderly passengers. 'Definitely different, darling,' he'd say. He called everyone darling when he wasn't calling them dear. 'They used to line up the hearses with the taxis when we arrived in port!'

'Today's menu, darling, soupe aux carottes, tarte aux poissons et petits pois écrasé, followed by pudding aux raisins.'

Tina stopped to think. 'Carrot soup and fish pie with mushy peas,' she said. 'But you lost me at the pudding!'

'Spotted dick, darling,' said Max. 'Doesn't translate well into French. I'm well on with the prep, but I've done nothing about emptying the dishwasher from yesterday.'

'No problem,' said Tina, and set to.

It was a busy lunchtime as Friday often was. In addition to their regulars of the homeless and out of work – or just plain strapped for cash – who came in for a free lunch, there were a number of shoppers who came for the friendly chat as much as the lunch and paid what they felt it was worth. Most of them were very generous and, as the cafe's organisers said, it all helped. The food was mainly close to its use-by from supermarkets, or otherwise donated. The staff gave their time. It was hard work, but much fun was had by all, staff and customers alike. Especially as the cafe had been much missed during the lockdown.

Even so, by three in the afternoon, Tina was shattered and more than ready to head for the bus and home. When she got there, she thought she could hear her neighbour's little dog barking, but it stopped when she opened her front door.

'I'm sure he'll be home soon, Jessy,' she called to the dog, and went in. She thought no more about it that night but was a little surprised to see the bike was still missing when her niece, Lois, picked her up on Saturday morning to take her to Wroxham for coffee and cake. She mentioned it to Lois, but she was dismissive of her aunt's concerns.

'Perhaps he's gone away for a few days,' she suggested.

'Not without his dog,' protested Tina.

'Or perhaps he's got a cold, or Covid, and he's staying in.' Lois really wasn't very interested in the movements of her aunt's neighbour.

'Then where's his bike?' objected Tina.

'I don't know, Auntie,' said Lois slightly irritably, so Tina changed the subject to a discussion about the previous night's TV. She was worried enough, though, to keep a special eye out for Phil that evening, and when she didn't see him return, she went and banged on his door. All this got her was a few barks, then nothing.

Worry kept her awake nearly all night and by morning she'd made her mind up. She tried the police first, using the non-urgent number, but they really weren't interested in a man who had only been missing, if at all, for a couple of days.

'What about the dog?' she asked. But they had rung off.

She tried peering in through windows but was too short to see much. After worrying some more, she made her mind up and rang the RSPCA. They were much more responsive, and sent someone round that afternoon, even though it was Sunday.

'One of our busiest days,' said the RSPCA man cheerfully, introducing himself as Dylan. He was tall and, shading his eyes, he too peered in at Phil's rather grubby windows. 'I can't see your neighbour,' he reported. 'But I can see a little dog. Looks like a Jack Russell. It's lying down in the doorway to the hall. Doesn't look too good. I think I need to report in.'

'Can we get in to rescue the dog?' asked Tina. 'But he'd never leave her to suffer. If she's in there then he may be ill upstairs.'

'Have you a key?' asked Dylan.

'No,' said Tina. 'We've always said we'd exchange keys just in case, but we never got round to it.'

'Then, no, I can't. I don't have power of entry. We need the police. I'll ring them too.'

Dylan was more successful than Tina had been. In short order he had reported the problem, and he had barely begun to drink the mug of tea Tina had given him when a patrol car pulled up outside, followed by a second.

'Gather you think you've a problem next door,' said the constable at the door. And, interpreting the quizzical expression on Dylan's face correctly, he added, 'Since you mentioned a dog, one of our dog handlers has come along as well. Luckily, she was nearby.'

Jenny Warren was getting out of the second vehicle as they spoke. Leaving an indignant PD Turbo, her springer spaniel partner, in her car, she walked up the path to join the first constable, Dylan and Tina on the doorstep.

'What's the problem?' she asked.

'This lady hasn't seen her neighbour for at least three days, and his dog is trapped in the house. I saw it from the window, and it doesn't look great. By all accounts it's a much-loved pet, so quite apart from the dog's welfare, we're worried about the owner too.'

Tina, feeling rather surplus to requirements, nodded her agreement, and opened her mouth to add her two penn'orth when Dylan spoke again. 'So, we'd like you to exercise your powers of entry and get me in,' he said.

Jenny and Constable Halstead exchanged glances.

'Let's have a look first,' he said.

They went round Phil's small semi-detached house, banging first on the front door and then on the back. Neither got any response other than one feeble bark.

'The dog sounds much weaker,' exclaimed Tina, now seriously worried. 'Phil would never leave her alone like that. He must be ill upstairs. Or...' She didn't want to voice the alternative.

'Let's do it,' said Jenny to Halstead. He nodded and turned back to his car to fetch the big red key.

They had one last attempt at getting a response to shouting and banging, and when none materialised, Halstead swung at the front door. It gave in without a fight. Jenny went first, with Halstead and Dylan hot on her heels. Tina, still hesitating on the doorstep, not sure what she should do, heard first Jenny's voice, then Dylan's, before Constable Halstead re-emerged into the hall and went upstairs. By the time he came down again, Jenny was standing on the doorstep, the small Jack Russell in her arms. It managed a feeble wag of its tail, but otherwise appeared almost moribund.

Halstead joined them on the step. 'Nothing,' he said. 'No sign of the owner, and no sign of a struggle or anything like that. Seems he just didn't come home. I've asked the office to check the local hospitals, and I'll secure the property. Not much else we can do here.'

'But Jessy,' exclaimed Tina in horror. 'What's happened to her?'

'Dehydration I think,' said Dylan. 'Her water bowl was empty and there was none she could reach anywhere else.'

'We need to get her to a vet, pronto,' said Jill. 'The nearest is Rollesby. I think they have an out-of-hours emergency service.'

'I should take her back with me,' objected Dylan.

'She may not last that long. She needs IV fluids fast. Look, I'll cover the bill, if necessary,' said Jill. 'Let's just save her life first and argue after. You ring Rollesby then follow me.' And she headed briskly for her car.

The big, new veterinary surgery was only minutes away, and warned by Dylan, the duty vet was waiting. The young man with a dark beard and big horn-rimmed glasses appraised Jessy with a swift glance and said crisply, 'Follow me.'

Jenny followed with Jessy, while Halstead and Dylan took seats in reception.

The vet examined Jessy rapidly, checking heart and lungs, gums, eyes and gently taking a pinch of the loose flesh on her belly.

'Dehydrated,' he said. 'IV fluids asap and then we'll see. It's a good job you brought her in quickly. I wouldn't like to see her go any further downhill.' He swept up Jessy in his arms and disappeared into a back room. Before the door closed behind him, Jenny saw a veterinary nurse was already preparing the line to administer the lifesaving fluids.

Back in reception, Jenny brought Dylan and Halstead up to date, then turned as the veterinary nurse appeared from the back.

'I'll cover any immediate charge,' said Jenny.

'No problem,' replied the nurse. 'Jessy is on our books anyway. We can bill her owner as normal.' A thought struck her. 'If he's OK, obviously. If he isn't, then we might need to think again. He adores his little dog. It wouldn't be like him to neglect her.'

'I'll keep you posted,' said Jenny. 'I'll drop by tomorrow anyway, to see how Jessy is doing.'

Outside, she looked at Halstead. 'Any luck with the hospitals?' she asked.

'Not so far. Looks as though we might need to log this as a missing person. I'll report it in.'

***

In Norwich on Saturday, Greg was visiting one of his least favourite places. It wasn't so much that he was nauseated by the smells and sights of the mortuary. Not usually, anyway. Frequent exposure had inured him to the most common. It was more that he found the contemplation of what was left after life departed just plain depressing. There was such a huge difference between a vital, active body with endless possibilities before it, and the silent, irrecoverable, unmoving mass of rapidly decaying flesh after the spark has departed.

He knew Dr Paisley thought differently. They'd had the conversation when she'd asked why he so much disliked attending a postmortem given that, to her certain knowledge, he'd neither fainted nor thrown up. A record not matched by all his colleagues.

She'd disagreed totally with his view, expressing her intellectual fascination with the extraordinary diversity of the human body and its incredible resilience. They'd agreed to differ.

Saturday morning, he heaved a mental sigh, girded his metaphorical loins and pushed open the door into the chilly space occupied by three steel tables with drains under and bright lights over.

Dr Paisley was waiting by the furthest table, the mostly skeletonised remains of Ormesby Body No 3 in front of her.

'Sorry we have to do this on a weekend,' she said to Greg over her shoulder. 'I'm completely backed up! I'm afraid I don't have much new to tell you either. Given the state of the remains, I can't be absolutely certain of cause of death, but I'm eighty per cent sure it was a stab wound to the back.' She pointed to marks on the skeleton's ribs. 'These marks fit the blade of the knife found under the garage floor, and a forceful blow here with that sort of knife would have caused damage to the underlying organs, possibly resulting in a collapsed lung or even heavy bleeding from the liver.'

'Would he have died quickly?' asked Greg.

'Probably not,' replied the doctor. 'In fact, those sorts of injuries are often survivable provided medical help gets there quickly enough. Which obviously wasn't the case in this instance.'

'And the timescale?' asked Greg. 'Are we still looking at around ten years ago?'

'That's right,' said Dr Paisley. 'Around that time. Can't be very precise, I'm afraid.'

Getting back into his car, Greg was hoping to be able to head for home when a voice message from Ned changed his plans.

'We've been looking at the material found in the two voids,' he said. 'Are you back in the office this afternoon? I'd like to take you through our findings.'

On my way. Greg texted Ned. Then rang Jill. 'Can you join me in the forensic lab?' he asked. 'Whatever they've got, it makes sense if we both see it first-hand. Is Jim in today?'

'No. He's on a day's leave,' replied Jill.

'Lucky sod,' muttered Greg as he put his car in gear and headed south.

Half an hour later, he was perched on a stool in the lab beside Jill, listening to one of Ned's bright new recruits delivering a complicated explanation on what he described as 'low copy number DNA'.

'Let me be sure I've got this right,' said Greg. 'A polymerase chain reaction, or PCR, is used to multiply the quantity of genetic material in a sample so specific genetic profiles or genes can be identified. And in low copy number DNA, you put the sample through repeated PCRs so you keep multiplying how much DNA you've got. A bit like breeding sheep. You get more and more sheep with each generation.'

'Close enough,' said Ned as his young expert took a breath to give Greg a more scientifically accurate description then let it out again.

'And this means you can identify DNA from very small samples. I thought you'd been doing that for a while.'

'We have,' said the enthusiast, unable to keep quiet. 'But it gets more and more sophisticated all the time. We can now pick up traces so small they might have been left just by someone touching something, like a doorknob, or a gun.'

'Or in this case,' said Ned, 'a knife handle and a Bible.'

'We have evidence that the same person touched the knife and the Bible?' asked Greg. 'Was it the elder Joanne Hamilton?'

'Yes, and no,' Ned replied. 'To be strictly accurate, we have two distinct DNA profiles on both the knife and the Bible. In addition to the one from the victim, that is. One is Joanne Hamilton senior. The other is an unidentified male.'

'Not Mr Hamilton?' queried Greg.

'No. Definitely in addition to the victim, although obviously his DNA is on the knife as well. Mainly on the blade, when he was stabbed. Mr A N Other left his DNA on the knife handle and also on the Bible. I think it's a reasonable bet he was the killer, or at least was involved in the killing, as we found the same DNA on the bloodstained clothing wrapped round the knife. And on this...'

Ned held out a small tray encased in an evidence bag, so Greg could see the contents. It appeared to be a small piece of white celluloid about an inch wide and six or seven inches long. It was stained both with blood and soil.

There was a silence as Greg looked at the exhibit. 'You know what that is, of course,' he remarked. Then looked up into the silence. 'You don't know?' he asked.

Ned shook his head, and the young PCR expert remained silent too.

'You weren't brought up by churchgoers,' Greg guessed. 'It's a clerical collar. Looks like our killer was a priest.'

7

Monday 7 September 2020 – back to work

'I suppose it's inevitable that you start work on the first day I have off for ages,' grumbled Greg.

Chris had already settled down at her laptop and, breathing slightly heavily from extreme concentration, was logging on to the police private network.

'Hang on,' she said distractedly. 'This is complicated. And I'm struggling to remember which password I should be using. It'll all come much easier when I've done it a few times. Great. I'm in. What was it you said?'

Greg sighed, smiled, and picking up the kettle decided there was too little water in it for two mugs of coffee and took it to the tap.

'I said, it's a pity you couldn't have postponed starting the new job until tomorrow, then we could have spent today together.'

'Sorry,' she replied. But he could see from her focus on the screen that her attention was already miles away.

'Don't mind me,' he said to the inattentive air. 'I'm going for a run, then I'll do some shopping.'

Over in Rollesby, on her way to a call-out in Martham, Jenny Warren checked her watch and decided on the spur of the moment to call in on Jessy the Jack Russell. Leaving Turbo monitoring arrivals and departures in the vet centre car park from his vantage point in the back of her squad car, she went into reception and explained why she was there.

'Oh, it was you brought Jessy in,' said the receptionist. 'Thank goodness you got to her when you did. Michael, the vet who treated her, he said she couldn't have gone much longer. A little dog like Jessy doesn't have much in the way of reserves. Come this way and I'll take you to her,' she said, indicating Jenny should follow her down the corridor to the treatment wards at the back of the building. 'Jessy is a great favourite here,' she went on. 'She's a lovely little dog. Have you found her owner, Phil Saunders, yet? He's besotted with her. He'd never have left her on her own on purpose. She's in here.'

She pushed the door open into a room lined with cages on three levels. Roughly half of them were occupied by dogs of various descriptions and sizes. A couple of them wuffed on seeing humans approaching, and a cocker spaniel lifted its head and emitted a long-lasting howl.

'Oh Lord, she's off again,' said the receptionist. 'I'll be really glad when her owner picks her up. She's only had a tooth out but she's carrying on as though she's had a leg amputated.' Jenny wasn't listening. She was looking round for Jessy and spotted her in a mid-tier cage behind the door. The little dog stood up and wagged her tail as Jenny approached.

'She's looking much better,' she said with relief, and held her hand up to the grill for Jessy to sniff. 'Good girl,' she said. 'Ready to go home yet?'

'She could go home now, strictly speaking,' said the vet nurse coming in through the door. 'But I gather she hasn't anyone to go home to, so we're holding on to her for the moment. But we will need to find another solution if we get busy.'

'I'll see what the news is about her owner,' replied Jenny. 'But I think the RSPCA will get involved if there's no other answer. I'd better be off,' she added, looking at her watch. 'I'm meant to be at the Martham Nature Reserve. I'll get back to you.'

Minutes later, Jenny was pulling up in the car park at Martham Boatyard alongside a squad car.

'Just a minute, Turbo,' she said to her passenger. 'I promise you'll be out of there soon, but I need to find out what's wanted.' Turbo, wagging his tail with slight disappointment as Jenny walked away towards the river, returned to his contemplation of the sheep grazing nearby.

A uniformed officer Jenny half recognised looked up as she approached.

'I don't think we're going to need a search dog after all,' he said. 'Constable Warren, this is Frank Gillan, he's a local boat engineer. And I'm Brian Foxton. I think we met once before. Frank here,' he said, indicating the bearded man in a baseball cap standing in the cockpit of a small boat floating below them on the river. 'He says he knows where the body is.'

'*The* local boat engineer,' corrected Frank with a grin as he wiped his oily hands on what looked remarkably like an old pair of Y-fronts. He noticed the direction of Jenny's gaze and flushing slightly, dropped the 'rag' into the bottom of the boat. 'Ready?' he asked.

'Frank has found the body that was reported yesterday then lost again,' Brian said.

'It was tourists that spotted it yesterday in the river, and they didn't have the nous to ring for help,' commented the local man with some contempt. 'Just left it where they saw it and came rushing back here.'

'Of course, by the time anyone went looking, it had floated away, and it was getting dark too,' added Brian. 'But, Frank...'

'I knew where the current would take it, so it wasn't exactly difficult to find. We can go there now, if you're ready.' He dropped the engine cover back in place, turned a key and the little boat started immediately. 'Come on,' he said, with some impatience. Jim and Jenny dropped into the boat, Jenny with a backwards look at her car, checking that she'd left a window open for Turbo.

'Sure we don't need Turbo?' she asked.

'Sure,' said Frank. 'It's only fifteen minutes or so down here, and it won't have moved any further. It's firmly wedged in the reeds. I didn't touch anything,' he added hurriedly. 'I know better than that, if only from watching TV.'

Sure enough, it was somewhat less than the specified fifteen minutes when the boat chugged round a long bend and Frank slowed the engine, turning them towards a large bank of reeds where the river divided.

'This is the edge of the nature reserve,' he said, as they drifted towards the reeds with the engine barely idling. 'The current slows here, and things tend to wash up. There it is!' He pointed. Brian and Jenny peered at what, from that distance, looked much like a bundle of clothes bobbing waterlogged by the reeds. As they drifted closer, Brian nodded, satisfied.

'It's a body alright. Can we get any closer without disturbing it?'

'No problem,' said Frank, and easing the throttle still further, he turned the boat in midstream, then edged carefully up alongside the reedbed, moving slowly against the current. They were soon alongside what appeared to be the body of an elderly man in overalls topped by a waterproof jacket.

Brian was getting his radio out. 'Good work, Frank,' he said. 'I'll call it in, and we'll get someone out here to recover it.'

'Recover *him*,' corrected Jenny, still peering at the casualty. 'Hang on, I think we might need the scenes of crime team. And the pathologist.' She took her phone out and snapped an image of the very obvious head trauma on the body floating on the turbid water. 'That could be accidental, but we can't assume it. Tell them we have a suspicious death.'

Brian hesitated a moment, then nodded and made his call on the radio. Jenny continued to watch the body rolling slightly against the reeds as he reported their find, then leaned over to take a closer look. The boat tipped as she did so.

'Careful,' warned Frank. 'This boat's too small to be stable while people walk about.'

'Sorry,' said Jenny. 'I was just taking a closer look at the man's legs.'

Brian looked over from his radio. 'They'll be here within the hour,' he said. 'The Broads Beat team are at Potter Heigham, as luck would have it. They'll bring the doc here and retrieve the body.' Jenny was still frowning down at the water.

'Did you find a bike anywhere?' she asked Frank.

'No. Why?'

'The body's wearing bicycle clips. Why would he be wearing bicycle clips if he wasn't riding a bike?'

***

Over at ECDF, or East Coast Drives and Fences, as the acronym was explained to him, Bill was standing in a large yard surrounded by piles of fence panels, wooden stakes and paving slabs. Judging by the pickup trucks and lorries coming and going, business was brisk notwithstanding the Covid restrictions.

'Don't really affect us now,' said the yard foreman cheerfully. 'Everyone's keen to get on with their renovations and as our work is mostly outdoors, it's all we can do to keep up with demand. Now, what was it you wanted to know?'

Bill tucked his warrant card back in his pocket as he followed the man with ECDF across the back of his jacket, over the yard and into the large barn. One corner had been screened off with panelling and glass to form an office. Bill took the seat in front of the desk indicated by the foreman and got out his notebook.

'When we spoke on the phone,' he began, 'I told you that we were trying to find the company that did some work in a garage in Ormesby roughly ten years ago. You said you could take a look back through your records.'

'So I did,' said the man, flicking through a big ledger sitting on his desk. 'What was the address again, and why us? What makes you think it was our work?'

'We'll be asking all the possible companies around here,' Bill reassured him. 'But we started with you because one of the neighbours thinks they might have seen your sign outside the property we're dealing with. I agree it's a bit vague, but we have to start somewhere.'

'Ten years you said,' said the man, turning over a wodge of pages. 'That should be round about here.' He started running his finger down the ledger. 'I think you're in luck,' he said. 'May the seventh to the tenth, 2010. According to this, we put a concrete floor in a garage that had just an earth floor. The hardcore went in on the Friday, then the concrete on the Monday. The customer paid in full a fortnight later. A Mrs Hamilton, according to the invoice.'

'The work was done either side a weekend,' said Bill. 'Is that right?'

***

'I've got a date for the murder,' announced Bill, on reporting to Jim. 'It has to have been the weekend of the seventh to the ninth of May 2010. That's the only time the bloodied clothes and the knife can have been hidden under the hardcore. During that weekend but before the concrete was laid on the Monday.'

'It's certainly a date for when the materials were hidden,' agreed Jim. 'But it's a bit of a leap to say that's when the murder was. It could have been anytime up to that weekend.'

'Oh.' Bill was a bit deflated. 'Bugger. Yes, that's right, isn't it.'

'Good work anyway, Bill. It does narrow things down. Now we need to find out who the clerical clothes belonged to. That's your next challenge.'

8

Tuesday 8 September 2020

Greg's first port of call, on arriving in Wymondham, was Forensic Science.

'Morning, Ned. Anything new for me?'

'Morning, Greg,' he replied. 'How's Chris getting on?'

'Well, thanks,' Greg said. 'Currently buried ears-deep in data. Looking – she assures me – for patterns and repetitions. Anything more on the stuff recovered from under the Ormesby garage?'

'Not a lot,' said Ned. 'You already know that the blood on the clothes and the knife belonged to Fred Hamilton. And that some other male DNA was found on both as well. Presumably the killer's, or at least you could make a good case for it being the killer's. That's still where we're at.'

'And nothing else from Dr Paisley?'

'No. She thinks the knife is a match for the marks on Mr Hamilton's ribs, and that she can be fairly sure he was stabbed in the back, but can't guarantee that was the cause of death.'

'Bit vague,' complained Greg. 'All a bit "probably" and "fairly". What I'd give for some certainty. OK, thanks, Ned.' He turned to go and got as far as the door, when it flew open to reveal the young DNA expert.

'I've got something,' he said impartially to Ned and Greg. 'It's quite exciting.'

'Sit down and tell us what it is,' Ned instructed.

The young man hardly waited for his rear to hit the seat before he flourished a printout and then laid it on the table. 'This!' he announced. 'It's more low copy DNA. These results have just come through. We've got Joanne Hamilton senior's DNA on the Bible, so she definitely handled it. But we've also got traces of the male DNA we found on the knife and the clerical clothes.

'Reinforcing the idea that a vicar or minister of some kind was the killer, or at the very least witnessed the murder and/or the burying of the body.' Greg was thinking aloud. 'Either way he's a person of interest. Only snag is, it was all ten years ago, and there must have been a devil of a lot of ministers of various denominations in and around Great Yarmouth and Ormesby. We're looking for a blade of hay in a haystack.'

'At least when we find him, we can know if it's the right one,' said Ned. 'A quick DNA sample will tell us that.'

'We have to find him first,' responded Greg gloomily, and took himself downstairs to his team's main office. Somewhat to his surprise, the room was nearly deserted, with only Jenny in situ.

'Morning, Jenny. Where is everyone?' he asked.

She looked up from her desk. 'Jill's on a day's leave so she and Diana can meet with social services about the two Mirren kids, Jim and Bill are chasing down vicars, and Steve has tested positive for Covid, so he's isolating.'

'Not again!' exclaimed Greg. 'Still, it's good Jim's already on to the vicar search.'

'Have you heard what Bill found yesterday?' asked Jenny.

'No, I went straight up to Ned this morning,' replied Greg. 'Bring me up to date, would you?'

'He found the company who laid the garage floor, and they've given us a date for when the fabric and knife must have been hidden under it.' Jenny pointed at the whiteboard, which now had an additional legend reading '7–9 May 2010'.

Greg moved to stand in front of the whiteboard, and surveyed all the notes, photos and arrows that summarised what they knew about the case. 'Looks like Mr Fred Hamilton died sometime just before or over the weekend of the seventh to the ninth of May 2010, of a stab in the back, and that a minister of the cloth was in some way involved with the death and/or its cover-up, since his DNA is on the bloodstained fabric and the knife that's front runner for delivering the fatal blow,' he said.

'Or,' said Jenny. 'And this thought has only just occurred to me, Boss. The perp had been to a vicars and tarts party just before stabbing Fred Hamilton, and it's nothing to do with actual ministers at all.'

Greg swung round and looked at her. 'That would be a bit of a bugger,' he said. 'Were they still a thing in 2010? And would an elderly recluse be likely to hold one? We'd better do some checking. Add Joanne Hamilton's party habits to the list of questions we're asking her neighbours. Meanwhile, I'll check on Jim and Bill to see how they're getting on.'

Jim was in his office, with Bill sitting across the desk from him, both glued to phones. Bill was in mid-discussion with one finger in his other ear. Jim put his receiver down with a sigh of relief and stretched back in his chair when Greg came in.

'Heard about Bill's breakthrough?' he asked.

'Yes. Jenny just told me. How are you getting on with your vicar search?'

'Slowly,' said Jim. 'For the C of E, I started by searching Crockford's Clerical Directory. According to that, there are currently over one hundred and seventy full-time stipendiary clergy in Norfolk. Add to that the part-timers and the retired, and we are looking at a lot more. Obviously we can exclude the women, and I've tried to narrow it down by looking for male clerics who were based in the Ormesby Benefice in 2010. Then I added any based in a neighbouring benefice, such as Great Yarmouth and Acle. That's reduced our pool to seven, which is somewhat more practical. I'm just working on a schedule for interviewing them all about any potential contact with Joanne Hamilton senior. Bill is doing something similar with Methodist Church records and we haven't started on the Catholic Church yet.

'Margaret isn't going to like this,' said Greg gloomily. 'And I haven't shared Jenny's bright idea yet. He outlined Jenny's thought about vicars and tarts parties, but Jim was dismissive.

'In my experience they were pretty much over by the end of the nineties,' he said. 'Even in Norfolk! And I can't see the reclusive Joanne senior going to one, much less hosting one. I think we should press on with our clerical leads for the moment and see where we get to.'

'I agree,' said Greg. 'Have you asked our current Joanne if her mother had any church affiliations?'

Jim smacked his head with his hand. 'I can't believe I overlooked that!' he groaned, and reached for his phone again.

'Keep me posted, would you?' said Greg, and left Jim to his self-recriminations.

Less than ten minutes later, Jim had his head round Greg's door. 'C of E,' he said succinctly. 'At least, the answer was "nothing much, but if she had any affiliation at all, it was C of E. That's what she'd say if she had to list religion on a form".'

Greg couldn't have been more delighted to be interrupted. He turned away from the despised paperwork on his laptop and pushed it away across the desk with a sigh of relief.

'Let's get going then,' he said. 'We can start with your priority seven and see where that takes us. We'll take my car.' Feeling like truanting schoolboys, they hurried to the car park before a call from Margaret could detain them.

'OK, where to first?' asked Greg. 'What do we have on your list?'

'Two retired vicars, one who had the living in Ormesby in 2010 and one from Acle. One ex vicar, now rural dean, who was in Ormesby up to 2008. And four long-retired vicars who provided services from time to time in Ormesby and the surrounding villages.'

'OK. Get someone to make an appointment for us with the rural dean. Even if it's not him, he's a good place to seek information on all things clerical. And while they're doing that, let's start with the chap who had the living in Ormesby in 2010. Where is he now?'

'In sheltered housing in Acle.'

'Near the fire station?' asked Greg.

'Yes.'

'I know it. Let's head there. We might get some lunch off Chris, while we're at it.'

9

Cycle 3

Kain was having a good day, even though his best mate had cried off their planned day out at the last moment, pleading ill health and a possible dose of Covid. Looking at the cloudy skies, Kain thought it was more likely he'd feared rain. Lucas was ever a fair-weather cyclist. However, the clouds had drifted by without precipitation, and Kain had enjoyed his solo ride around some of the more picturesque Northern Broads.

He'd set off from his home in Hemsby around ten o'clock and joined the circular route – No 5 from Broads By Bike – in West Somerton, heading north on Horsey Road. He'd sailed past Horsey Windpump, having visited it on a number of occasions, but decided to take a break at Waxham Barns and got himself a takeaway coffee. That occasioned an unscheduled stop shortly after Sea Palling to unload, as discreetly as possible, the surplus fluid.

By lunchtime he was at Hickling Broad and decided to treat himself to lunch at the Pleasure Boat. A pint and a sandwich in the garden by the water went down very nicely. *More fool Lucas*, he thought, and was very tempted to have a second pint. Only the thought of yet another unscheduled toilet stop dissuaded him, and he climbed back on his bike to complete the circuit through Potter Heigham and Martham.

He was having such a good day, that in Martham he decided on an impromptu side trip down to the River Thurne. He was pedalling gently through the woods on the infelicitously named Cess Road when he heard the roar of a diesel engine behind him. He barely had time to take in the proximity of a pickup moving dangerously fast for the narrow road, when it surged alongside him. In seconds he was spinning through the air as his bike crumpled under a heavy wheel. Then his head met a wayside tree and that was the last he would ever know. His day out, his impromptu side trip and his life were all over.

The driver got out, surveyed the results of their action and the road, empty in both directions, then bent and with some effort and a lot of grunting, hauled the body a few yards into the wood. Returning to their vehicle, they tossed the bent bike into the back, glanced sideways to where the body was hidden in a bed of nettles, then drove on to the car park on the riverbank.

At this time in the afternoon there were still people about: returning canoes, mooring small craft and, in one instance, completing the revarnishing of a cabin cruiser. The pickup driver got out a newspaper and a flask of tea, then appropriated a bench seat by the water.

An hour or two later they had the riverbank to themselves. The boat hire business had closed for the day, and the few tourists had departed. One last look around, then it was the work of moments to haul the bike out of the back of the vehicle and half push it, half carry it to the water's edge. A varied collection of small cruisers and yachts was moored along the bank. The bike was dropped into the water between a small launch and a rather badly maintained yacht. It fell with a barely audible gurgle and a few bubbles, to disappear beneath the muddy waters.

10

Later on September 10

Arriving at Linnet House, Greg and Jim bumped into a lady in blue scrubs going off duty. Greg stepped forwards as she bent to unlock her car door.

'Sorry to bother you,' he said. 'We're police officers hoping to have a word with one of your residents. Do you know who we should speak to about gaining entry. I realise you are still operating under a lot of restrictions.'

She turned to regard him with friendly blue eyes over her mask. 'It depends who you want to see,' she said. 'The frailer residents in the main building are still being kept away from outsiders. Those who don't need medical care and live in their own homes – it's up to them whether or not they are shielding. Many of them are. Who was it you wanted to speak to?'

Greg looked down at the note in his hand. 'Mr Thurlow,' he said. 'He's a retired vicar, I believe.'

'Oh, Roy Thurlow. He's one of our owner residents. You'll find him in the ground-floor flat over there.' She pointed. 'Do you mind telling me what you want him for? I wouldn't want him to be upset. He's hale and hearty for his age, but he is quite elderly you know.'

'So I believe,' said Greg. 'We just want some information relating to a current case. An informal chat, that's all.' *At this stage*, he added to himself, feeling slightly disingenuous.

'I'd come with you,' she said, 'but I'm just going off duty and it's been a long shift.'

She hesitated, but Greg replied, 'No need. We won't keep him long. Thank you for your help.'

He and Jim walked briskly in the direction she had indicated, and as they paused by the front door of a ground-floor flat, Jim glanced back.

'She's on her mobile,' he said. 'I'd guess she's calling the management.'

'No problem,' replied Greg. 'Come on, let's see how we get on.'

There was a long pause before the doorbell was answered, then the dark green door swung open to reveal a tall, spare man in grey flannels, dark grey shirt and the sort of patterned, woolly jumper worn by Frank Spencer in *Some Mothers do 'Ave 'Em*.

'Can I help you?' asked the man civilly, leaning on the stick which explained his slow approach to the door.

Greg introduced himself and Jim, both holding out their warrant cards. 'We'd just like to talk to you about a current case,' he explained. 'Although we've only begun to investigate it now, it concerns events which happened in Ormesby in 2010.'

Both men were watching Mr Thurlow closely, but neither could detect any reaction other than polite interest.

'You'd better come in,' he said, and preceded them slowly down a short passage and into a pleasant living room. At one end was a chunky riser recliner leather armchair, well placed for viewing a large wall-mounted TV, and with a cantilever table strategically placed alongside, currently bearing a cup of coffee and a plate of biscuits.

'I'm sorry,' said Greg. 'We seem to have interrupted your coffee.'

'No problem,' said Mr Thurlow, waving them to the sofa at right angles to his chair. 'Can I get you a coffee?'

'How about Jim here makes the coffee while we start our chat,' suggested Greg, foreseeing a long wait if their host did the fetching and carrying. 'He's quite civilised in a kitchen, I promise you.'

'If you don't mind, that would probably be more convenient,' agreed the elderly man. 'I don't get about very quickly these days, as I'm sure you've noticed. Bring the tin of biscuits in as well,' he added, raising his voice to reach Jim in the kitchen. 'And you'll find fresh milk in the fridge.'

While sounds of a boiling kettle reached them through the open door, Greg turned to Mr Thurlow. 'The time we're interested in is the summer of 2010 in Ormesby. I believe you were the vicar there at that time.'

'Sounds about right,' agreed Mr Thurlow, taking a sip of his coffee. 'I'd have to look it up to be sure of the year. It's surprisingly hard to remember exactly where you were in a particular year when you've moved around a lot.'

'That's where you were according to Crockford's,' said Jim, coming in with a couple of mugs in one hand and a tin full of shortbread in the other. 'I took you at your word about the biscuits. I hope that's OK.' He sat down next to Greg and put the two mugs on the coasters waiting on the coffee table before them.

'If Crockford's says so, then that's where I was,' said Mr Thurlow with a disarming grin. 'It's never wrong. I find I remember people and events a lot better than years. For example, I can see a wedding in my mind's eye and recall exactly what the bride said when she tripped over her train, but I couldn't tell you which year it happened.'

'What did she say?' asked Jim, intrigued.

'Shall we just leave it that it wasn't exactly suitable for the Lord's House,' replied Mr Thurlow with another grin.

'That could be a useful sort of memory to have,' said Greg, taking them back to the subject. 'If we can agree you were the incumbent in Ormesby in 2010, do you remember a parishioner of yours named Joanne Hamilton?'

Mr Thurlow leaned back in his chair while he thought. 'I can't say I do,' he said. 'Was she a churchgoer?'

'We don't know for sure,' said Greg. 'It seems likely she was only an occasional attendee.'

'I'm not great on names either,' admitted Mr Thurlow. 'Do you know anything else about her that might jog my memory?' Both detectives were watching him closely. Neither could detect anything in his demeanour other than a good-humoured willingness to assist.

'She lived in a bungalow not far from the village hall,' replied Greg. 'As far as we know, she was a bit of a recluse. But she was getting on in years and you might have visited her in your parochial role?'

'We have a photo of her in her younger days,' added Jim, producing a photocopy from his pocket of one of the framed photos they'd found in the bungalow. As far as they could tell, it depicted the elder Joanne Hamilton at a party, probably in her late fifties.

Mr Thurlow took the photo and scrutinised it carefully, then shook his head and handed it back. 'Sorry. It's not reminding me of anyone,' he said. 'But it was a big parish and I had responsibility for two others as well. I don't recall her at all. But on the other hand, the visiting of the sick and needy was shared between me and my two assistants. One of them might remember her.'

'Do you have any contact details for them?' asked Jim.

'Only one of them. I'm still in touch with my old deaconess, Milly Gent. But she's old in both senses of the word,' he added. 'And a bit confused these days. She's living in a home for the elderly in Great Yarmouth. The other was a retired clergyman. I mean he was already retired in 2010, although he wasn't all that old. He had some health issues, and he'd left an inner-city parish to retire to the countryside. If I remember correctly, stress may have been part of the problem. Anyway, he wasn't keen to do much in the way of services, but he did do hospital visiting and the like.'

'Do you have any idea where he might be now?' asked Greg.

''Fraid not. We lost touch long since. You could try Crockford's again,' he suggested with a smile.

'True,' said Jim. 'What was his name?'

'Ah, now there you have me. I said I wasn't great on names. I think it was something like Bert. Or perhaps Will? Sorry I can't help more than that.'

Back in Greg's car, the two men looked at each other. 'I think we can cross him off our list,' said Jim.

'Agreed,' said Greg. 'No reaction at all to the year, the place or Joanne Hamilton. He'd have to be a real actor to keep that up. We needn't worry about Milly Gent either. Wrong gender. And it seems unlikely we'll get any useful information from her if she's "confused". Which I take to be a polite way of saying she's suffering from dementia.'

'Depends how far advanced it is,' objected Jim. 'Sometimes they remember the distant past better than the more recent.'

'Still inadmissible in court, though,' replied Greg, starting the car. 'We could pay her a visit as a last resort, but I think we'd do better to focus on the others on your list and Bert or Will. If we can find him. Let's go and grab a bite of lunch with Chris. We're only five minutes away. Then we can head back to HQ and see if we're getting anywhere with the rural dean.'

Chris looked up in surprise as the two men interrupted her focus on spreadsheets. Bobby was rubbing herself on Jim's legs, back arched and tail curled, but Tally contained her reaction on their entry to a quiet grunt and a shuffle of her wings.

'Hi,' said Chris. 'What brings you two here?'

'The hope of lunch,' said Jim, sitting down in a chair opposite. 'How're you doing, Chris? Found us anything interesting?'

'There was me thinking you were asking after my health. Until the last sentence, that is,' replied Chris.

'No need to ask. It's obvious you're in rude health,' responded Jim.

'Have you eaten?' asked Greg practically, dropping a kiss on the top of her head.

'Not recently,' said Chris. 'I got interested in the stats I've been looking up. I think there's still some Camembert in the fridge, and bread in the bread bin.'

'That'll do,' said Greg and headed for the kitchen. 'I'll have a bit of a forage and see what else we've got.'

'So, what trail are you following?' asked Jim.

'Nothing specific. I'm still getting my head round all the data that's out there. One thing did intrigue me, and that's the number of missing people who seem to set off on bike trips and don't return. There've been three in the last couple of months. Now, I know that bikes have shot up in popularity during lockdown, but it doesn't seem the ideal choice of vehicle for a disappearing act. Then I looked up accidents involving bikes and found that Norfolk is outside the norm for the number of cyclists killed in accidents. Numbers have risen sharply over the last year. From seven in 2019 to ten already this year, while numbers have dropped in other counties. Weird, isn't it?'

Greg reappeared with a tray bearing plates, knives, cheese, butter, bread and tomatoes. 'Pickle and coffees coming up,' he said. 'Anything for us in what you're finding, Chris?'

'Oh, I shouldn't think so', said Chris. 'As I said, I'm just getting my head around the databases, to see what I can find. Funny though, isn't it?'

Driving back to Wymondham, Greg glanced sideways at Jim and asked, 'What do you think of Chris?'

'Looking good to me,' said Jim. 'Not that I'm any expert either on head injuries or pregnant women, but on both counts, she looks blooming to me. So long as she doesn't overdo it...'

'When have you ever known Chris *not* overdo it?' asked Greg. 'But thanks, Jim. You've confirmed what I was thinking. I just wanted to check I wasn't being overconfident.'

Jim was looking down at his phone. 'Sorry,' he said, 'I've just got a text to say the rural dean is available for a chat tomorrow afternoon, if it suits.'

'Where?' asked Greg.

'Norwich. Seems there's been some sort of clergy conference, and we can catch him at the cathedral before he goes home.'

'OK, say we'll see him in Norwich at around 4pm. If there's a private room we can use, then we can come to him at the cathedral, or if not, we'll need to see him at the Norwich police station. In the meantime, I guess there's a lot we can be getting on with, back at the office.'

Jim rang the number listed in the text message, and after a swift conversation, rang off. 'They say there's a room we can use at the cathedral,' he said. 'And we can park near the Song School. Apparently, he's too busy to be trekking across Norwich to the police station.'

'Oh, one of those,' said Greg. 'OK. That's sorted for tomorrow.'

When Greg got back to his office, the first thing he found was a note on his desk from Jenny, asking to see him in private.

Odd, he thought, stood up to head down to the incident room, then thought the better of it and picked up his phone. If Jenny wanted a personal chat, she presumably had a good reason.

He was just going through the postmortem report on Fred Hamilton again, to see if there was anything he'd missed, when Jenny appeared in his office.

'Thanks, Boss,' she said as she closed the door behind her.

'Take a seat, Jenny,' he replied, putting the paperwork down. 'What can I do for you?'

She sat down in the chair across the desk, looking a little embarrassed. 'I'm sorry to take up your time,' she said, 'but I wanted to tell you myself, not just in an email or message. I'm going to be transferring to another team.'

'I'm sorry to hear that, Jenny,' said Greg. 'Is there a problem I can deal with? You are a valued member of our team, as I hope you know.'

'It's not that sort of problem,' said Jenny. 'And not something you can help with, I'm afraid. It's partly Turbo and partly me. Turbo is nearly nine now, and the decision's been made. It's time he retired. As you know, he has had an issue with lameness recently, and he's getting a bit grumpy. The vet says it's arthritis, and our instructor says he should retire. After all this time, I can't bear he should go to live anywhere other than with me, but if I keep him then I have to leave the dog handling team. I couldn't leave him at home and go off with another dog every day. Poor Turbo would pine. So, it's time we both moved on. Turbo will become a pet in his retirement, and I'll go back to uniform. Greg opened his mouth to say something, but she intervened swiftly. 'It's not a bad move for me,' she said. 'I've loved being a dog handler and all the work I've done with your team, but it's time I had a change too. And maybe I'll get a chance at sergeant.'

'I don't know what to say,' said Greg. 'You'll be missed, both of you.'

'It's good timing too,' said Jenny. 'The policies have changed a lot since I first started as a dog handler. Everyone works in two-man teams now. Or perhaps I should say two dogs plus two handlers. The whole resource is based here in Wymondham, and you'll get whatever two-dog team is most suitable for your needs, depending on the reason for the call-out. You know, explosives, or drugs, or violent offender. Whatever. The response times are really fast, day or night, so I hear.' She grinned suddenly. 'It's been fun, Boss,' she said. 'But all good things come to an end.'

She stood up to go. 'I've taken up too much of your time,' she added. 'But I wanted to tell you personally before you got the formal notification. That'll come through very quickly now.'

'When do you leave?' asked Greg, giving way to the inevitable.

'End of the week, if that's OK with you,' she said. 'No point delaying anything, and there are new graduates from the dog training school joining the team all the time. All thirsting for a chance to get stuck in and show what their dogs can do.'

11

Evening: 10 September

Fran enjoyed her evening dog walks. It was cooler for a start, and in this hot summer weather, better for her dog, Buddy. Like all springer spaniels, Buddy was constitutionally incapable of taking it easy. He had only two speeds: stationary and flat out. So early morning and evening walks it was, with the later wander in the fading light definitely the one she enjoyed the most. Quieter roads also meant she dared let Buddy off his lead, which was a bonus. *On* his lead meant *he* was walking *her*, and generally at a pace considerably in excess of her preference. Now, down the quiet turning which led to the Ormesby Broad, she could let him loose and enjoy watching him rummage in the hedgerows.

Occasionally he would startle a rabbit into a panic across the fields, and sometimes a pheasant would take off with a clatter of wings and a lot of squawking. On one memorable occasion he had emerged from the damp ditch with a large grass snake writhing in his mouth, and it had taken some persuasion and bribery with gravy bones from her pocket to persuade him to let it go.

This evening had been blessedly free of reptiles and rabbits, but a mile or so down the road, Buddy had become very interested in something in the ditch. So much so, he had refused to return to Fran, even after much offering of gravy bones, backed up by threats to 'spifflicate him' if he didn't do as he was told. Sighing heavily, Fran had scrambled over the rough verge to see what was so exciting.

At first it looked like just an old, abandoned bike. Even allowing for Buddy's dislike of bikes, the level of interest he was showing looked odd. He was circling the bike at a safe distance, making an odd noise, half growl, half whine.

Fran was just about to give a tug on the bike, to pull it out of the ditch, when her brain computed what her eyes were seeing. Suddenly all the fragments of vision fell into place, as though a kaleidoscope had twisted. She realised the shape on the edge of the ditch was a shoe, and that it contained bones, while lying under the bike was the rest of a body, face down in the dust at the bottom of the dry dyke. The foot bones seemed to have been detached from its leg, and her first thought was to hope, with a profound intensity, that it hadn't been Buddy that had separated the two. Then she turned to one side, was sick on the grass, and shakily moved back to the road, fumbling for her phone.

She sat down on the verge with a bit of a bump and, trying to focus her swimming eyes on the small screen, dialled 999. Spotting his mistress at ground level, Buddy abandoned his circling and came over to stick his nose in the nearest ear. She took a firm hold on his collar as she reported the finding of a body.

The next fifteen minutes were the loneliest of her life. There was no traffic on the quiet road, and she just sat on, without moving, her back to her grisly find and her arm round Buddy's neck. And that's how the first response car found her.

The car with blue lights flashing pulled up beside her and a uniformed constable got out, pulling on his peaked cap.

'Are you Fran Rix?' he asked. 'I'm Constable White. You called in a body?'

'That's right,' said Fran. 'It's in the ditch, behind me.' She pointed over her shoulder without turning round. 'My dog found it. Forgive me for not getting up. I'm still feeling a bit shaky.' She hung on to Buddy, as he demonstrated every desire to bounce all over the constable with his usual exuberant welcome.

'OK, you stay there for the moment,' he said. 'My colleague...' He nodded at the driver just emerging from the police car. 'She'll take down your details. I'll just have a look at this body.'

He walked over the rough verge behind Fran, and she heard his footsteps come to a halt, a sort of cough, then he was back on the edge of the road. 'Definitely a body,' he said to his colleague. 'We'll need the specialists. Can you look after Ms Rix here while I call it in?'

'Sure,' said the other officer, a comfortable-looking woman, a buxom shape straining out of her uniform in several directions. 'Come on, Ms Rix, or can I call you Fran? Let me give you a hand up, then come and sit in the car for a bit while we deal with the formalities. Can we put the hound on the lead?' she asked as Buddy tried to say hello to her too. 'I think that might be better.'

'Oh, yes. Of course. Sorry,' said Fran, taking the blue lead from round her neck and clipping it to Buddy's collar. She accepted the proffered hand up and went to sit in the back seat of the car, carefully avoiding looking behind her.

Constable White had just finished on the radio. 'They say secure the scene, keep out of the way and wait for reinforcements,' he said. 'We need to know,' he added to Fran, 'did you touch anything?'

'No, not at all,' she replied. 'As soon as I realised what I was looking at, I backed off and came back to the road. I was sick,' she remembered with a blush. 'And I wondered if Buddy might have touched the ... the foot. But thinking about it now, I don't think so. He was nervous of it and circling it at a distance.'

'Why did you go over to the ditch in the first place?' asked the female officer. 'Sorry, I should have introduced myself. I'm Vicky Allen.'

'Because Buddy wouldn't come back,' answered Fran. 'He was obviously interested in something by the ditch, and he wouldn't come back. Last time it was a snake. So I went over to see what was so exciting and to get hold of him.'

'Do you walk down here often?' asked Vicky.

'Fairly often,' said Fran. 'But not recently. I've been walking Buddy on the beach mainly, but I thought, today, that it would make a nice change to walk somewhere a bit shady, so we came down here instead.'

'When did you last walk this road?' asked Constable White, seeing where Vicky was going.

'Probably August sometime,' said Fran. 'I tend to walk down here when the schools are out and the beaches are busy, then go back to the beaches when term starts.'

'Can you be any more precise than that?' asked Vicky.

'Probably the bank holiday weekend at the end of August. Sorry, can't be more exact than that.'

'That's helpful,' said Vicky, making a note. 'Now, if you're OK to wait a little, either we or one of our colleagues will run you home. As soon as the promised reinforcements arrive,' she added, looking at her partner with a raised eyebrow.

'Shouldn't be long,' he said. 'In the meantime, I'll get some crime scene tape out. You stay with Ms Rix.'

Fran was never sure exactly how long it did take. She stayed in the car with the door open, Buddy sitting on the verge alongside, on the end of his lead, while she chatted to Vicky Allen. She realised afterwards that she'd answered quite a lot of questions about her lifestyle, work, relationships and dog-walking habits in the course of the conversation by the time another police car and a forensic services van pulled up alongside. Vicky got out of the car to chat to the new arrivals, then the white-suited contingent deployed to the ditch while the sergeant from the second car issued orders about closing the road. Then Vicky came round to Fran and Buddy and leaned down to talk to her, one hand on the roof of the car.

'We're going to need a formal statement from you. But this is hardly the place. How about we take you and Buddy home and take a statement there? Is that OK with you? It's just a formal statement of how you came to find the body,' she added reassuringly.

Fran struggled out of the car. 'That's fine by me. I live on the edge of Ormesby. But are you sure it's OK for Buddy? He's not very clean,' she said, looking at his soil-covered paws.

'It's no problem,' replied Vicky. 'You get him in the car with you, I'll collect my colleague, and we'll be on our way.'

Fran's bungalow was only minutes down the road. Once Buddy was watered and settled down with a bone, Vicky, and George White sat facing Fran across a low coffee table. Fran looked much calmer now she was back on her own territory with her normal domestic routines around her.

'Do you live alone?' asked Vicky.

'Yes,' said Fran, sipping her tea and looking as though she'd have preferred the 'something stronger' she'd offered the police officers. Unfortunately, they'd declined, and she didn't feel able to hit the booze alone.

'Do you have a friend or relative handy who might come round?' asked Vicky. 'You've had quite a shock, and some company might be a good idea.'

'I've good neighbours,' replied Fran. 'If I need company I'll pop round. But I'm OK for now. What was it you wanted to know?'

Vicky had her notes open. 'You already told us how you came to be walking Buddy down that lane and when you last walked down there. You described how Buddy attracted your attention to the body in the ditch. I've only got a couple more questions really, then we'll get this typed up at the station and someone will pop round with a copy for you to sign.'

'Just to be clear, did you touch the body or the bike?'

'No,' said Fran with a shudder.

'Did you see Buddy touch or move any part of the body or the bike?'

'No,' said Fran again.

'Did you recognise the person in the ditch?'

'No,' said Fran. 'It ... they were face down and I didn't notice anything else.'

'What about the clothes or the shoes?'

'No,' said Fran. 'As soon as I realised what I was looking at, I got out of there quick.'

'And the bike?' asked George.

'No,' said Fran, then opened her mouth again before closing it on words unsaid.

'Were you going to add anything?' asked Vicky. 'Did you think of something?'

'Not really. Well, sort of,' said Fran. 'I think I might have seen the bike there in the ditch some days before. But I was driving by, not on foot. I go that way sometimes, to get to the garden centre in Rollesby. I have this vague recollection I saw an upside-down bike on the edge of the ditch and thought something like *more fly-tippers!* Then thought no more about it.'

'Do you know when that was?' asked Vicky.

'No, no idea. No, hang on,' said Fran. 'If it was a garden centre visit, I'll have paid with my credit card. That would show when it was.' She fetched her lightweight waistcoat with the multiple pockets from where she'd dumped it on returning home, and rummaged for her phone. Some screen tapping and heavy breathing followed, then she held it out to Vicky and George, showing them the screen. 'There,' she said. 'It was

Friday the fourth of September. That's when I went to the garden centre.'

'Just to be clear,' said George, pausing in his note-taking. 'You saw the bike in the ditch on Friday the fourth of September as you drove by. Are you sure of that?'

Fran paused for thought. 'I'm sure I saw *a* bike in the ditch on that road, on that day,' she said, 'because I clearly remember the thought about fly-tipping and that's when I went to the garden centre. But I couldn't swear it was that bike, or precisely that bit of ditch.'

'That's fair enough,' said Vicky. 'Thank you for all your help. We'll be back with a statement for you to sign, and we may have a few more questions, but that's all for now.'

12

11 September

Greg was ploughing through paperwork again when Jim appeared in the doorway with his signature bacon roll clutched in one hand and a coffee in the other.

'Seen the report in from the Yarmouth team last night?' he asked.

Greg breathed in the tempting aroma of bacon with a sigh. 'Don't bring that thing in here,' he growled. 'Chris prodded my six-pack last night and termed it "porky", so I'm on a diet. Which report?'

'The one about the body in the ditch,' said Jim. 'I had an idea...'

'Wonder if it was the same one as me,' said Greg. 'After three. One, two, three...'

'Ask Chris about her disappearing cyclists,' they chorused, more or less together.

'Already asked her,' said Greg, slightly smugly. 'She'll get back to me. It could be a hit and run of course, not necessarily one for us.'

'It could,' agreed Jim, taking a bite of bacon butty in contravention of the recent ban. 'But something doesn't sit well with me. For the bike to be on top of the body, well that's odd for a start. And the ditch is quite a long way from the edge of the road. If it was an RTA they would have to be hit very hard, to land in the ditch instead of on the verge. And the driver who hit them would have to know what they'd done. It would be the worst sort of hit and run.'

'What does Ned say?' asked Greg.

'Nothing from them as yet, apart from the basic info: ie, a woman, dead for some time, no ID on the body, face down in the ditch, a bike lying on top of her. The postmortem is scheduled for this afternoon and hopefully some more from Ned as well.'

'I marked it as one to watch,' agreed Greg. 'We'll catch up with Ned later. Then we're off to interview the rural dean at the cathedral song school.'

Jim got up to leave then paused at the door. 'Chris was right,' he said. 'More Party-7 than six-pack,' then ducked the screwed-up paper thrown at him and left, chuckling.

Greg had barely settled back in front of his laptop, trying not to think about the persistent scent of fried pig, when Jill popped her head round his door.

'Hi, Boss,' she said. 'Something's come up I wanted to ask you about. Jenny got involved in a missing person case the other day, mainly because she was nearby, and a dog was involved. Since then, she and Turbo were called to look for a body in the water near Martham. In fact, it seems Turbo wasn't needed, because a local waterman knew where things tend to wash up, and sure enough, that's where they found the body. The thing is, Jenny noticed that the body was wearing bicycle clips, and her missing person had a bike that's also missing. She realises it's a long shot, but she wondered if there was any chance they might be one and the same.'

'Has she checked whether any ID was found on the body?' asked Greg, his mind partly on the report in front of him on the screen. 'Hang on, you're saying this is a missing cyclist?'

'I suppose I am,' said Jill.

'In that case, can you do some checking for me? Get all the details of Jenny's missing person and chase up the forensics and postmortem results on the Martham floater. See if they're a match. And check with Chris to see if they're on her database of missing cyclists. If either or both turn up a yes, start the wheels moving to see where that person entered the river, and find the bike. Let me know where you get to.'

'Will do, Boss,' said Jill, and withdrew her head from the doorway.

***

They were on their way into Norwich and the cathedral song school before Greg managed to catch up with Jim again. Driving in convoy, so both could head home after the interview with the rural dean, the hands-free conversation was interrupted by frequent failures in signal, much to the frustration of both.

'What was that you just said?' demanded Greg for the third time. 'You broke up.'

'I said,' bellowed Jim, in an illogical assumption that greater volume equalled greater connectivity, 'I spoke to Ned and he's not at all happy about the cyclist in the ditch. He says there's no way the bike could have landed on top of them by accident. He's certain it was put there after the hit and run. And he says that the velocity needed to propel someone from cycling on the road to lying in the ditch was considerable. He doesn't think it can have been an accidental glancing blow. It's possible, only if someone was driving at reckless speed, but unlikely.'

'Driving at reckless speed isn't exactly unusual,' objected Greg.

'No, but Ned thinks the scenario's unlikely. And he's certain about the bike.'

'OK. Anything from the pathologist?' asked Greg.

'Not yet. How about Chris?'

'She thinks the details are possibles for two of her missing cyclists.'

'Two!' exclaimed Jim.

'Ah, you don't know yet about Jenny's case.' Greg brought him up to date swiftly. 'So, she thinks she's got possibles for the body at Martham and the one in the ditch. She's emailing me the details. We can take a look when we arrive at the cathedral.'

Navigating Norwich and the one-way streets was simple enough. Greg was used to them by now. Moreover, when he first arrived in the city, he'd shared a rented house near the cathedral with his (now ex) singer wife. The streets, the Close, and the great stone arch by which the latter was accessed were all familiar from a past life that seemed to have belonged to someone else.

Parked alongside Greg in the last space available, Jim appeared to have read his mind. 'You used to live near here, didn't you?' he said.

'Just down there,' said Greg, pointing vaguely. 'Very expensive but very select neighbours.'

'The views are better where you are now,' said Jim, turning to survey the impressive bulk of the eleventh-century cathedral. 'I know this is considered timeless and beautiful by many,' he said, 'but give me the river at sunset every time.'

'You prize God's creativity over man's efforts in praise of him?' asked Greg.

'Every time,' said Jim again. 'Anything through from Chris yet?'

'Not yet,' replied Greg, checking his phone again. 'The signal's not great here either.' The two men rounded the corner to enter the cathedral by the south door.

'Where did he say we should meet him?' asked Greg

'We go through here, I think,' said Jim as he led them through the cathedral shop and pushed on a door marked private. 'He said this door would be left open for us. Here we go.'

They found themselves in a corridor with a pale wood floor and multiple doors opening off, with little clue as to what was behind them. The first door revealed only an empty room, set up with a circle of chairs facing a blackboard and lectern. He was luckier second time around. This one opened to reveal a room set out as for a meeting, with a man sitting in the 'Chairman' position, apparently reviewing his notes. He rose as they came in, revealing himself as a well-fed man in his early sixties, sporting a crew cut and face so well-shaven it seemed to be polished. He held out his hand.

'I'm Harold Willis,' he said. 'You must be Detective Chief Inspector Geldard and Detective Inspector Henning. Which of you is which? You can call me Father Harold.'

Both policemen held out their warrant cards for inspection as Greg introduced them.

'Thank you for agreeing to meet us, Father,' he said. 'As I think has been explained to you, we are looking for some information relevant to a death which occurred around ten years ago.'

'How can I help?' asked the dean.

'We understand that you held the living in Ormesby up to 2008, before your appointment as rural dean,' said Greg. 'That's a little before our time frame, but it would be helpful to know if you have any recollection of a lady, living in a bungalow near the village hall, by the name of Joanne Hamilton.'

'That's rather a tall order,' complained the dean. 'It's correct, I was in Ormesby before I moved on and then took up the rural dean role. But that's over twelve years ago now, and twelve busy years if I may say so. I'm sorry, I don't think I can help you there. I met a lot of people at that time, and I've met a lot since, but I don't recall that name.'

'In that case,' said Greg. 'Perhaps you can help us in your role as rural dean. I understand that means you are responsible for the welfare and so on of the many clergy in your area.'

'That's right,' said the dean. 'Mainly their spiritual welfare, but, of course, that's inevitably impinged by other, more practical matters.'

'Then, perhaps you could put us in contact with the clergy who worked in the Ormesby area in the few years leading up to and including 2010. We've already spoken to Mr Thurlow, who had the living after you, and he mentioned a number of retired, or semi-retired, clergy who assisted him with services, visiting parishioners, and so on – given that I understand he was looking after a whole group of churches, not just one.'

'That would be correct,' responded the dean. 'Sadly, we don't have the financial resources to supply a vicar for every parish, nor do we have clergy in sufficient numbers either. So it's routine for a vicar to be responsible for several churches and parishes, and they would certainly struggle if it wasn't for the voluntary assistance of deacons and deaconesses, lay readers and retired clergy.'

'So, who was it assisting Mr Thurlow around ten years ago?' asked Greg slightly impatiently.

'As to volunteers from the community, I wouldn't know,' answered the dean. 'But for retired clergy still licensed to provide services, those I can look up for you. Now, if there's nothing else...' and he started to shuffle his papers together.

'Can you look it up now?' asked Greg, indicating the laptop open in front of the dean. 'I assume the records are all on a database these days.'

He sighed heavily. 'Well, I suppose so,' he said. 'Although I am in a bit of a hurry and my secretary—'

'We really would appreciate the information as soon as possible,' said Greg. 'If you wouldn't mind.'

The dean sighed again, sat down in front of his laptop and glared at it for a moment before tapping some keys. There was a lot more glaring, sighing and tapping over the next few minutes. Greg was left with a clear impression that the cleric's reluctance had a lot more to do with his lack of familiarity with the workings of the database than it did with his busy schedule. Greg and Jim sat on, patient and silent, succumbing only once to the temptation to exchange an eloquent glance.

At last, he looked up from his struggles. 'There were three retired clergy in the area who are recorded as having offered their services to the Flegg churches and indeed, in one instance, to the Bure to Yare Benefice as well. They were Inskip, Lloyd and Goddard. Inskip has since fully retired and is recorded as living in a church-sponsored care home in Ipswich. Goddard died two years ago. Lloyd is still in this area, and as I understand it, volunteers with a charity for the homeless in Great Yarmouth. That's the lot, I'm afraid.'

'Perhaps you could let us have their contact details and addresses,' suggested Greg. 'Do you know either of these men?'

'A little,' said the dean. 'Mr Inskip is in his eighties now, and I'm sure I've met him a couple of times at least. I know Lloyd a little better. He retired quite early from an inner-city parish. In the Midlands, I think. Quite a stressful posting I believe. But he seems to have taken on the visiting role with some enthusiasm. He was a volunteer chaplain at the local hospital for a while, as well as assisting Mr Thurlow. According to my spreadsheet, he's working with the homeless, as I said.'

'Thank you for your assistance,' said Greg, rising to his feet. 'DI Henning here will take down the contact details. Jim, I'll see you outside in a moment.'

When Jim joined him in the car park, Greg was leaning on his car, his phone pressed to his ear.

'Thanks, Chris,' he said. 'We'll follow that up.' Then rang off as he spotted Jim approaching.

'Got those addresses?' he asked.

'Yes, no problem,' said Jim. 'Are we headed there now?'

'In the light of what I've just been told, I think we need to divert via the mortuary,' replied Greg. 'It seems Dr Paisley has something to tell us.'

13

Postmortems

Slightly to Greg's and Jim's surprise, Ned was waiting for them along with Dr Paisley when they arrived at the mortuary.

'This has been a joint effort,' said the doctor briskly. 'Come on through and I'll explain what I mean.'

They followed Dr Paisley through the swing doors, and both covered their faces in an involuntary gesture as the smell hit them. It wasn't the worst Greg had experienced, but he reckoned it was up there in the top twenty.

'Greg, meet our new forensic anthropology team,' said Dr Paisley, oblivious to the stench and waving to a couple in white coats perched on stools by the furthest table. Drs Tobias Blackwood and Harper Vaughn, both from Cranfield, in accordance with the new contract for forensic anthropology.'

A plump man with a goatee beard stepped forwards, holding his hand out. 'Toby is fine,' he said, and Greg had to hide a grin, as the man's resemblance to a Toby jug was marked.

'And I'm Harper,' said the dazzling apparition by his side. She had long blonde hair tied up in ponytail, but that was without a doubt the last time Greg was to think of a horse in her vicinity. Her face was a perfect oval and perfectly symmetrical, while her white coat bulged in all the right places and was the shortest Greg had ever seen, revealing long, bare, tanned legs that were undoubtedly raising his blood pressure. Memories of their predecessors, George and Mildred, faded into mist and blew away. Dr Paisley coughed, and Greg realised his jaw had dropped. He shook Harper's hand hurriedly and closed his mouth as Dr Paisley bent a sardonic gaze in his direction.

'Now that introductions are over,' she said drily, 'perhaps we can get on with hearing their conclusions.'

'Oh. Yes,' said Greg. 'Good. Yes. Right.' He realised he was making an idiot of himself and turned to the Toby jug with relief. He also realised that Harper was well used to men reacting like that in her vicinity, and that it made no more impression than a gnat bite. He stamped, mentally, on his hormones and concentrated on what he was being told.

The sight of the body on the table brought him sharply down to earth. It was mostly skeletonised, but not quite.

'Not great, I know,' said Dr Paisley, noting their recoil. 'Toby and Harper had the worst job though, recovering the bones. The body had pretty much liquefied, except for the fragments of flesh still adhering to the bones, as you see.'

'Teeth and nails have, of course, begun to fall out, but we recovered all the teeth, as far as we know.' Toby took up the narrative. 'This means that there's not a lot for us to work on as regards cause of death, and we've relied heavily on Ned's observations added to our own at the scene, and the photographs his team took.

'As far as time of death is concerned, Dr Paisley and I agree on at least a couple of weeks ago, probably not a lot longer than that.'

'Which fits with the evidence from the lady who found the body,' interrupted Jim.

'Quite,' said the Toby jug, with slightly obvious patience. 'It's a woman, aged between forty and sixty, a little dental work, but not a lot. A few of the teeth we've recovered had been filled. Perhaps that might help with ID, and we've got DNA samples we can use for comparison if you can identify a possible victim.'

'And the cause of death?' prompted Greg, as Toby seemed to have gone off track.

'Oh yes. As I was about to say before I was interrupted, this was a bit of a conundrum. There are some marks on the lower tibia that we're pretty certain are down to animal interference. We also found damage to the right knee consistent with a hard blow by a blunt object at or immediately before the time of death. But neither would have caused her death. And then Harper here came up with an interesting theory. I'll let her explain.'

'It's the position of the body in the ditch that gave me the clue,' she explained. 'She was found face down in the ditch with her torso and legs higher than her head. The ditch was dry, and given the weather we have been having, it would have been dry when she fell into it, or was propelled into it, so it's unlikely she drowned. I think she died because, in that position, she couldn't breathe properly. She would have lost consciousness quite quickly, and after that, without assistance, death was inevitable. In other words, the most likely cause of death was postural asphyxia.'

Greg switched his gaze to Dr Paisley, who nodded. 'It's consistent with Ned's observations too,' she said.

Ned stepped forwards. 'If I'm reading the signs at the side of the road correctly, she was hit forcibly by a vehicle, so hard that the collision propelled her off the bike and over the verge until she ended face down in the ditch, with her torso and legs higher than her head, as Dr Vaughn has said. There are some marks in the vegetation that suggest she rolled after she left the bike. The bike ended up on its side on the verge and then was picked up and thrown on top of her. There's also what looks like a tyre mark on the very edge of the verge.'

'Fingerprints on the bike?' asked Greg.

'One set of prints all over the handlebars, which are probably the victim's,' answered Ned. 'Some blurred marks on the frame that probably belong to a perpetrator wearing gloves.'

'What sort of vehicle are we looking for?' asked Jim.

'Nothing low slung and sporty,' said Ned. 'Whatever hit the bike had a fairly high, sturdy bonnet, like a small van or a four-by-four. The tyre mark, such as it is, supports that too.'

'If someone had helped her out of the ditch, she would have survived?' asked Greg.

'Correct,' said Dr Paisley. 'Now, come and look at our second victim. Thank you, Toby and Harper,' she added. Leading the way to the second, occupied, table, she pulled back the sheet. Greg and Jim approached with caution as the two anthropologists turned to leave.

'We'll be in the office, writing up our report,' said Toby over his shoulder. 'When you've finished here, perhaps we could get to know each other a little, since we're likely to be working together a good bit. How about lunch in the canteen? If you have the time...'

Greg glanced at Harper's legs again and decided that they probably had time.

The body on the second table was blackened, and there had clearly been a lot of insect activity, not to mention fish.

'I hope you have your Vicks handy,' said Dr Paisley, noting their recoil, although she herself seemed largely unaffected by the aromas.

Greg wondered if a pathologist's sense of smell became stultified by frequent exposure to decomposition or if they, as a breed, just had deficient olfactory capabilities. He thought the latter would be a convenient adaptation.

'This is the body that was found caught in a bed of reeds in the river near Martham,' said the doctor. 'I originally did this postmortem on the eighth of September and the body would normally have been moved on by now, but there was some hold-up on identification, and as it turns out, that was lucky. You see, there are some disturbing similarities...'

'Do you still need me?' asked Ned. 'Because if not, I should be getting on.'

'I'll catch up with you later,' promised Greg. 'Thank you.'

'This one is male,' continued Dr Paisley, dragging their attention back to the body. 'A little older than the other, probably late sixties to seventies. As you know, decomposition is slower in water than on land, but even so, I think this victim had been in the river for less than a week. Plenty of time for the gases to bring him to the surface, but not long enough for the skin to slip completely.

'This man was hit on the right side, hard enough to produce damage I can see in the remaining tissues here and here' – she pointed – 'but close enough to death that there is little bruising. He also acquired three broken ribs and a broken wrist on the left side, plus a blow to the right side of his head. But none of these were the ultimate cause of death. From examination of his lungs, I'd say he drowned in the river. The water in the lung tissue is consistent with river water.'

'Why trauma on both sides?' speculated Greg.

'That's a question for you, detective,' replied the doctor. 'But if it was me, I'd be looking for a place where a low wall divides a road from the river. The injuries are consistent with a cyclist being hit by a car and knocked into a wall, before falling into the river. Of course, the fall into the river could have been a separate incident, but it was close in time to the other injuries, so perhaps not. You already know the victim was wearing bicycle clips.'

'You mentioned a problem with identification?' said Jim, looking into the tray containing minimal belongings. 'Odd there's no house keys, or money.'

'No ID at all on the body. Nothing other than what you see,' replied the doctor. 'A reusable cigarette lighter but no cigarettes, a pencil and that notebook, but all it contains are what look like measurements in inches. There is some dental work, which might help. But what's bothering me is the similarity between the two cases. Two cyclists, apparently killed by exceptionally ruthless hit-and-run drivers. And within days of each other.'

Greg looked up sharply. 'Thank you, Doctor. We have a couple of missing persons who might match these details. We'll check those out asap.'

Back in the car park, Greg got out his phone. 'We might need another chat with that waterman,' he said. 'He was pretty accurate on where the body would end up after it was spotted near Martham. Perhaps he can tell us where it came from. Where is the source of the Thurne anyway?'

'The source is sometimes described as being a small brick pump house between Horsey and West Somerton, but, in fact, it gets water from all sorts of places: Martham Broad, Horsey Mere and Hickling Broad to name but three. But I don't think we'll need the waterman's expertise this time,' replied Jim. 'I can think of one place straightaway that matches the doc's description of a low wall between a road and the river, and that's the old bridge at Potter Heigham.'

'Surely that's in the wrong direction,' objected Greg. 'If the river rises in the northeast, it's flowing the other way.'

'You're forgetting the tides,' said Jim. 'At high tide the water comes under that bridge at Potter Heigham at a rate of knots. It could easily carry a body upriver.'

'I asked Jill to look for the bike,' said Greg. 'Point her at that bridge, will you. And Chris has just texted me again. Our man from Martham Broad is almost certainly a Mr Phil Saunders from Potter Heigham, and if he was on his way home, it's entirely plausible he entered the river from that bridge.'

Greg checked his watch. 'I think we'll leave interviewing our elderly clergymen until tomorrow, starting with Mr Lloyd. Can you—' He was interrupted by his phone buzzing. 'It's Chris again. Can you give me a minute, Jim.'

Chris was already in full flow when he turned his attention back to his phone.

'...so I think we have a major problem brewing,' she said.

'Whoa, hold on, Chris. I missed the beginning of your sentence. What's a problem?'

'The missing cyclists. Weren't you listening? I thought you'd just been to the mortuary. I agree with the doc. It's looking very much as though two of our missing cyclists have turned up dead after a hit and run, with some evidence that both incidents were deliberate. We have at least three more missing persons that fit the pattern, and a heap of cyclist mortality that bucks the trends of other counties. I think we have someone out there targeting cyclists.'

14

Next day: 12 September 2020

Greg surveyed his team, gathered for an early start in the incident room. Chris and Jim sat near the whiteboards at the end of the room. Ned and his deputy, Yvonne, lurked at the back behind Jill, Steve, Bill and Jenny.

'Thanks for coming in early,' he started. 'I think you are all aware of at least some of the recent developments, but the point of this morning is to make sure everyone is on the same page. We need to decide how we divide our resources, since it looks as though we have two major murder enquiries on our hands.'

He was interrupted by the door opening behind him, and Margaret entered the room.

'Just got your message,' she said. 'Sorry I'm late. Don't mind me, I'll just sit in.' She headed for the back row, where Steve leaped to his feet to offer his seat. 'Thank you,' she said, settling herself down and fluffing her hair with one hand. 'OK. Please do carry on, Greg.'

Steve perched himself on the table behind him, and picked up his mug again, being careful to hide the inscription he felt unsuitable for the eyes of a chief superintendent – *I used to fart to hide the cough, now I cough to hide the fart* – in the palm of his broad hand.

'OK,' said Greg, picking up the thread. 'I'm going to take the historic case first.

'We've now ID'd the third Ormesby body as Frederick Hamilton, husband of the elder Joanne Hamilton. He died around ten years ago, which would make it 2010, and was buried in the garden in a shallow grave under a patch of lawn. At around the same time, some materials were hidden under the concrete floor of the garage. These included fragments of fabric that appear to be clothing that would be worn by a clergyman, and a knife. Both carry DNA traces that are matches for Frederick Hamilton and another, distinct DNA source. The creation of this cache of materials is dated to the weekend of the seventh to the ninth of May 2010, fixed by the date when the floor was first hard-cored then concreted over. A further void was found near the doorway from the garage to the hall, and this contained a Bible which also carries the same DNA as the bloodied clothing and the knife.

'Joanne Hamilton says her mother was "Anglican if anything". Clearly this doesn't rule out other denominations, but we've prioritised exploring the C of E link and spoken to the vicar who was in Ormesby in 2010. He's not looking promising, and was happy to let us have a DNA sample, so it should be easy to rule him out. We still have leads to a couple of retired clergymen who helped him out at that time, and interviewing them is our next step. If they can also be ruled out, we'll have to spread our net wider.'

Margaret coughed to indicate her desire to chip in. 'If that's the case, we may need to reconsider handing this one over to the cold-case team,' she said, 'depending, in part, on what you're about to tell us next.'

A stubborn expression passed over Greg's face, but he forbore to comment. 'I'll come back to resource allocation at the end,' he said. 'Now let's turn to the most recent case. I'll let Chris bring you up to speed with the data.'

Chris briefed swiftly on the statistical data relating to accidents and deaths involving cyclists, the comparison between Norfolk and other counties, as well as between the current year and previous years. There was a little shuffling of bums on seats, as those not in the know wondered where this was going.

'You're wondering why I'm boring you with this,' concluded Chris correctly. 'I'll tell you.' She stuck a photograph at the top of an empty whiteboard.

'This is Ann Cooper, aged sixty-three, reported as missing by her neighbours on the second of September. They said she regularly went out for a bike ride, and her bike was missing, so they thought she'd failed to return from a ride. However, they weren't certain when they'd last seen her. No further action was taken.'

She added a second photograph, clearly taken in a mortuary, of a body in an advanced state of decomposition. 'This body, which I shall call Body A, is of a woman, found a couple of days ago, face down in a ditch on one of Ann Cooper's regular cycling routes, by a dog walker. Or to be more specific, by the dog. The dog walker hadn't walked that route since August but had driven down it on the fourth of September and remembers noticing a bike in the ditch as she drove past.

'There is evidence that Body A had been hit hard by a van or four-by-four, knocked across the verge and into the ditch. The bike was dropped on top of her – it didn't get there by accident. The doc says she died at least ten to twelve days ago and thinks she died of postural asphyxia. No accident reported. No CCTV in the area. It's a quiet lane with, at the moment, little passing traffic.

'Then there's this man.' A third photograph went up on the board. 'Philip, or Phil, Saunders, aged seventy, but still working as a self-employed carpenter. He was reported missing on the sixth of September by his next-door neighbour when she became concerned about his dog, apparently abandoned without food or water, very much contrary to his normal practice.' Chris glanced at Jenny. 'Jenny was involved in rescuing the dog, I believe. The last known sighting of Saunders was at a cottage in Repps, where he'd been hanging some doors. According to the householder, he set off home to Potter Heigham on his bike, after dark, on the third of September.

'On the seventh of September a body was reported to be floating in the River Thurne. Jenny and Turbo were deployed to assist in the search, but Turbo wasn't needed because a local man knew where flotsam and jetsam tended to wash up, and sure enough, Body B, the body of an elderly man, was recovered from a bed of reeds and taken to the mortuary. As it happens, the same mortuary as Body A. As Jenny had observed, Body B was wearing cycling clips, although no bike has been found. The doc reckons he had been dead a little less than a week and the cause of death was drowning in the river. But Body B also has the beginnings of bruising on the right side and a head injury plus broken ribs and wrist on the left side, consistent with a cyclist being struck by a high-bonneted vehicle and knocked sideways into a solid obstacle, like a wall, before falling or being pushed into a river. And as Jim pointed out, the old bridge at Potter Heigham fits the bill for this incident. At high tide anything entering the river at the bridge would be carried along the Thurne to the reedbed where Body B was found.

'In other words, we have two bodies in the morgue which, while not yet definitively identified, show every sign of being the bodies of Ann Cooper and Philip Saunders. The doc spotted some similarities between the two deaths. She is concerned that both appear to have been killed by a hit-and-run driver who subsequently concealed their bodies and/or their bikes.' Chris paused before she added, 'And we have at least four other cyclists missing from this area. One of them went missing only two days ago.'

Greg stepped in before questions could erupt. 'Your theory is that someone driving a four-by-four, van or similar is targeting cyclists, knocking them off their bikes, concealing their bodies and leaving them to die?'

'Yes,' said Chris. 'Exactly that.'

Jill had her hand up. 'If true, why hasn't this come to light sooner?' she asked.

'Because standard procedures don't call for much action on missing persons unless they are children or vulnerable in some other way or have been missing for a long time.

Sometimes not even then. When the missing person is a fully functioning adult, they're assumed just to have exercised their right to self-determination and taken themselves off somewhere. Unless a relative makes a lot of fuss. All the missing persons we have on record are just that – recorded then forgotten about,' responded Chris.

Steve was waving his hand in turn. 'Couldn't these two cases just be accidents?' he asked. 'Just hit and runs by someone, not even necessarily the same someone, who hit a cyclist and then legged it because they didn't want to get into trouble? Not nice, and almost certainly death by dangerous driving, but not murder, which I think is what you're suggesting.'

Ned cleared his throat and stood up at the back. 'Possible,' he said. 'But I don't think so. It doesn't fit the evidence for Body A nor our preliminary findings at Potter Heigham bridge. Specifically, the angle and speed at which the vehicle hit the cyclist, and the likelihood it's the same vehicle or type of vehicle. If these were accidents, you'd expect the angle to be much shallower and the vehicle to be braking. There's no sign of that in either location. And by the law of probabilities, you'd expect different makes and models of car to be involved.'

'I didn't know you'd been to the bridge,' exclaimed Jim. 'That's quick work.'

'I've a team there now,' said Ned. 'As soon as I got your heads-up last night, I organised to go there at first light. This is only a preliminary conclusion, as I said, but it does look as though Body B entered the river from that bridge. I'll have more detail later today.'

'The other thing that's bothering me,' chipped in Bill, 'is why didn't anyone spot Body A sooner? Not to put too fine a point on it, it must have been stinking that road something shocking for at least a week.'

'It's a question we need to ask neighbours,' agreed Jill. 'It's described as a quiet road, so maybe there weren't many people going down it. And maybe those who did, didn't want to get too close to what they may have thought was a dead animal. But there's not much point speculating. We need to ask the questions.'

Greg clapped his hands together to get their attention. 'OK, folks. The first thing we need to do is finalise the identification of Bodies A and B. Jill, can you chase that up? DNA from homes to compare, neighbours, family or friends to identify property, belongings, clothes etc – you know the drill. If you could combine that with getting some help from uniform with a door-to-door, that would be great.

'Second, we need to follow up on the other missing cyclist cases Chris has identified. Have any turned up since? For those still missing, where were they going? Has anyone searched their usual, favourite or intended routes, particularly any on quiet and unfrequented roads? Has there been any activity on phones or credit cards? Let's see if we can narrow down the current list to any that are a particular worry.

'The vehicle. We don't have much to go on yet but is there any CCTV that might show any common vehicle movements between the Potter Heigham bridge and the lane where Body A was found? Have any local garages been fixing a van or four-by-four with the sort of damage you might get after hitting several bikes? Bill and Steve, you get started on the missing cyclists – Chris will point you in the right direction –

and get some civilian help scrutinising CCTV for the vehicle. Boss – you did say there might be some extra resource?

'Jim, I'd like you to oversee the activity on this case, reporting to me, and everyone to report their findings to Chris to collate.

'I'm going to go and interview our elderly clergymen and, while we still have Jenny, I'd like her to accompany me.'

Margaret stood up to leave. 'It's been very enlightening – I'm glad I sat in,' she said. 'Yes to the extra uniformed and civilian resource while you get a grip on the cyclist case. But, Greg, if nothing breaks soon on the Ormesby body, I think you should hand it off to cold cases and concentrate on the cyclists. When this gets out, it's going to be explosive. You have a week, then you need to see me.'

'No pressure then,' muttered Greg as she left the room. He beckoned to Jenny across the hubbub. 'We'd better get going,' he said.

15

Out and about

Waiting for Jenny in his car, Greg heard a ping on his phone. Text from Margaret. He grimaced as he scrolled.

Cold case is not an abandoned case. Just saying you need to prioritise. Ormesby 3 has been dead 10 years. Cyclists may be dying now.

He closed the phone. *She is right, of course. But I am so close. I can taste it.* He turned sharply as Jenny got into the car.

'OK,' he said. 'We'll be off then.'

'To Yarmouth, is it?' she asked.

'Yes. Our Mr Lloyd lives in a semi not far from Lawns Avenue.'

'Handy for the magistrates' court then,' she replied. 'If he turns out to be the guilty party, that is.'

'True. We're going to go in softly on this, Jenny. We have no evidence he *is* directly involved, so our first questions need to be about Mrs Hamilton and whether he knew her. If he did, we can be more probing about their relationship, and we will, in any event, ask if he's willing to provide a DNA sample. It's important you watch his reactions carefully. If he was involved with the death, this may be something he's been dreading for ten years.'

'Is he expecting us?' asked Jenny.

'Yes. The office rang him this morning to check he'd be in. But as far he knows, this is a general enquiry relating to the homeless charity he's working for.'

They parked the car two or three doors away from their destination, then got out and looked around them.

'Nice quiet street, not particularly wealthy neighbourhood,' was Greg's summation as they walked towards No 5 and rang the doorbell.

The man who stood on his doorstep, blinking at them in the strong morning sun, looked every one of his seventy-two years. What hair remained was grey, matching exactly his grey shirt and grey trousers, and he had a pronounced stoop. The hand he held out to them shook a little, but his smile was warm.

'Come in, come in,' he said in a friendly voice that still held a trace of his Welsh roots. 'The kettle's just boiled. Perhaps you'd like a cup of tea, or coffee?'

Greg and Jenny put away the warrant cards they'd been holding out and followed Mr Lloyd through a dark hall into a sunlit sitting room. It was plainly furnished with age-worn G-Plan furniture. The sofa cushions had seen better days, but the rest of the suite and the accompanying tables and cabinets were a testimony to the longevity of 1950s design.

Having taken their orders for one tea, milk one sugar, and coffee, black no sugar, Mr Lloyd bustled away to come back in short order with three mugs clutched precariously in one hand and a plate of biscuits in the other. He surmounted the challenge of putting everything down without spillage with some difficulty, then sat in the chair opposite the sofa.

'Sit down, do,' he said. 'How can I help? I hope none of our chaps have got themselves into trouble. Or at least,' he amended with a rueful grin, 'no more trouble than usual.'

'It's a problem a bit further away, and a bit longer ago that we need your help with,' said Greg. 'By the way, do you mind if Constable Warren here takes notes? I find it helpful.'

'That's fine,' said Mr Lloyd. 'But I don't yet understand why you're here.'

'I'd like you to cast your mind back to 2010 and your time in Ormesby,' replied Greg. 'Perhaps you could start by explaining how you came to be there.'

'That's going back a bit,' said Mr Lloyd, taking a sip of his tea. Greg noticed that the hand holding the cup had a pronounced shake.

'I came to Norfolk when I retired from a living in Stoke-on-Trent. It was a big, inner-city parish in Hanley. One of the five towns of the Potteries, you know,' he added. 'I think I arrived in Norfolk in 2005.'

'You must have been quite young to retire,' said Greg. 'I thought parish priests went on forever. Judging by the age of your archbishops, anyway.'

'I did retire early,' admitted Mr Lloyd. 'I found my ministry in Hanley very stressful. Some of the parishioners were delightful, don't get me wrong,' he said hurriedly. 'But there was a difficult crowd of lads. They weren't churchgoers, but something I did got their backs up, and they targeted me. They made my life a misery, to be blunt. And it wasn't getting any better. In fact, their actions were escalating, and I thought someone was going to be injured, or even killed if they went on the way they were going. Of course, the more I tried to tackle them, the worse it got and, in the end, I had a breakdown.'

Even the recollection was visibly disturbing the old man, now almost crouching in the chair across the coffee table from them. Jenny was beginning to feel guilty about worrying him, when Greg said, 'I'm sorry to remind you of upsetting times. You came to Norfolk, then, for a break?'

'Yes,' said Mr Lloyd on a deep breath. 'It was considered I should retire on health grounds, and a quiet, rural location was recommended. A friend had links to Norfolk and suggested that not only was it a quiet place, but also a cheaper place to live. Rents and so on. So I moved to Ormesby in the first instance, then later to here.'

'It was Ormesby I wanted to ask you about,' said Greg, leaping on the opening. 'Did you move there in 2005?'

'Yes, that's right,' replied Mr Lloyd.

'And I gather that when you were there, you helped out with things like hospital visiting and so on, although not with church services.'

'Yes, that's right,' said Mr Lloyd again. 'To be honest, my faith had taken a bit of a knock in Hanley. I didn't feel certain enough of what I believed to be advocating it from a pulpit. But my wish to help other people hadn't diminished. Visiting those who were sick or in trouble was something I could manage and it made me feel useful. Later, when I moved here, I started to volunteer with the homeless, and I still do what I can.'

'When did you leave Ormesby?' asked Greg.

'I'm not sure exactly,' said Mr Lloyd. 'It must have been around, now let me see, around 2009, I think.'

'The clergyman who had the living in Ormesby in 2010, Mr Thurlow, says you were still helping him then,' said Greg. Jenny was watching their subject closely, but as far as she could see neither his expression nor the shaking changed noticeably.

'Well, if Roy Thurlow says I was there then, I probably was,' said Mr Lloyd. 'He's bound to be right. I'd need to look up when I moved here to be sure.'

'We might ask you to do that,' said Greg. 'Just to be clear on dates. But when you were in Ormesby, did you know a Mrs Joanne Hamilton? She lived in a bungalow in the centre of the village. Near the village hall.'

'Gosh! Asking me to remember one name from ten years ago is asking a lot,' said Mr Lloyd. 'I acted as one of the hospital chaplains as well as visiting parishioners in their homes. Joanne...? What was it?'

'Hamilton,' said Greg. 'I thought the name might have been brought to your mind recently because of the press reports about a body found in Ormesby. I think there's been quite a lot about it on the news. Did you know Joanne Hamilton?' he asked again.

'I don't think so, no,' said Mr Lloyd. 'It doesn't ring any bells, I'm afraid.' He looked Greg in the face, then his gaze fell sideways to the coffee table. 'More coffee?' he asked.

'No thank you,' said Greg. 'But I would be grateful if you could look up when you moved here. If it isn't too much trouble.'

Mr Lloyd hesitated a moment, then got up and headed towards one of the cabinets. He stumbled slightly as he made his way across the room, and Greg half rose. But the elderly man recovered himself and pulled open a drawer. There were a number of cardboard folders in it, and after some shuffling of them, he selected one. Back in his seat, he went through the chosen folder, and after a moment pulled out several sheets of paper stapled together.

'My original rental agreement on this house,' he said. 'You'll see it's dated September 2010.'

Greg took it off him and checked the date. 'That's fine,' he said. 'Just one other thing. Do you mind if we take a DNA sample, just for elimination? It's a very simple procedure, quite painless. We just—'

'I know how it's done, but no thank you,' said Mr Lloyd firmly. 'You have nothing to exclude me from, so I see no reason to give you a sample. Now, if you don't mind, I have things I need to be getting on with. I need to be getting off to work.' He stood up, and started pushing papers, rather randomly, into a briefcase.

Greg watched for a long moment, then stood to leave. 'Thank you for your time, Mr Lloyd,' he said. 'We may have some other questions in due course, but that's all for now. Thank you for the coffee too.'

Out in the car again, Greg looked at Jenny. 'Thoughts?' he asked.

'I don't know what to think,' she said. 'Is the refusal to give a DNA sample suspicious? I don't want to think it's him; I thought he was a kind, very genuine old boy. But I did think he was lying when he said he didn't know Joanne Hamilton. He denied it a couple of times and looked away when he said so. And at the very least, he must have seen some of the stuff in the media recently.'

'He moved from Ormesby not long after Fred Hamilton died, according to the evidence from when that garage floor was laid,' said Greg reflectively. 'But to play devil's advocate, I suppose we can't assume his reluctance to give a sample is evidence of guilt. But I agree with you about the lie. Hold on, here he comes now.'

They watched as the old man in grey came out of the front door of No 5 and headed down the garden path, then turned right towards the roundabout on the road near the racecourse. Reaching that, he turned left and walked briskly out of their sight, in the direction of the busy Lawnswood Avenue.

Jenny had twisted in her seat. 'He's left his front door open,' she said. 'That's odd.'

Greg started the car. 'Let's see where he's going,' he said.

By the time Greg turned the car left, Mr Lloyd was more than halfway towards the junction with the main thoroughfare into Great Yarmouth. There was the occasional stumble as he walked, but his pace was rapid and his hands were empty.

'I'm getting a bad feeling about this,' muttered Greg, and the powerful car suddenly surged forwards as he hit the accelerator. The car and Mr Lloyd reached the junction at roughly the same time, just as a heavily loaded oil tanker came into view, heading towards town. After that, everything seemed to happen at once. Greg performed an emergency stop, Mr Lloyd stepped forwards, Jenny wrenched the passenger door open and almost fell out of the car as the air was rent by the simultaneous sound of an air horn and heavy-duty hydraulic brakes.

16

Getting started – Wymondham: 12 September

Jim checked his notes and looked round the room. Chris was already deep in her spreadsheets with Steve and Bill. *They'll be OK for a minute.* He went over to where Jill was having a quick word with Jenny.

'Isn't the boss waiting for you?' he said pointedly to Jenny.

'Damn. Yes. I'm off. I was just passing some contact details to Jill for Phil Saunders's neighbour. I'm off now.' She waved a goodbye as she headed for the door.

'I'll start with…' said Jill, then realised she was talking to a deaf ear, as Jim had his phone pressed to the other one.

'That's good,' he said. 'Thanks for that.' Ringing off he turned to Jill again. 'We've got two uniforms to help with the house-to-house, and it's the same two that responded to the call-out when Body A was found, so at least they have some background in the case. Give me a minute to update Chris, and I'll be with you.'

'While you do that, I'll brief our civilian assistants on getting hold of the CCTV footage and what to look for,' replied Jill.

On the other side of the room, Steve and Bill were cheering up as it became apparent their task was more action and less computer-based than they'd feared.

'Chris, how're you getting home now Greg has shot off?' asked Jim. 'I take it you're not driving yet.'

'Not yet, no,' said Chris. 'It's a bugger, but on the other hand, I'm not going anywhere at the moment. I've just agreed with Steve and Bill that I'll prioritise the missing cyclists to follow up, and they'll do the legwork.'

'The area we're focussing on isn't a million miles from the boss's gaff,' added Steve, 'so one of us can drop Chris home when she's ready.'

'But are you OK?' asked Jim. 'I understand the pressures, but I'll never hear the last of it if you overdo things. I thought you were supposed to be easing yourself back by working from home.'

'Bollocks to that,' said Chris inelegantly. 'This is the most alive I've felt since that nutter whopped me over the head with his shillelagh.'

'I thought it was a cricket bat,' said Jim.

'Whatever,' said Chris. 'Don't fuss, Jim. I'm fine.'

'What about…?' Jim nodded significantly at Chris's middle.

'My little stranger?' she responded. 'I don't think you need to be so discreet, Jim. I'm sure the whole station knows. It's fine. If I'm happy, he, she or it is happy. Now get on and leave me to do the same.'

She turned back. 'Right, you two. This is what I think we need to do first. As I said, there are at least four recently missing cyclists on our books. I think we should start with those, before we go further back in our dataset. They are, in date order:

'Ben Lyell – twenty-five-year-old father of two. Went missing on the fifteenth of August. Last seen at his workplace in Wroxham. Never got home at the end of the day.

'Carol Hodds, fifty-two, assistant at a care home in Rollesby. Lives alone. Was reported missing when she failed to turn up for work on the eighteenth of August.

'Shirley Crabtree – not *the* Shirley Crabtree, the wrestler,' she added.

'You into women's wrestling, ma'am?' asked Steve with a bemused expression.

'Not women's wrestling, men's,' replied Chris. 'You know, Big Daddy. Oh, never mind. Google it. And since when have I been "ma'am"?'

'Since you got promoted and stopped being sarge, ma'am,' said Bill.

'Well drop it. Boss will do. Anyway, back to Shirley, aged forty-eight, reported missing by her husband when she failed to return home from what he called an exercise ride. And finally,

'Kain Smith, twenty-three, set off on a bike ride, supposedly with his mate Lucas Willis, on the tenth of September, only Lucas says he cried off because rain was forecast. Reported missing by his mother yesterday, after he failed to come home from what she assumed was a night's clubbing with Lucas.

'There could be other reasons for any of these folk to have gone missing, but they fit the emerging profile. Start with

Lyell, and work your way forward. Report to me when you have any answers. Here're the addresses and contact details for the relatives or whoever reported them missing.

'What're you waiting for,' she demanded rhetorically, and they made themselves scarce.

'God, I've missed this,' she said aloud, and turned back to her spreadsheets and phone.

Jill had already settled her two assistants in front of a large map pinned to the wall. One male, one female, one fair and stout, the other dark and skinny, they were both staring earnestly at where Jill was pointing.

'You'll have already noticed that the main road linking our two locations, here and here' – she pointed at Potter Heigham and St Michael – 'where the two bodies were found, is the A149. There are lots of cameras on that road even though there are none either on the old bridge or the side road where Body A was found. So start with the A149. There's a good chance our vehicle moved along it at some point. If you find anything of interest, branch out onto other roads where camera coverage is good, for example the A1062 and the A1064, and see if you can trace it to a particular location. Then we can get the foot soldiers to follow up. You have the key dates and the vehicle description.'

'Such as it is,' muttered Fair-and-Stout.

'Clear?' Jill asked, and they both nodded. 'Good. I'll leave you to it for now. Ring me if you find anything particularly interesting, otherwise I'll catch up with you at the end of the day.' Jill turned to find Jim behind her.

'OK?' he asked.

'All good. Do you want me to start on the house-to-house, or with the IDs?' she asked.

'Can you organise the house-to-house near Ann Cooper's place first? Then see who or what you can pick up that will assist in her ID while you're at it. I'll go for a chat with Phil Saunders's neighbour. Ring if you need me.'

Tina Booth was a bit flustered to find a burly detective inspector on her doorstep, but Jim's local burr soon put her at her ease.

'I'm sorry to bother you,' he said again, once ensconced in a comfortable old armchair by the window, a mug of tea in front of him and a generous plateful of homemade shortbread by his side. 'This shortbread is wonderful by the way,' he said. 'Much better than the bought stuff. However, to work. I gather I'm lucky to have caught you in.'

'I do volunteer in a community cafe,' she said, neglecting to mention that the admired shortbread had, in fact, been baked by the cafe's chef. 'But not today. How can I help? Have you found Phil?'

'We think we've found him,' said Jim. 'But I'm sorry to say it's bad news. We found a body in the river that we think is him. I'm sorry. Were you close?' he asked as the lady opposite him wiped away a tear.

'Not really,' she said, sniffing. 'I'm sorry, I'm being silly. We were good neighbours, but no more than that. We usually only saw each other in passing. I'm sorry about the little dog though. She and Phil were inseparable when he wasn't working. It was lovely watching her greet him when he came home. What will happen to her?'

'I'm afraid I don't know,' said Jim. 'But of course we don't yet know for sure that the body we have is Phil. That's where I was hoping for help from you. Do you know if he had any relatives? It's clear that he lived alone next door, and we haven't been able to find any address book or letters that might give us a clue.'

'I think he had a son in Australia,' said Tina. 'I'm sure he mentioned a son. But I don't think they had any contact with each other.'

'If that's so, then we'll need to contact the son. He'll be next of kin, assuming there's no wife anywhere,' said Jim.

'I think his wife died,' said Tina, taking some shortbread for herself. 'It was before my time here, but the lady I bought this place off said she'd been to the wife's funeral. The son didn't come over for it. I remember her being a bit shocked about that.'

'Do you know how long ago that was?' asked Jim.

'The funeral? At least eight years, because I've been here that long.'

'We can check official records for the wife and son,' said Jim. 'But it doesn't sound as though any relatives are easily contactable. This is a difficult thing to ask you, Mrs Booth, but would you be able to help us with the identification of the body? Maybe just to rule Phil Saunders in or out? I'm going to have a look round his house for anything that might give us a DNA sample, but DNA analysis takes time, and you could help too, if you were willing.'

Tina swallowed her shortbread in a hurry, and asked, 'Do I have to look at a dead body?'

'Possibly not,' said Jim. 'I would ask you, in the first instance, to look at the clothes and tell me if you think they were Phil's. Are you willing to help?'

'I'll help if I can,' she said rather uncertainly. 'But I'm not sure I'm up to looking at a body. Won't it be...' She paused while she sought for an appropriate term, then settled for '...a bit nasty?'

'Let's see how we get on with the clothes first,' said Jim. 'If you're willing to come with me now, you go and get your coat on while I take a look round next door. Then I'll come back and drive you into Norwich. That sound OK?'

It didn't take Jim long to find both a used toothbrush and a hairbrush with hair still in it. He bagged both, then turned his attention to an old bureau. As he'd expected, this was where Phil Saunders, carpenter, kept his paperwork. There was a neat file of invoices, most of them marked 'paid', and a pile of notebooks which, on a quick flick through, seemed to contain details of various jobs. Another file contained a dog's vaccination certificate and microchip details. Phil seemed to take his ownership of Jessy seriously, which fitted with what Jim had been told. He made a mental note to tell Jenny she'd need to let the RSPCA know if Phil was confirmed as Body B, then picked up his evidence bags and locked the door behind him. He stripped his plastic gloves off then knocked again on Mrs Booth's front door. It opened immediately to reveal the lady ready for travel in a neat brown jacket and clutching a brown handbag.

'I'm a bit nervous about this,' she confessed as he settled her in his car.

'That's normal,' he said. 'But don't worry too much. I'll be with you every step of the way and you can just say if anything is too much for you.'

When they arrived at the mortuary, the staff were ready for them. The curtains were drawn on the viewing room, and the clothes they had removed from Body B were laid out on a table.

'Take your time,' said Jim. 'And take a good look. But don't touch anything.' His warning was unnecessary, as Tina Booth approached the table with extreme caution, her hands clutching her handbag behind her back.

She moved fairly swiftly past a dark jacket and work trousers, then paused to look closely at the left trouser leg, where Jim could see a white mark on the cuff. She moved on to a red-and-green checked shirt with short sleeves and paused again, then turned to Jim with decision made.

'I think they're Phil's clothes,' she said. 'He got paint on his new work trousers the first time he wore them, and I remember commiserating with him. I think that's the white mark on his trousers there.' She pointed. 'And he had a shirt like that one. I've seen it on the washing line many times. He always hung it outside to save having to iron it. Or so he said.'

'Does that mean he *is* dead?' she asked. 'Did he drown? Was it an accident?'

'It looks as though it is Phil, and yes, the doctor thinks he drowned,' said Jim, hoping she wouldn't notice he hadn't answered the last question.

'I don't have to look at the body, do I?' said Tina. 'I really don't want to. I've only seen a dead body once and that was in a hospital. Quite different.'

'No, I don't think we need you to look at the body,' replied Jim. 'I think you've given us enough. I'll take you home now.'

On the phone to Chris after dropping Tina Booth off, he said, 'Obviously her evidence isn't definitive, but it's enough for us to work on now, and the DNA will confirm things later.'

Chris had barely put the phone down on Jim when it rang again. This time it was Steve.

'I don't think the Lyell chap is one of ours,' he said. 'I called at his workplace in Wroxham. It's a greasy spoon where he was employed as a cook. I suspect he'd say chef but cook seems more accurate. Either way, he'd been sacked. According to the owner, he was given a month's notice the week before, but he was playing silly buggers and on the Friday he was late, slow and rude to a customer. She was on the verge of telling him not to bother to come in on the Saturday, but, instead, gave him a pep talk, pointing out that if he wanted a good reference he needed to buck his ideas up. He was late again Saturday morning, and she'd had enough, so she told him to collect his things and clear off.

'His wife didn't know about the sacking, and they have two youngsters, both under three, so she's tearing her hair out and alternating between thinking he's run off, or dead. At the moment, it's a fine line between which she'd prefer.'

'Why did his employer give him notice?' asked Chris.

'Too little work and too many overheads,' replied Steve.

'And his wife, were there stresses at home that might cause him to run off?'

'Apart from two small kids?' asked Steve. 'No, she says not. And I will say, there're photos of him with the kids all over the house.'

'Any activity on his credit cards?' asked Chris.

'As far as the wife knows, they only have the one on a shared account, and she says not. She says they have to be really careful with money and find just one credit card is safest. But I suppose he could have another she doesn't know about. He hadn't told her he'd been sacked.'

'Just to sum up,' said Chris. 'Here we have a young man who was effectively made redundant at short notice, has a wife plus two small children to support, no evidence of family disputes, no evidence of subsequent credit card usage and you think he's made it away on his toes with just a bike and his chef's whites? Doesn't that sound a bit shaky to you, Steve?'

'Put like that,' said Steve, his blush almost visible down the phone, 'well, yes, it does.'

'Go away and do some more work on this,' ordered Chris. 'At the moment it sounds more like a breakdown or a suicide than a runaway, but you definitely haven't excluded the possibility he is another victim of our cyclist killer.

'Have you spoken to neighbours? Or traced his route home? Or checked CCTV to see where he went that Saturday morning? What time did he leave the cafe?' she added.

'I'll get on to it, Boss,' promised Steve, and rang off before his blush became incandescent.

Chris put her phone down with a sigh, and leaned back in her chair, stretching. Backache seemed to be arriving to keep the little stranger company. She had a strong feeling that pregnancy had a few more downsides than she'd yet discovered. *Perhaps I should go to the antenatal classes.* She pushed the thought deep within her mind. Nearly as deep as she'd pushed the invitation in her handbag, so Greg wouldn't spot it.

She looked up as the phone rang again. Bill this time. Hoping it wasn't going to be another example of lazy investigation, she answered it.

'Can rule out Shirley Crabtree,' Bill began. 'She's turned up in a shelter for battered wives. Describes husband as controlling and bullying. So-called exercise rides were his idea, and he forced her to go on them, describing her as a fat slob. The bike rides were the last straw, and eventually she planned her escape, using the bike to get to the shelter and despatching her favourite clothes and jewellery to the same place via Royal Mail parcel service. Smart lady! She had the postman collect the parcel the morning that she left on the bike, while her husband was at work. She says he kept her too short of money for her to take a taxi, so she used his PayPal account to set up the delivery then she pedalled off on the bike. I think he's known all along what had happened but was too embarrassed to admit it.

'She's now suing for divorce and applying for jobs, so I don't think we need to worry about her, Boss.'

'Good, that's one less,' said Chris, rubbing her lower back. 'How about Hodds and Smith?'

'I haven't got on to Smith yet. Hodds is still a possible. She lives alone in Fleggburgh, on the northern edge. Her neighbours say she used to cycle to work through the back lanes to the care home in Rollesby. Her coworkers tell the same story. Say she often extolled the virtues of fresh air, exercise and quiet country lanes. They *are* quiet too. I've driven the two most likely routes and passed nothing. Unfortunately, I didn't find anything either. There are no obvious places where a body could be lying in a ditch or similar. There are a couple of places where an energetic and reasonably fit person could have taken a body and disposed of it in or near one of the Trinity Broads. If you're happy, Boss, we could get a dog team to check out, for example, Town Dyke, which leads to Lily Broad, and the areas near the car park at Filby Bridge, to name but two.'

'I'll get that organised,' said Chris, scribbling. 'Can you get on to our last candidate, Kain Smith?'

'Wasn't he on Steve's list?' asked Bill.

'He was, but Steve's still busy with Ben Lyell. Let me know how you get on, and I'll get back to you about a dog team. Realistically, it won't be until tomorrow.'

17

Aftermath

Greg leaped out of his car and raced to the pavement. The oil tanker in front of him was still rocking with the force of its sudden stop. Behind it the driver of a battered Ford Escort was struggling out of his seatbelt. New dents in its front bumper suggested he'd been a bit slow on the brakes.

Greg arrived at the front of the lorry, more or less at the same time as its driver.

'He just walked out. I had no chance. No warning. Nothing.' The grizzled man in overalls was gabbling, white as a sheet from shock.

In front of the lorry, so close to the front wheel that the front of the cab overhung them, was the entangled mass of Mr Lloyd and Jenny. Greg had already tapped 999 on his phone when, to his immense relief, he saw that Jenny was starting to move. As she extricated herself, her jacket caught on a fragment of bumper and tore, then she rolled clear of the old man and stood up.

'I think he's alright,' she said to Greg. 'Nothing worse than bruises anyway.'

Greg was speaking into his phone. 'Ambulance, please,' he said. 'I'm a police officer. DCI Greg Geldard. I've just witnessed an attempted suicide, and we need an ambulance ASAP. She's asking, "Is the casualty breathing?" ' he said to Jenny, then went to bend down to Mr Lloyd, who was lying still, half under the lorry cab.

Jenny beat him to it. 'Yes, he's breathing and conscious,' she said. 'I don't think the lorry hit him. I think he's just shocked.'

'What about you?' asked Greg. 'Did it hit you?' The driver started expostulating again, but Greg shushed him with a raised hand.

'Shaken but not stirred,' said Jenny with a feeble grin, then winced as she twisted to answer him.

'You'd better get checked out as well,' said Greg. 'Look, you go and sit in my car for the moment. I'll stay with Lloyd until the ambulance gets here.

'And Jenny, that was one of the bravest things I've ever seen. Mad, but brave.'

At that moment a patrol car pulled over from the opposite lane, blue lights flashing. A couple of uniformed officers unfamiliar to Greg got out and came over, pulling on their caps. 'What've we got here, sir?' asked one.

Still crouching next to Mr Lloyd, Greg reached into his pocket for his warrant card and held it out. 'DCI Geldard,' he said. 'This is a person of interest in one of my cases. I think he was attempting suicide. I've requested an ambulance, for him and for my colleague too. She's in my car.' He pointed.

The lorry driver interrupted. 'He stepped out in front of me,' he insisted. 'The woman was trying to hold him back. I did my best to stop—'

'And a very good best it was,' said Greg. 'Your speed of reaction very probably saved their lives. Look, these two officers will take a statement from you, and your contact details, then you can be on your way if you're OK to drive. You've had a shock too.

'Can you deal?' he said to the uniformed officer standing over him.

'Will do,' he responded, his notebook already in his hand. 'I gather the lorry didn't hit the casualty?'

'I don't think so,' said Greg. 'But we'll wait for the paramedics before we move him.' He placed a restraining hand on Mr Lloyd, who was starting to raise his head. 'Just wait for the paramedics,' he instructed.

The second officer was already dispersing the small crowd that had started to gather, and intercepted the indignant Ford owner intent on collecting insurance details from the driver of the lorry. 'Give us a moment, sir,' he was saying. 'Then we'll get that sorted for you.'

The ambulances, two, arrived shortly after, and Greg resigned Mr Lloyd into their care with a sigh of relief. 'Where're you taking him?' he asked.

'The James Paget,' said one, just as his colleague from the second ambulance came over from his conversation with Jenny.

'We'll be taking DC Warren into the Paget too,' he said. 'She should have an X-ray to check her hip is OK. I think it's just bruising, but we need to be sure.'

'Absolutely,' said Greg. 'I'll follow in my car.' He turned to the first man to say, 'I'll need to talk to your patient as soon as the doctors allow it. Perhaps you could mention that?' As he spoke, the tanker driver and the victim of the sudden stop from the car behind shook hands and got back in their respective vehicles. The two uniformed officers came over to Greg, with the satisfaction of a job completed written on their faces.

'Assuming you're happy, they can get on their way,' said the first, a slightly older man who seemed to be taking the lead. 'There's no damage to either vehicle that would prevent them driving and we have statements and contact details.'

'Thank you,' said Greg. 'Can you forward both to me, and I'm happy for you to get the traffic moving again.' He glanced at the queue of cars and vans moving slowly by in the one remaining lane. 'I imagine this lot will be pleased,' he added. 'Before you leave though, can you secure the property at No 5, Lacon Street. The tenant left in a hurry and failed to lock the door.'

'Will do,' said the constable.

As Greg went back to his car, realising belatedly that it was sitting on the roadside with the passenger door open and the keys clearly visible on the central console, the tanker moved off, followed at a safe distance by the slightly battered Ford Escort. The two constables collected the cones they'd used to guide the traffic and got back into their patrol car to head back into Yarmouth, via Lacon Street.

All over, he thought. *Thank God Jenny's OK.* He started his car and realised that the steady flow of traffic in front of him, newly released from the jam, was not going to let him into the flow anytime soon. Sighing, and tempted to put his blue lights on, he decided against setting a bad example and did a U-turn towards the coast road to bypass the slowly unwinding queue.

***

By the time he arrived at the James Paget Hospital, both ambulances were parked outside the non-Covid emergency entrance. Leaving his car creatively parked in the over-full car park, partly on a grassy bank, Greg went through to the triage team, pulling on a mask with one hand while waving his warrant card with the other.

The nurse on duty was both efficient and helpful. 'Your colleague DC Warren has gone down to X-ray,' she said, consulting the screen in front of her. 'She'll likely be there a while. There's a bit of a backlog. Multi-car pileup on the Acle Straight. The other patient you asked about...' She tapped a few keys. 'He's in cubicles. I'll get someone to take you through. According to what I have here, he's likely to be discharged if there's anyone at home to keep an eye on him.'

'There isn't,' said Greg. 'At least, I don't think so. I need to have a chat with him. Is that OK?'

'Can't see why not,' said the nurse. 'But the doctor will have the final say.' She beckoned to a passing care assistant. 'Can you take Chief Inspector Geldard through and let the doctor know he wants to talk to the patient in cubicle four? she asked.

Greg followed the dumpy shape in blue scrubs down the aisle in the centre of the waiting room. As he'd expected, with any Covid-suspicion patients in their separate A&E, most of the casualties waiting seemed to be clutching minor injuries. Those that weren't obviously bloodstained were either peering into bowls with a wary air, or simply looked stressed. Having recently sat in Addenbrooke's, waiting to find out what had happened to Chris, Greg could sympathise.

A cough – the attention attracting sort, not Covid – drew his eyes to a tired-looking young man in green scrubs waiting at his elbow.

'You want to speak to the patient in cubicle four?' he said without preamble. 'A Mr Irwin Lloyd, is that right?'

'That's right,' confirmed Greg.

'Well it's OK with me. If I knew he had someone at home to look after him he'd be out of here. We've checked him over, and frankly he's safer at home than in hospital. I believe he's trying to organise a friend or neighbour as we speak.'

'Thank you,' said Greg.

Irwin Lloyd was indeed on the phone as Greg went in but rang off as soon as he recognised his visitor. He put the phone down on the bedside table with a hand that shook, then he looked up.

'I imagine you have more questions for me,' he said in a voice that quavered. 'I've been dreading this day for over ten years.' Then he leaned back on the pillow, tears trickling down his face.

Greg took a seat by the bed, unable to avoid a sense of pity, and took out his phone. Setting it to record, he looked again at the old man before him. He seemed to have aged another ten years since their conversation earlier that morning.

'Mr Irwin Lloyd,' he said, 'I'm going to record this interview and I'm going to administer an official caution.' He did so, then added, 'I also need to tell you that if you want a lawyer present, then I'll postpone all my questions until we're down at the station and one has been found for you. But if you prefer, we can carry on now. It's your choice.'

'Am I under arrest?' asked Lloyd.

'Not yet,' said Greg. 'But it's only fair to warn you that, depending on what you tell me and what other evidence comes to light, I may need to arrest you.'

There was a long silence while the man in the bed thought. Then he sniffed, reached for a tissue from the box on the table and blew his nose.

'I'll talk now,' he said. 'It's been long enough. You want to know who killed Fred Hamilton. It was me.'

They were interrupted by the cubicle door opening. Greg turned round to tell whoever it was to push off, then realised it was Jenny. She was walking stiffly but otherwise seemed to be OK.

'Got the all-clear, Boss,' she said. 'I thought you could do with a hand.'

'DC Jenny Warren has entered the room,' said Greg for the recording, and turned back to Lloyd, praying that the disturbance wouldn't have knocked him off track.

'The constable who saved my life,' he murmured. 'I hope you're not going to be disappointed. It probably wasn't worth it.' Jenny took a seat on the other side of the bed and got out her notebook.

'You just admitted to killing Fred Hamilton,' said Greg. 'Could you describe the circumstances, please? What exactly happened?'

'I went into Jo's kitchen from the garage and found her grappling with her husband,' said Lloyd. 'His back was to me, and he had her by the throat. I remember her face was congested, sort of red and blue at the same time, and she was pushed up against a kitchen cupboard. I shouted something, I don't remember exactly what, and I pulled at his arm. His left arm. He elbowed me in the face, shook me off, and went back to throttling Jo. I was seeing stars. I thought he'd broken my nose, and I went to grab him again, then Jo sort of sagged towards the floor. I saw a kitchen knife on the worktop, grabbed it and stabbed him in the back.

'I want to say that it was the only way to stop him,' he added tiredly. 'But after years of thinking about it, I don't think that's strictly true. I was trying to stop him hurting Jo, but I was also frightened he was going to hurt me. I'm not a very brave man. The knife was a convenient solution to both problems.'

'What happened next?' asked Greg.

'I helped Jo up off the floor and through to her sitting room. Then sat down next to her on the sofa, holding her hand. I fetched her a glass of water and went back to holding her hand. She couldn't speak at first, but when she could she just croaked, "Thank you".

'I got up to reach for the phone. I said something like, *We need to ring the police and explain what happened*. But she caught my hand again and pulled me back. She said no, several times, and she was getting upset, so I said, "OK, let's take a few minutes." I picked up a throw from the back of her sofa and used it to cover him up. Then I went back to holding her hand again.

'We must have sat like that for an hour or more before I started to say that we must dial 999. She put a finger on my lips, then sort of croaked at me, "No. He's not going to ruin your life as well as mine." I started to speak, and she shook her head. She said the same thing again.

'Slowly over the next hour or two, she opened up about how he'd treated her, both when they lived together and after they'd separated. All the cruelties. All the hate. I knew they hadn't been happy. I knew she was afraid of him. But she'd never told me the details before.

'She was absolutely determined to keep it secret. What had happened, I mean. She talked and argued all through that afternoon and into the evening. Then she persuaded me to help her pull the body from the kitchen to the garage.

'We wrapped him in the old throw and pulled him along the floor. Then she set to with a mop and cleared up the mess. I was pretty messy too. We both were. Thinking back, I realise I must have had blood on me from when I … when I stabbed him. There was more by the time he was in the garage. Jo looked at me and said I ought to change before we did anything else. She rummaged around a bit then came up with a big loose jumper and some jogging bottoms and held them out to me. My shirt was sticky with blood and there were smears on my trousers too. It was revolting. So I did what she said and changed. I felt pretty ridiculous in her clothes, but at least they were clean.

'I was reeling with tiredness by then, and every time I tried to say anything about the police, she shushed me. In the end she swore me to secrecy and sent me home. She said she'd think about what I'd said to her and see me in the morning. If I still felt the same, she'd ring the police then.'

18

Slow progress

It was late afternoon by the time Chris got hold of the dog section.

'What precisely are we looking for?' was the first question from the despatcher.

'Dead bodies,' said Chris succinctly. 'Somewhere between one and six weeks old. Any chance of a cadaver dog?'

'That might be a problem,' was the cautious reply. 'We've only got one in Norfolk. I'll see what I can do. And where, exactly?'

Chris gave him the Ordnance Survey grid references for Town Dyke and Filby Bridge. 'They seem the most likely places for a body to be dumped after an incident on the back roads between Rollesby and Fleggburgh. If you have any other ideas, we'd be glad to take them on board.'

'You realise that on the longer timescale, and on the assumption the bodies are in the open, we'll mainly be looking at bones,' said the man.

'Is that a problem for the dogs?' asked Chris.

'Shouldn't be, unless the bones have been scooped up and moved. If they're still in situ, then there'll be plenty of decomposed material associated with the site for the dogs to work on. If the bones have been moved, we might still find the location. They can usually track a disturbance. We'll see how it goes.

'OK. I've tasked Constable Philips with Meg, and Constable Scouller with Pat.'

'Two dogs?' asked Chris, surprised.

'Two dogs and two handlers,' confirmed the despatcher. 'They're an experienced team. They'll be on site 09.00 tomorrow. Barring any high-priority emergency call-outs, of course, and they most often affect the GP dogs or the explo teams.'

'General purpose?' queried Chris, correctly deducing the meaning of GP in this context.

'That's right,' said the despatcher. 'They'll be with you tomorrow. Who should they report to?'

'Assume DI Henning, unless I contact you again,' said Chris, wishing it was her.

In Wroxham, Steve was busy spotting CCTV cameras. The marina and Broads Holidays were fruitful sources. The many establishments of Roys of Wroxham were also minded to be helpful, but unfortunately didn't keep their recordings for long enough to be useful. Some of the smaller establishments serving the holiday trade were his last resort, and the craft and glassware shop was a surprising success. At first, when he discovered the exterior camera was a dummy and the only live one was that intended to deter shoplifters, he thought he was out of luck. It was only on the insistence of the shop assistant that he viewed some of the footage from the camera behind the till, and discovered she was right. It did indeed provide a good view not only of the shop interior, but also through the large plate glass windows on to the street beyond.

'I think I've got something, Boss,' he said to Chris on the phone. 'I've seen what looks like Ben Lyell pedalling up the main street at 07.16 on the morning of the fifteenth of August. At least, I've got a chap who looks like Lyell, dressed in chef's whites, pedalling a dark-coloured mountain bike in the direction he'd have been headed if he was going home.'

'You've got the footage, I take it?' said Chris.

'Yes. I thought maybe we could get the chaps reviewing traffic camera footage to look for a bike along the route he'd have been taking back to Horning, given we now know the time.'

'I'll have a word,' said Chris. 'Good job, Steve.'

She put the phone down, realising as she did so that she was approaching the end of her energies, really could do with going home, but had no means of getting there other than a taxi. Greg and Jenny were, as far as she knew, still at the James Paget Hospital, interviewing the elderly clergyman. Jim was somewhere between Norwich and Potter Heigham with Phil Saunders's neighbour, Tina. Bill was on his way back from Fleggburgh, and Steve was in Wroxham. That left Jill. Where the devil was Jill? She massaged her temples with a weary sigh, leaned back in her chair and closed her eyes. She'd ring Jill in a minute, then it'd have to be a taxi home, unless Greg reappeared. Just for a moment, she wished she'd stayed at home and joined the briefing meeting by Zoom. That way she could have been relaxing with Bobby and Tally now. She didn't realise it, but she was unconsciously stroking her, very slightly, rounded belly as she relaxed. *This is all your fault*, she said mentally to her little stranger. *I hope you're not going to be this exhausting when you're out and about.*

Jill was, in fact, debriefing her uniformed assistants, standing in a huddle round her car. They had, they assured her, completed the house-to-house.

'Although,' said Constable White, 'it was more of a farm-to-farm, than house-to-house, in places. Apart from her nearest neighbours, I spoke to a breeder of alpacas, a smallholder with chickens, a tree surgeon with a backyard full of logs, and a scruffy devil who claimed to be living off the grid. As far as I could see, it seemed to be an excuse for not washing very much,' he said, wrinkling his nose.

'What about you?' asked Jill, turning to the other constable.

'I got the mainly bungalow section,' she replied. 'And therefore, mainly the elderly and retired. At least half of my interviewees were deaf, judging by how much shouting I had to do, and probably wouldn't hear the last trump, let alone anything to do with a neighbour several doors away.'

'Did you learn anything useful?' asked Jill, her patience hanging by a thread.

'Nothing from my lot,' said the inquisitor of the deaf. Constable White seemed more engaged and flicked through his notes a second time.

'The off-the-grid merchant said he'd sold Ann Cooper foraged mushrooms and wild garlic earlier in the year. The tree surgeon said he saw her on her bike pretty regularly but couldn't remember the last time. He also knew her fairly well, having sold her firewood in the winter. It seems she had a policy of buying locally. The alpaca breeder hasn't lived here long, and said she didn't know her at all. But she does have a Land Rover Discovery, which is the sort of vehicle we're looking for, isn't it?'

'Something along those lines,' agreed Jill. 'Did it have any damage at the front?'

'Couldn't see the front,' said White. 'It was parked half in and half out of a small barn, with a trailer attached to the back. I thought I'd better check with you before I did any more poking about. There're lots of Land Rovers about, after all.'

'OK, thanks for your help,' said Jill. 'Write up your reports as soon as you get back to base and let me have them ASAP. I'll go and have a quick chat with the alpaca breeder. Name?'

'Tristan Smith,' was the reply. 'But it *is* a woman, despite the name.'

Jill drove back down the winding road towards Ormesby Broad, a distant memory jumping up and down in her head. The name was ringing a bell, but she just couldn't think why.

The barn that was her destination, and other farm buildings, were set well back from the road, clustered near to a neat cottage. Jill paused at the end of the drive to get a feel for the place, and realised that 'neat' was the word that kept coming to mind. All the paddocks that she could see were well fenced, weeds controlled, and the grass either mowed or grazed to such a uniform height that, if shorter, it could have been a bowling green. The buildings were immaculate: wood either painted or stained, and brick- or blockwork well pointed. The cottage looked like a child's drawing, with windows to either side of a central doorway. The only thing missing was a plume of smoke from the central chimney. The resident alpacas viewed her inquisitively as she got back in her car and drove up to the neatly gravelled yard between the cottage and the buildings.

As Jill got out of her car, a woman, apparently of late middle age, came out of the building nearest the cottage, brushing shreds of wool off her jeans.

'Good morning,' she said in a pleasant voice with a faint accent that Jill couldn't immediately place. 'Can I help you?'

'Morning,' said Jill. She held up her warrant card. 'I'm Detective Sergeant Jill Hayes. I'm following up on the conversation you had this morning with one of my colleagues.'

'The nice young man who's scared of alpacas?' asked the woman with a smile. 'Sorry, I shouldn't laugh I know, but my girls wouldn't hurt a fly, and even Geronimo is pretty harmless. Unless you're another male alpaca.'

'Geronimo?' queried Jill.

'My stud male. The big grey over there.' She pointed to a paddock containing an aristocratic-looking grey alpaca with a smaller white companion. 'But you haven't told me how I can help?'

Jill was edging round the Land Rover as she talked, hoping to get a clear view of the front.

'I believe you are Tristan Smith,' she said. 'We're making enquiries relating to the death of Ann Cooper, one of your neighbours.'

'I'm sorry,' said Tristan. 'But as I already told your colleague, I didn't know Ms Cooper. I haven't lived here very long. I moved here from North Yorkshire only six months ago.'

Jill realised she could place the accent after all. It was similar to that Greg occasionally exhibited when talking about his previous posting. She edged a bit further round the vehicle.

'So you hadn't met Ann Cooper?' she asked.

'Not to my knowledge,' said Tristan. 'Look, if there's something you want to look at, just say so. I've nothing to hide! You don't need to keep sidling about.'

'Then you won't mind me looking round your Land Rover,' said Jill, slightly embarrassed.

'Be my guest,' said Tristan, waving a hand.

Jill walked round the vehicle, insofar as she could with the substantial livestock trailer attached to its towbar. She paused at the front, noting scratches and a dent in the nearside front bumper and bent to take a closer look. Then asked, 'How did you come by this damage?'

'Novice trailer tow-er at the last show I went to before Covid,' replied Tristan. 'It was at the Great Yorkshire in fact. She was aiming at a space on the other side of my car, got completely screwed up about which way she should turn the steering wheel, and scraped my nearside. She put a dent in my trailer too,' she said, pointing to a mark. 'She was so apologetic I couldn't be too mad with her. I told her the best trick when reversing was to take it very slowly and remember that the back of the trailer goes in the same direction as the bottom of the steering wheel. She thanked me, but drove off forwards. I think she'd lost her bottle by then. I've never got round to getting either of them fixed up.'

Jill stood up and looked also at the dent in the trailer. 'Thank you,' she said. 'Do you mind if I have a bit of a look round your outbuildings?'

On the phone to Chris, to bring her report up to date, she explained, 'I was looking for bikes, given that Phil Saunders's is still missing, and I found one. But it's a ladies bike, so I don't think it's the one Phil Saunders was riding. Everything else looked OK. The other sheds were either storing animal feed or looked like they were used as animal shelters in winter. One was set up for weaving. I rather liked the look of the rugs she's making,' she said. 'Notwithstanding the damage to the Land Rover, I doubt she's our bike killer.'

'Good to be thorough though, Jill,' said Chris. 'Log it anyway. Where are you headed next?'

'Back to the office,' said Jill. 'See you soon.'

***

At the James Paget, Greg and Jenny were still listening intently to the wavering voice of Mr Irwin Lloyd.

'How did you get home from Ormesby that night?' asked Greg.

'In my car. I drove home.'

'And what happened to the clothes you'd taken off?'

'I left them at Jo's. I forgot about them to be honest. In fact, I never saw them again. When I drove back the following morning, I was thinking about the conversation we needed to have with the police. I was wondering how I could explain why we'd behaved the way we had. How on earth we could explain the delay in reporting the death. Whether I'd be arrested, and how I'd deal with being in prison. I was winding myself up into a right state, to be honest, by the time I arrived at Jo's. When I went in, I glanced through the door into the garage, but I couldn't see anything. So the first thing I said to her, when I got into the kitchen, even before good morning, was, "Where's the body?"

'I remember she was filling the kettle at the tap. She didn't even turn round. She just said, "Buried".' He stopped talking and looked up at the ceiling. He seemed to be remembering the moment.

'What did you do, when you found she'd buried your victim?' asked Greg, deliberately brutal.

'Nearly passed out,' said Lloyd. 'I was so shocked; I didn't know what to do. I just sat on the kitchen chair and gaped, probably for several minutes. She carried on making the tea, then put a mug in front of me on the kitchen table. "I've put lots of sugar in," she said. "You've had a shock." I just stared at her, with anger building inside me for the first time. I said something like, *You've done what?*

'And she said, "I've buried him in the garden. That's an end to it. I told you I wasn't going to see you go to prison for saving me, and I meant it. He's dead and nothing will bring him back, and I'm damned if he's going to haunt me for the rest of my life. No one will care. No one will even notice he's gone. He lives alone. I'll get rid of his car, and that's that. All you have to do is keep quiet."

' "I can't do that," I said.

'And she said, "You have no choice. His blood and your fingerprints are on the knife. His blood is on your clothes. You might have taken a chance on a self-defence plea if we'd reported it last night, but the odds weren't good, not with a stab in the back. I've saved you from yourself", she said. "Irwin, just go home for now, and think about it. You'll come to see I'm right." '

'What did you do next?' asked Greg as Lloyd showed signs of drying up again.

'I went home. I thought about it. And I realised that what I mainly felt was relief. I've felt guilty about that ever since.'

'When did you next see Jo?'

'I didn't. I told you I was a coward, and I was cowardly about that too. I kept meaning to go over and see her, but after a week or two passed, I realised I never wanted to see her again. Whatever I had felt, it just died that night, along with her husband. Then I tried to pluck up the courage to tell her, and I couldn't even manage that. In the end, I wrote to her. I said I wished her well, but that I couldn't forgive myself for what we'd done, and it was better that we never met again. I wrapped the letter up with a Bible that I'd bought for her earlier and never got round to giving her, then I posted the parcel and started looking for somewhere else to live. And some way to live with myself.'

'We found your clothes,' said Greg. 'Hidden under the floor of the garage. We also found a Bible. But we think it was hidden later than the clothes.'

'So, although she threatened me about the clothes, she had probably already hidden them,' said Lloyd, tears trickling down his face. 'Perhaps she did mean to protect me, after all.'

'We'll never know,' said Greg. 'But now we need to take that DNA sample, if you're willing this time. And Irwin Lloyd, I'm arresting you on suspicion of the murder of Frederick Hamilton...'

Out in the foyer, waiting for the arrival of transport to take Irwin Lloyd to Wymondham, Greg turned to Jenny.

'That business about the clothes... She may have been trying to protect him but, if so, why not just burn them and disinfect the knife?'

'Because she hadn't made her mind up what she would do if he let on about the body?'

'Something like that,' agreed Greg. 'I think they were an insurance policy in case the body came to light. I don't think she was as motivated by care for him as he'd like to think.'

'One other thing occurs to me, Boss,' remarked Jenny. 'We know Fred Hamilton wasn't the biological father of the younger Joanne. Maybe he had reason to be jealous!'

Greg nodded. 'It's worth bearing in mind. Ah, here's the transport team. We've got the OK from the doctor, so as soon as they're away, we'll get back to Wymondham. And thank you, Jenny. I'm sorry your last day with us was so eventful! But well done. We got a result and Margaret will be pleased.'

19

Evening: journeys home

Chris was still hesitating over ringing for a taxi when she got a call from Greg.

'I'm on my way to Wymondham now,' he said. 'Be with you in five minutes. Are you OK?'

'Bit tired,' she replied. 'Perhaps I should have stayed home and joined the briefing by Zoom, but, on the other hand, there've been a lot of developments today. I'll be glad to get home though.'

'And tomorrow you stay there,' said Greg firmly. 'See you soon.'

By the time Greg and Jenny got to the incident room, word had spread, and they were met by applause, led by Jim.

'In the bag?' he asked.

'Assuming the DNA test comes back positive, yes,' said Greg. 'At present we haven't got much more than Lloyd's confession, so we need the supporting analysis if the CPS is to take a case to court. Fingers crossed. One thing still puzzles me, and that's what happened to Fred Hamilton's car. I'd like to dot that 'i' if we can.

'How about the cyclist case? Chris has told me we've confirmed the identities of Bodies A and B, but what else have we got?'

'We've ruled out one of the possibles,' said Jim. 'And we're still following up on the other three. A dog team is booked for tomorrow morning to take a sniff around a couple of priority sites and the CCTV team are scrutinising footage both for the cyclists and possible aggressor vehicles. Slow progress so far.'

'Did I hear you say that Body B has been identified as Phil Saunders?' asked Jenny.

'Yes. The next-door neighbour's testimony was pretty definitive. Again, we're waiting on DNA analysis, comparing the body to hair I took from his hairbrush, but there's little doubt.' Jenny looked thoughtful and went back to packing up her remaining belongings at her desk.

'Did you have a particular reason for asking?' asked Greg.

'The little dog,' said Jenny. 'His Jack Russell. I thought I might adopt her if he really was dead. She was a charming little dog, and Turbo is going to need a companion when I'm at work.'

'Will he take to another dog?' asked Jill.

'Oh, I think so,' said Jenny with confidence. 'He loves having a dog to play with, and a neutered female would be ideal. I'm going to ask the RSPCA if they'd be happy for me to give it a try. Unless, of course, there are any relatives of Saunders's that are going to have a say.'

'I doubt there's any that will object,' said Jim. 'According to the neighbour, there's only a son in Australia and he hasn't visited in an age, so he's unlikely to be interested. You should probably ask him though. I've got contact details so I can break the news to him. I'll pass them on once I've spoken to him. I was waiting for the DNA first, just in case there's a mistake.'

Greg was going over the key updates posted on the whiteboards. He paused over one, then turned to ask, 'Where's Jill?'

'Here,' said Jill, entering the room. 'I was about to ring you when I realised you were in the office. Congrats on your arrest.'

'Thanks,' said Greg. 'I've just been looking at your summary here' – he pointed at the board – 'about the house-to-house around Ormesby Broad. Did you really talk to a Tristan Smith? Was she an alpaca breeder?'

'Yes, how did you know?' asked Jill.

'If it's the same one, and there surely can't be two women with that name, she was involved in the case that first brought me to Norfolk. The body in the World War Two bunker on a Yorkshire farm.'

'I knew that name rang a bell,' said Jill with relief. 'But I don't remember any details. Was she a suspect in that case too?'

'A suspect? No. She was just unlucky enough to buy the farm where a murder had been committed. Is she a suspect in this case?'

'Suspect is a bit strong,' admitted Jill. 'But she was a neighbour of Ann Cooper, and she has a dent on the front of her Land Rover.'

'I might have a chat with her tomorrow, after the dog team's search,' said Greg. 'Meantime, everyone home. It's been a good day.' He turned to check Chris was ready, but she was already on her way out of the door.

'See you all tomorrow,' he said. 'Jim, a quick word, if we can, then I'm off too.'

By the time he'd arranged things with Jim, checked that there was nothing new waiting in his office and hurried down to the car park, Chris was already sitting in his car, eyes closed and head back on the headrest. As he put his hand on the car door, his phone rang again. He answered it, hand still on the door, and a voice he recognised asked, 'Is Chris with you?'

He took his hand off the car and turned away to respond. 'She's in the car,' he replied. 'I'm just about to drive her home.'

'Before you do, listen to me,' said Chris's mother. 'Did you know she's been ignoring invitations to antenatal check-ups?'

'No,' he said. And took a step or two away. 'How do you know?'

'I asked her about it,' she said. 'I knew she should be attending appointments, and when I offered to take her, she just said, "Don't fuss, Mum," so I asked her point-blank. You need to do something, Greg.'

'I didn't even know,' he protested. 'They must have come in the post when I was out of the house. She hasn't said anything to me either.'

'If you ask me,' said Jane Mathews, in the tone that said *I'm going to tell you what I think whether you ask me or not*, 'she's in denial about this baby. And the way you're carrying on, I'm beginning to think you are too.'

'That's a bit unfair,' he said. 'I'm thrilled about the baby. But I don't know what you expect me to do at this stage. It's a bit early for me to be coming over all paternal. And Chris is my priority. She always will be.'

'Then you need to get your head around the fact that you'll soon have a competing priority, and do some planning,' she recommended. 'Chris is how many months pregnant? Three?

Four? She should be having all sorts of tests and screens. And it's not long, you know, before your baby arrives. Then you'll both know it! Neither of you will be able to just carry on as though you've bought a puppy.'

'She had a lot of tests while she was in Addenbrooke's,' he said defensively. 'And we've both been busy. We haven't had much chance to get a grip on what else is needed.'

'That's precisely my point,' she almost shouted. 'You need to get a grip now and decide how you're going to cope with a baby as well as two busy careers. I'll help where I can, but you can start by persuading her to engage with the prenatal stuff. Otherwise, you'll be heading for a disaster.'

Greg put his phone in his pocket, feeling as though he'd been steamrollered, and turned back to the car.

'You look shattered,' he said to Chris as he got into the driving seat. 'You've overdone it, haven't you?'

'Probably,' she said, without opening her eyes. 'But if anyone can tell me how I'm to know, in advance, at what point behaving as normal becomes overdoing it, I'd be grateful. At the moment it's trial and error.'

'Well try erring on the side of caution,' he recommended, and put the car in gear, deciding to tackle the bigger issue once they were home.

Chris, at Greg's bidding, collapsed in a heap on the sofa when they got home. A Marks and Spencer ready meal supplied quick and easy sustenance, and once both cat and parrot were fed, Greg suggested bed.

'Go on,' he said, hauling her to her feet and pointing her at the stairs. 'Shower and bed. I'll be up in a minute.'

Bobby was let out for a night's hunting along the riverbank, Tally had settled, head under wing, on her perch and the doors were locked. Then Greg hesitated by Chris's handbag. The temptation to check it for NHS appointment letters was terrible. For just one second his hand reached out, then he snatched it back. *That way lies disaster*, he thought. *If we can't talk about it, we're sunk.* And he too headed for the stairs.

By the time he'd showered and towelled his hair dry, Chris was sitting up in bed flicking through TV channels. She looked brighter than she had all evening. He decided to take the bull by the horns.

'Your mother's been on to me,' he said, deciding the straight approach was probably best. 'She says we're both in denial about the baby and we need to get our act together.'

'I thought it wouldn't be long,' said Chris, her eyes still fixed on the TV.

'What's this about missed hospital appointments?' asked Greg.

'She mentioned that as well, did she? They weren't hospital appointments. Just the GP.'

'Still important,' said Greg.

'I didn't have the energy,' Chris said, becoming defensive. 'You're always telling me to slow down. Now you want me to add in extra stuff.'

'Not extra, just priority,' said Greg. 'What you've been doing with the intelligence has been great. Groundbreaking. But it shouldn't come ahead of your health or our baby's.'

Chris twisted in the bed to look at him, the TV forgotten. 'Are *you* going to put the baby first?' she demanded. 'I don't see you cancelling work to go to a GP appointment with me.'

'I didn't know you had any,' said Greg, exasperated. 'You hid them from me.'

'Because I knew you wouldn't put them first.'

'You didn't give me a chance!' Voices were rising to the point where a squawk from Tally, annoyed at being disturbed, became audible.

Greg tried to calm down. 'Are we having our first row?' he asked.

'Looks like it.' Chris still wasn't to be placated. 'Nothing about this situation is normal,' she burst out. 'I come round from a coma, and you tell me I'm pregnant. Normally it would have been *my* privilege to tell *you*, to be greeted with cries of delight, flowers and celebrations. And I'd have had chance to get used to the idea before I needed to tell you. It shouldn't have been like this.'

Greg was silent for a while, thinking about what on earth he could say next. He reached out to take her hand, and when she snatched it away, he recaptured it and held it to his heart.

'I'm truly sorry,' he said. 'I don't know what to say. When they told me in the hospital, I was too worried about you to celebrate the baby. It ... he, or she, was just something else to panic about. At that point I didn't know for sure whether you would live, and if you did, whether you'd be...'

He hesitated, and she supplied, '..brain-damaged.'

'OK, yes. If we're going to be blunt, brain-damaged. Then you recovered, amazingly, and I had chance to think about the baby for the first time. As a real baby, I mean, a prospective person made of half you and half me, rather than just an abstract concept. And I started to get excited about us being a family. But then *you* got excited about *work*, and I started to worry all over again about whether you were doing too much, and it never seemed the right time to do the baby talk.'

A silence fell. Outside a muntjac barked, and was answered by another a little further off.

Chris squeezed his hand. 'Truth is...' she said, and hesitated. He waited patiently, sensing that it wasn't the time to rush his fences. 'Truth is, I'm terrified,' she confessed. 'So I'm hiding in what I know, which is work. I'm terrified I'm never going to feel properly strong again. I'm terrified of being stuck at home, bored out of my mind. And I'm terrified I won't love the baby. That I might resent it, and I'll be a rubbish mother and disappoint you, and you'll stop loving me. And that's before we get on to the whole subject of having to push something the size of a football out of a bit of me that I'm convinced isn't designed for it!'

Greg let go of her hand, put an arm round her shoulders and pulled her into his chest. 'Let's take those one at a time.

'First, I won't stop loving you. I couldn't. You're embedded in my soul, part of me.

'Second, there's no reason you need to be stuck at home, bored. We can afford some help for you, so you can go back to work part-time if that's what you want. I can't have the baby for you, but I can help make sure you get what you want.

'Third, I think this baby will be lucky to have you for its mother, and I have no doubt at all that, if it takes after you even a little, it'll be both lovable and exasperating in equal measure. Boring, it definitely will not be.'

He kissed the top of her head. 'And I'm sorry, both that I didn't realise how you were feeling, and that I've been so buried in work. I'll do better, I promise.

'Come on. Let's go to sleep, and we'll sort out those appointments in the morning.'

As they were settling down to sleep, a final thought struck him. 'There was a fourth,' he added. 'When it comes to the business with the football – you're on your own.'

She poked him in the ribs. Hard. 'That's what you think,' she murmured.

20

13 September 2020

As the starting pistol for phone calls to the doctors' surgery didn't fire until 8am, Greg rang from his mobile at the start of his journey to Filby Bridge. He was waiting in a telephonic queue when he arrived in the car park by Filby Broad. No one else had yet arrived – apart from the uniformed officers keeping the general public away with crime scene tape and stern instructions to any inclined to ignore it – so he carried on holding. As luck would have it, the phone was answered just as the dog team arrived.

'Hello, it's DCI Geldard,' he shouted down the phone, and out of the window, 'I'll be with you in a minute.'

'I can't hold, I'm sorry, sir. You'll need to ring back later,' said the phone.

'No,' said Geldard. 'No, please don't ring off. I wasn't talking to you. I've been waiting for ages. I need an appointment for my...' He hesitated. '...wife, Chris Mathews, to have her prenatal appointment. She's sorry she missed the last.'

There was a heavy sigh from the receptionist, a pause and then she replied, 'I have a cancellation this afternoon. At 17.00. Can you do it?'

'Yes,' said Greg, mentally crossing his fingers. 'We'll be there. Thank you.' He took a few seconds to text Chris with the appointment details. *I'll pick you up at 16.40* he promised, then turned his attention to the two officers unloading a couple of springer spaniels from their van.

'Constable Philips,' the first introduced himself. 'And Constable Scouller,' introducing the short, fair-haired woman with the second spaniel. 'This is Meg, and Scouller's got Pat,' went on the burly man with faded brown hair and a greying beard that didn't match the hair very well. 'Shall we get started?'

'Thank you,' said Greg. 'I was expecting … oh here she is. This is DS Jill Hayes. We're all here now.'

'In that case,' said Philips, 'please stand over there, sir, and keep out of the dogs' way. Ready Fi?' he asked his colleague.

'Ready,' she said. Turning to her dog, Pat, she released him from his lead and gave a quiet instruction. Philips stood back, Meg still on her lead and whining slightly, clearly keen to join in. Both officers watched Pat closely.

'Missed a bit over there,' said Philips to Scouller, pointing. She turned to see where he was indicating, nodded and redirected Pat to the area of undergrowth so far unchecked. A couple of pink-footed geese emerged and set sail across the Broad with an indignant wag of their tails. Pat stayed steady to his task, impressing Greg more than a little.

After what seemed a short time, Scouller called Pat to heel, and Philips released Meg.

The search procedure was repeated. Correctly interpreting Greg's look, Scouller explained, 'It keeps the dogs fresh and interested if we don't work them for too long.'

As Meg completed her stint, also without success, they all moved forwards some yards, followed by Greg and Jill. It didn't take them long to complete a search of the car park in the woodland, the surrounding area and as far along the bank of the Broad as it was realistically practicable to carry or drag a body. Nothing.

'Do you want us to go any further?' asked Philips.

'No, I think that's far enough,' said Greg. 'Very fast work. It would have taken us days to do a search without dogs.'

'That's rather the point,' said Philips with a grin. 'Over to the next site?'

Greg nodded. 'Thank you.' Back in the car park, he told the uniformed officers they could remove the tape and head back to the station. 'Thank you too,' he said.

At the next location, the uniformed team had closed the side road all the way from Narrowgate Corner to the junction with Fleggborough Road. They came across 'Road Closed' warning signs well before they came up to the barrier over the road. Greg held his warrant card out of the window as a constable he vaguely recognised came over.

'Drive on, sir,' he said. 'We'll hold the tape up for you.'

'DS Hayes is just behind and the dog team behind them,' said Greg.

'Got yer, sir,' said the officer.

By the time Greg pulled up, where three or four traffic cones had been left by the roadside, Jill was behind him with the dog van hot on her heels. He got out of the car and walked over to the cones.

'Not an obvious spot to dispose of a body,' he said, looking at the hedge that led across the fields towards a belt of trees.

'Those trees are hiding Town Dyke,' said Jill. 'And that leads, straight as a die, down towards the Broad. That's why we thought it was worth investigation.'

Philips and Scouller unloaded Meg and Pat and walked along the hedge towards the trees. Meg was checking the hedgerow as they went and flushed a couple of pheasants. She too stayed steady to her task, although she did look at Philips with a pleading expression.

As they reached the trees, the shallow ditch beside the hedge suddenly became a substantial dyke. Philips called Meg to him, while Pat took over the search. This time, the result was different. Pat froze, and sat, his nose pointing at the dyke in front of him, a few yards along from the accompanying humans. Scouller went to investigate, pulling a tennis ball out of her pocket as she did so.

'Well done, Pat. Good boy,' she said, and threw the ball back into the field behind her. Pat bounded after his reward with joy in every leap, and Scouller looked at Greg.

'He's found a body, at least,' she said. 'Whether it's the one you were looking for, who knows?'

Greg went forwards as far as Scouller, then stopped. He could see crumpled fabric, what looked like a coat over pale lavender scrubs. And bones.

'Call it in, Jill,' he said. 'We need Ned and the doc. No one go any closer until they've had a look.' On the phone to Chris, he reported, 'From a distance, looks like it could be the care worker, Carol Hodds.'

'The one that went missing on the eighteenth of August?' said Chris.

'That's the one. We'll know more when Ned gets here. I'll still collect you at 16.40, don't forget,' he added. 'Jill's here and she can look after things for an hour or so, if necessary.'

'Where did you find the remains?' asked Chris. 'Filby Bridge or...'

'Town Dyke,' said Greg. 'And not very far along, either. But it's a remote location. I doubt many people would know it was there, unless they were local. That might narrow things down for us a bit. Filby Bridge was always a bit of a long shot, unless the body had been buried, and that doesn't fit with what we know about the MO.'

Greg went over to thank the dog handlers. 'Glad we could help,' said Constable Scouller, looking round from putting Pat back in their van. 'Anytime.'

They had barely driven off, when their space on the road was filled by a white van marked 'forensic services'. Ned's team were spreading out along the hedgerow and dyke.

'Given your description and the fact that these remains have been out in the open for nearly a month, I've made the call to Cranfield,' said Ned. 'The doc is on her way, but it's likely another job for the anthropologists.'

'Well at least the Cranfield pair are close to normal,' said Greg, a tad grudgingly. 'Compared to George and Mildred that is. Sense of humour a bit on the black side, but otherwise surprisingly sane.'

'You're just prejudiced,' said Ned. 'They're really quite nice people, you know.'

'I'll take your word for it,' said Greg. 'I'm still struggling with the memory of Toby's and Harper's conversation over lunch. If I'm eating a chicken leg, I don't need details of their last visit to a mass grave as accompanying entertainment!'

'You shouldn't have enquired what they'd been up to recently,' reproved Ned. 'That was just asking for trouble. Good legs though,' he added.

'Really? Never noticed,' said Greg.

As they spoke, a couple of Ned's folk staggered past with a large parcel, clearly containing one of the ubiquitous blue forensic tents.

'It's going to be a bugger getting that up,' said Greg, 'given the location. Depending on timing, I may have to leave you to it for a while, Ned. But Jill is here, and Jim is on call. I have an appointment I have to meet, but I'll catch up with you before the end of the day.'

Keeping out of the way of the busy forensic folk, Greg was sitting in his car, catching up with emails, when Jill knocked on the side window. Beckoning her to get in, he put his phone away.

'All OK?' he asked.

'So far,' she said, 'although no one's turned up a bike yet, so that's still missing, like Phil Saunders's bike.'

'Anything on the other missing persons? We've two still unaccounted for, haven't we?'

'That's right,' she said. 'The most recent one, the young lad, Kain. And the chef from Wroxham. Steve's got the chef on CCTV pedalling out of town. I don't think we've spotted anything since then. Bill's on the Kain case, but I haven't had an update recently.'

'And then there's our Mr Lloyd,' said Greg. 'We'll be needing to charge him soon. But as far as I know, we're still waiting on the DNA results.

'Jill, we all need a proper catch-up tomorrow, but, for now, can you chase Bill? I'll have a word with Jim. With luck the Cranfield team will be here before I need to leave.'

Jim was embroiled in a testy conversation with Irwin Lloyd's solicitor.

'You do realise you need to charge him or release him very soon?' he was saying.

'You do realise your client has confessed,' said Jim, hanging on to his patience by a slender thread. 'And you don't need to teach me my job, I'm well aware of the timescales.'

'He made that confession without the benefit of legal advice—' complained the dark-suited solicitor.

'Which he was offered, as I'm sure you know,' interrupted Jim.

'Ah, but how sure are you that he was competent to make that decision?' asked the solicitor. 'He's an elderly man, you know, and easily confused.'

Jim glowered at him, perceiving the direction of travel without difficulty. 'I'm expecting some DNA results very soon,' he said. 'Then we'll see.' He sat down at his desk and booted up his laptop. 'They may be here now, if I only had chance to check,' he muttered at the solicitor's departing back. Unfortunately, they weren't.

Jim was still checking messages and thinking of bacon butties when Bill appeared at the door.

'Can we have the dog team again?'

'Where this time?' asked Jim.

'I've been given the route that Kain's mate reckons they were planning to cycle that day. He cried off because of the weather, but he thinks Kain may well have gone on that ride on his own. It's a circular route taking in West Somerton, Horsey, Sea Palling, Hickling and Potter Heigham. If it's OK with you, I thought I'd drive the route, keeping an eye open for possible body-dumping sites and asking around at cafes, pubs, etc, where he might have stopped.'

'Sounds like a plan,' agreed Jim. 'Let me know how you get on. We can get the dog team in again if you can narrow it down to a realistic search area. Where's Steve got to?'

'Last time I saw him, he was bothering the two lassies checking CCTV,' said Bill. 'He's not a happy bunny. I think Chris put a flea in his ear.'

'Then he probably deserved it,' said Jim without sympathy. 'I'll catch up with him later.'

21

Further investigations

Greg was beginning to check the time slightly nervously, when the doc arrived at the dyke.

He joined Dr Paisley at the roadside and offered to carry her bag. 'The terrain is a little challenging,' he said, referencing the hedgerow, the ditch and the deep dyke.

'No problem,' she said, but relinquished her bag into his care notwithstanding. 'How many more of these are you going to find for me, Greg?'

'Possibly two more, and after that, who knows?' he admitted. 'Chris identified four that matched the pattern closely. One of those has been found alive and well, albeit in a women's refuge. This is one of the four. We're still investigating the other two.'

'And that's in addition to the two I've already seen?' asked Dr Paisley, and stopped walking to look him in the eye. 'When are you going to announce that we have a serial cyclist killer on the loose?'

'That's the Chief Super's call,' said Greg uncomfortably. 'Until we found this body, all we had was speculation and stats.

And we still don't have much else to be frank. Unless you find something interesting.'

'No pressure then,' said the doc, and resumed her journey towards the blue tent. 'How's Chris by the way? Is she getting on OK?'

'I think so,' said Greg. 'We have an appointment for some antenatal checks booked for today. After that we'll perhaps know more.'

'How far is she along?' asked the doc.

'Three months, or thereabouts,' replied Greg.

'You won't find out a lot then,' said the doc. 'It's too soon to tell the gender of the baby, if that was what you were hoping.'

'I don't give a damn what sex it is, so long as it's healthy,' said Greg cheerfully as he held the flap of the tent open.

The smell arising from the remains laid out before them was not pleasant, but by no means as strong as it would have been a few weeks before. The body was still clearly recognisable as such, albeit there was little left within what had been lilac-coloured scrubs, other than bones and sinew. The ground beneath the body was covered in a dark sludge and some of the smaller bones of the feet and hands were missing. The skull had lost its teeth and hair. The doctor took multiple photos of the remains, muttering into her phone as she did so.

When she straightened her back, Greg stood back to allow her to leave the cramped tent.

Out in the fresher air, she took a deep breath and said, 'I can't do much more here. I'll have a chat with the Cranfield team and get back to the lab. I think they'll want to see the remains in situ, so the bones will have to stay put for now. What I can see is consistent with death having occurred around four weeks ago. And also consistent with it being a woman, but the forensic specialists will give you a definitive judgement on that. There's been some minor disturbance of the smaller bones, most likely animal, so they'll probably want to have a look around for them.'

'Cause of death?' asked Greg without much hope.

'Can't tell from here,' she replied briskly. 'Leave it to the Cranfield team.'

'By the way, didn't you say something about having another appointment?' she looked significantly at her watch.

'Oh God, is that the time?' said Greg. 'Thanks, Doc.' And he vanished precipitately in the direction of his car.

He was indeed five minutes late picking up Chris, who looked at the clock meaningfully but forbore to comment. They were exactly on time for the appointment when they pulled up outside the surgery, and Chris went in while Greg found somewhere to park. By the time he rushed into the waiting room, she was sitting by an open window, book in hand.

'I've checked in and they're running ten minutes late,' she said to Greg. 'You can get your breath back.'

Greg remembered, with a start, to turn his phone to silent. 'What are they looking for at this check-up?' he asked Chris.

'Not sure. I expect they'll tell us,' she said calmly.

By the time they were invited into the treatment room, Greg was on pins and trying to hide it. The doctor, a pleasant-looking woman in her fifties, took in the relative states of the prospective parents at a glance.

'No need to get into a tizz,' she said to Greg. 'This is a routine appointment and not a very exciting one at that. We'll listen to baby's heartbeat, take a blood sample for testing and do a scan. Your wife had lots of the routine screening tests done when she was in Addenbrooke's, so we're mainly checking for risk of things like Down's syndrome. I'll also be able to give you a clearer idea of the baby's due date. OK so far?'

'Yes,' agreed both Chris and Greg.

'First of all,' the doctor went on, 'how are you feeling, Chris? You had a pretty rough start to your pregnancy!'

'I get tired more quickly than usual,' admitted Chris. 'But I don't know how much of that was the blow to the head, and how much it's down to being pregnant.'

'Much sickness?' asked the doctor, looking down at her notes.

'No, not really. I seem to have been lucky there. I did get some morning sickness, but it seems to have worn off lately.'

'You have been pretty lucky then,' agreed the doctor. 'OK. On the couch, and let's have a listen to junior's heartbeat.'

When they left the surgery, flushed with good news (so far ... as the doctor cautioned) and the excitement of seeing their baby on a scan for the first time, they were laden with good advice and stern injunctions – mainly about not doing too much and 'paying heed to what your body is telling you'. As soon as felt decent, Greg turned his phone back on and was not greatly surprised to find it buzzing with messages. The most urgent seemed to be from Jim, so he rang him as he got back into his car. Chris was pulling on her safety belt when the phone switched to the car speaker and Jim became audible to her too.

'...chance of you getting back here this evening?' he finished up.

'After I've dropped Chris back home,' replied Greg, and rang off. Looking right for oncoming traffic, he said, 'I'm sorry, I'm needed back at HQ. The DNA results are through on Irwin Lloyd, and we need to interview him again before we charge him. Time's running out, so I can't leave it until tomorrow. On top of that, Margaret is fretting about the cyclist cases, so I need to be sure I've got all our ducks in a row before I see her in the morning.'

''Twas ever thus,' said Chris. 'No worries. Get yourself something to eat though, will you. I imagine you're going to be late home.'

''Fraid so.' He spared a hand from the steering wheel to pat her knee. 'You OK?' he asked. 'Everything looked good, didn't it. Starting to get excited yet?'

'I could see you were,' said Chris. 'But yes, it did start to feel more real when we heard the heartbeat.'

Heading out from Acle just after six meant Greg had the advantage of going in the opposite direction to most of the rush hour traffic. Unfortunately, that advantage disappeared when he joined the A11, and his speed dropped markedly for the rest of the journey to Wymondham. It was closer to seven than he'd have liked before he galloped into the incident room to find Jim contemplating the whiteboards at the end.

'Some developments here too,' he said, indicating the summary of the cyclist cases.

'Lloyd first,' said Greg. 'Before we run out of time. Is his solicitor here?'

'Yes. With him now,' replied Jim.

'OK. Let's do it.'

Irwin Lloyd was indeed already sitting in the interview room alongside his dark-suited solicitor.

Forgotten his name again, thought Greg, taking his seat alongside Jim. *Something like...*

'Gregson. Solicitor.' said the suit opposite, for the benefit of the tape and, as it happened, Greg too.

Jim and Greg completed the necessary introductions and a pause fell while Greg took thought.

'Mr Lloyd,' he said at last, 'when we spoke before, we established that you knew Joanne Hamilton in 2010 and you admitted that you entered her kitchen just in time to witness her husband, Frederick Hamilton, attempting to strangle her. You further admitted that you snatched a knife up from the kitchen table and stabbed Mr Hamilton, causing his death.'

The solicitor interrupted. 'My client made this admission under duress and without the benefit of legal advice,' he said. Mr Lloyd looked uncomfortable but kept quiet. Greg ignored the interruption and carried on.

'You failed to report the death at the time, in compliance with Mrs Hamilton's wishes, but stated that you planned to do so on the following day when she'd had chance to calm down. You changed out of your bloodied clothes and went home. But when you returned to the property you found that Joanne Hamilton had disposed of the body overnight. Buried, she said, in the garden, and you agreed to keep the death secret.' Greg paused.

Irwin Lloyd looked at his solicitor and muttered, 'No comment,' rather reluctantly.

'As we told you,' went on Greg, 'Joanne Hamilton concealed the bloodied clothes in a contemporaneous cache under the garage floor.'

'No comment,' said Lloyd again, with another glance at his solicitor.

'We now have the results of the DNA analysis of the clothes and the knife,' said Greg. 'Do you know what low copy number DNA is, Mr Lloyd?' When, as anticipated, Lloyd shook his head, Greg went on. 'Low copy number DNA refers to those cases where a DNA sample is very small, such as may occur when someone touches an item. The science is now so far advanced, that we can multiply the quantities of DNA picked up, until they can be analysed with accuracy. We did that with the samples taken from the clothes and the knife. The samples on the clothes weren't that small actually, because you had worn them. The knife was more challenging, because you had only handled it.

'Your DNA was found on the bloodied shirt and trousers, and on the knife, which was also covered with Frederick Hamilton's blood.'

There was a silence.

'I believe the alleged weapon was a domestic knife, which my client could have handled at any time,' said the solicitor.

Jim opened his mouth to argue the point but was interrupted by Irwin Lloyd.

'No, it's no good,' he said, in a voice so tired Greg winced. 'I know I told you I was confused and pressured when I made my confession, and that was true. I'd just tried to kill myself. But the confession was true too, and I can't carry it on my conscience any longer. I stabbed Frederick Hamilton to stop him killing Joanne. And I connived at the hiding of his body. Can I go back to my cell now?'

'In just a moment,' said Greg gently. 'We have a few more questions. You've told us about the death. We have it on record twice now, and this time with your solicitor present.' He wanted to be sure that was in the bag. 'But I'd like to know a bit more about what led up to that point. What was your relationship with Joanne Hamilton?'

There was another long silence. So long, that Greg began to think he wasn't going to get an answer. But then Lloyd stirred and said, 'I was in love with her.'

***

Bill, meanwhile, was driving in a big circle. At Potter Heigham he'd joined the route Kain had planned to take and wasted over an hour fruitlessly questioning shopkeepers and cafe owners near the river. Carrying on to West Somerton, he'd taken careful note of any area that looked possible both for an unnoticed RTA and a body dump, stopping whenever he spotted a location even vaguely likely. *I don't want Chris on my back too for sloppy investigation!*

At Horsey he stopped to question more cafe owners, with the same result as Potter Heigham. He was getting absolutely nowhere when he called in to Waxham Barns.

To be honest, he was mainly after a caffeine boost for his rather dispiriting day and showed the bloke with a ponytail but no hair on the top of his head the photo of Kain, with little hope of success. To his surprise, Ponytail gave it a second glance after his first, rather dismissive, one, took the photo out of Bill's hand, pulled a pair of reading glasses out of his shirt pocket and gave it a thorough scrutiny before asking, 'Was he on a bike?'

'Yes, he would have been,' replied Bill, hope sparking in his eyes.

'Then, yes, I did see him,' said Ponytail. 'He nearly came a cropper right in front of me here.' He pointed. 'That's why I remember him. He turned away on his bike, with his coffee in one hand, and didn't notice the car coming up behind him. I don't think the driver was very aware of their surroundings either. Anyway, words were exchanged. And then he cycled off.'

'What was said?' asked Bill. 'Did you hear?'

'Oh, you know, the usual. The driver was a female dog, the cyclist was born out of wedlock and had some sexual habits that didn't call for anyone else to participate,' said Ponytail with a grin.

'Did you notice what sort of car it was?'

'Not really. Some sort of four-by-four, I think. But they might have it on the CCTV,' he added, pointing at cameras on the outside of the building.

Bill looked up with a rising excitement, and shot off into the barn, leaving his coffee behind. *Perhaps I could solve this in one fell swoop. Victim and Perp on one camera shot!* Ponytail held up the coffee with a shout on his lips, then put it behind him on the counter, in case he should spot Bill on his return journey to his car.

It took Bill a little time to run the office manager to earth, and a little more before he managed to convince her that his need to see the CCTV was urgent. But eventually he was sitting in front of an elderly desktop reviewing the footage for the relevant day. He stabbed a finger at the screen in his excitement, then turned to the young woman.

'I need a copy of this,' he said. 'From here to here.' He showed her the note of timings he'd made in his notebook. Then left her to scratch her multi-plaited head in an agony of indecision while he rang Jim.

'I can see Kain clearly, and he's definitely having an altercation with the driver of a Land Rover. Then he pedals off.'

'And the Land Rover?' asked Jim.

'It parks a little way along and the driver gets out and goes into the barn. It's a woman, like the coffee vendor said, but that's all I can see.'

'Have you got the number plate?'

'Partly,' said Bill. He read two letters and a number across to Jim. 'I've had a look at other footage, but I can't see the number any better than that.'

'And Kain definitely leaves?'

'Yes. I thought I'd carry on round his route to see if I can find evidence of him anywhere else.'

'Yes. Do,' said Jim.

The video footage in the bag, and his enthusiasm newly fired, Bill set off towards Sea Palling. More waving of the increasingly dog-eared photo didn't produce anything useful, until he got to Hickling. There he got another nibble from the man behind the bar in the inn.

'Looks familiar,' he said, holding the photo up to the light. 'On the other hand, he's not very distinctive looking, is he? Sort of generic cyclist type. And we get quite a few of them.'

'Can you say one way or the other?' asked Bill, disappointed. 'Or do you have any CCTV that might be helpful?'

'Not sure I can, and, yes, we do have CCTV, but we only keep it for a day or two,' said the barman, raising and dashing Bill's hopes in one breath.

'Could you put a percentage on how sure you are?' asked Bill, in one last desperate attempt to salvage something.

The barman waggled a hand as though balancing something first one way, then the other.

'I'd say about sixty per cent sure,' he said, cautiously.

Back in his car, Bill rang Jim again. 'Disappointing,' he said. 'But I do think there's a good chance he got this far and then carried on round the circle towards Potter Heigham, Hemsby and home. I'll keep going and I'll keep looking.'

Unfortunately, when he'd finished the loop, he was none the wiser. No further sightings (or quasi-sightings) and no body. He turned his car for home.

***

Lloyd stirred in his chair and looked across at Greg.

'I'd been asked to visit her in hospital,' he explained. 'That was how we first met. She was being treated for something gynaecological. I didn't ask too many questions. As a hospital visitor, you know when not to ask questions you might not enjoy the answers to!' He managed a wry grin. 'But she seemed to appreciate my visit, and when she went home, I carried on visiting. We just hit it off straightaway. We never had any trouble finding things to talk about, and before long I persuaded her to come to a coffee morning with me.

'That was a mixed success. She was always a very private person and preferred a quiet conversation one to one, to anything more sociable. She said as much to me, more or less, so I asked her if she'd like to have lunch with me one day. Lunch became dinner. Quite a few dinners, both out and at her place. After a while, dinner came to include...' He hesitated. 'She asked me if I'd like to stay the night,' he said almost inaudibly. 'And I did.'

'I asked her to marry me,' he said, still in a very quiet voice, 'but she said she couldn't. That, although she regarded herself as divorced from her husband, Fred, she wasn't legally divorced because he'd refused. Because he was catholic.

'I didn't say anything right then, but I went away and made sure of my facts. Then one evening I sat her down and said that she could still get divorced, with, or without, Fred's consent, if she wanted to. They'd already been separated more than five years. There was nothing to stop her, if that was what she wanted. I got the impression that she was nervous of Fred's reaction. That she already knew that divorce was a possibility, but that the status quo had been acceptable, until I came along.'

He paused again, for so long that Jim opened his mouth to say something, but shut it when Greg gave him a look. They sat in silence for what seemed like a long time, before Lloyd carried on.

'She agreed about the divorce. She did want to marry me,' he insisted. 'But she said she had to tell Fred first. She wrote to him. The next thing I knew, I was looking at his back as he tried to choke the woman I loved. That's why I agreed to keep quiet that first night. I felt guilty. None of it would have happened if I hadn't pushed her for the divorce just so I could square my conscience. About sleeping with her, that is.

'Ironic, isn't it?' he added with a twisted smile. 'After all that, I couldn't go on. I couldn't even see her, without the dead man rising up in my mind. I tried to contact her, to explain how I felt, but between her anger and disappointment and my fear, I got nowhere. In the end I took the coward's way out. I wrote to her, and I sent her a Bible. That was my goodbye.

'So I lost Joanne, I lost my home and I ended up with a worse crime on my conscience than lust, the *worst* crime. It's a relief to admit it all. To lay it down at last. Which is why,' he said, looking at his solicitor, 'I don't care what happens to me now. I'm sorry that, in my panic, I misled you. But my life was over the moment I stabbed Fred Hamilton. It's just taken me ten years to realise it.'

22

14 September 2020

At Greg's request, they were all congregated in the incident room well before eight in the morning. The room reeked of bacon and coffee, as Greg noted with a grin. Bill, Steve and Jill were grouped at one end of the room, arguing over video footage playing on a screen in front of them. Jim was studying the whiteboards at the other end, while Ned stared out of a window, deep in a conversation on the phone pressed to his ear.

'Attention everyone,' said Greg, after a cough and the rattle of a pen on his mug had failed to produce the silence he sought.

'Officer on deck,' added Jim, then shut up quickly as Greg bent a mock-severe gaze in his direction.

'We've a lot to do and too few people to do it, so let's not waste any time,' went on Greg. 'It's been a good couple of days, in terms of progress made, but I wanted to make sure we all know exactly where we've got to, and the implications.

'Let's deal with the Fred Hamilton case first. I think you all know that DNA evidence confirmed the clothing and knife found hidden at the scene had been worn and handled by

Irwin Lloyd, retired clergyman. Well done to Ned's team for getting the confirmation to us so promptly. What some of you may not know is that when Jim and I had a final interview with him last night, he confessed to stabbing Fred Hamilton. He's been charged with murder, and it's now with the CPS.

'Now the cyclists. When we met last, Chris outlined her concerns about missing persons who met a specific profile, ie cyclists who had failed to return from a bike ride, or failed to make it home on their bikes, without any known reason for disappearing, all within a relatively small geographical area, and all within the past three months.

'You all know that the two bodies found by accident, Phil Saunders and Ann Cooper, fit into this pattern. You also know that we found a third body yesterday, tentatively identified as Carol Hodds, the missing care worker.

'One of the mispers highlighted by Chris, Shirley Crabtree, has turned up safe and well. That leaves two unaccounted for: a young man, Kain Smith, who went out for ride around the countryside on the tenth of September and a chef, Ben Lyell, on his way home from Wroxham after being made redundant.

'Folks, we have two major priorities competing for our attention and resources. We need to find Smith and Lyell, dead or alive. And we need to find and stop this maniac killing cyclists. I asked Margaret for more resource this morning, and we *will* get some help from uniform with family liaison and the more labour-intensive tasks like searches and door-to-door. But the detection is going to be down to us. The people in this room.

'So, what leads do we have? And where do we go from here? I want to hear your suggestions.'

They all looked at each other, but Jill was the first to speak up. 'I think we need a closer look at Tristan Smith,' she said. 'She has the right sort of vehicle and it has dents, albeit she had an explanation of sorts for those. But also, she moved here relatively recently. The timing would fit with when these deaths began.'

Greg looked sceptical, but agreed. 'OK, you look into Tristan Smith,' he said. 'You know I don't see her as a strong prospect, given what I know of her from my earlier contact. But that shouldn't prejudice a new investigation. See if you can rule her in or out. Anyone else? Bill?'

'There's evidence that Kain Smith did go on the circular bike ride he'd outlined to his mate. I've interviewed people who saw him, and he's on CCTV at Waxham Barns. I've driven the route and I can't spot anywhere near the road that a body could lie hidden and unnoticed. I thought my next step should be exploring possibilities further off-road with the dog team. Perhaps at Hickling to start with. That's the last place he seems to have been seen. I know that's a bit vague,' Bill admitted. 'But, Boss, this is the most recent of the cases. It's only been a few days—'

'And there's still a chance we could find the lad alive.' Greg completed the sentence for him. 'OK. You have my authority to call in the dogs.

'Now, what about the chef – Lyell? Anything new, Steve?'

'Got him on CCTV leaving Wroxham, and possibly on the A1151 after that, but not clearly. Still trying to narrow it down,' said Steve, embarrassed by his relative lack of progress.

'OK. Let me think about that. Anything we've missed?'

'The bikes,' said Jim. 'We haven't found either Saunders's or Hodds's bikes. Cooper's was found with the body, but not the other two, so presumably they were taken from the scene.'

'You're thinking, by the killer?' asked Greg.

'Possibly,' said Jim. 'I think we should look for bikes when we check out possible suspects like Tristan Smith and any others that come along.'

'Noted,' said Greg. Then a further thought struck him. 'Where's the best place to hide a bike?' he asked rhetorically. 'In with a lot of other bikes,' he answered himself. 'And any bike not locked down would disappear pretty quickly. Bikes get nicked more than most things. Check the CCTV at places like railway stations for anyone leaving a bike from a four-by-four.' He stopped to look through his notes. 'Steve,' he said. 'I think we'd better park your misper for the moment. We're spread too thin. You help Bill on the Kain case. Someone needs to have another chat with his family, and it'd better be you. See if you can get any more intelligence on where he might have gone.'

There was a susurration in the room as everyone prepared to make a move but hesitated, waiting for Greg's dismissal.

'The thing that's bothering me,' he said, thinking aloud, 'is motive. The basics are always means, motive and opportunity. We know a bit about means and opportunity, but sod all about motive. Why is he, or she, doing this? What on earth could inspire this sort of malice?'

'You were probably right in the first place, Boss,' replied Jim. 'You referred to a maniac. That is probably what we're dealing with here.'

'If we are, then they may already be known to the health services. I think a chat with the Mental Health Trust may be in order.'

23

Kain Smith

Steve found Mr and Mrs Smith in much the state he'd expected. Although relieved that their fears were being taken seriously, they had correctly surmised that the arrival of a family liaison officer was not a good sign.

The young man in uniform who opened the door was also clearly finding the circumstances stressful. 'It's my first time,' he hissed to Steve as the latter wiped his dusty shoes on the doormat. It bore a dog's face and the words 'You're just visiting. The house is mine'.

'Is there a dog?' asked Steve, mindful of some other occasions when a resident dog had been over possessive.

'Yes, but it's a soft little thing,' said the constable. 'I'm Jack Reed. Pleased to see you. Have you any news for the family?'

'No, I'm afraid not,' said Steve. 'I'm here to see if I can get any more information from them about Kain's plans for the day.'

Mrs Smith was sitting on a leather-look sofa in the lounge, hugging an elderly-looking Cavapoo. The woman was probably in her late thirties but looked approximately sixty. Mr

Smith was pacing up and down in front of the bay window, clenching and unclenching his fists. Both turned to look at Steve with a mixture of hope and dread. Both looked away as it was immediately plain that he was not the bearer of any tidings, good or bad.

'Mrs Smith, Mr Smith,' he said. 'I'm Steve Hall. I'm sorry to bother you, but I'm hoping that you might be able to help us with some insight into the route your son might have cycled.'

'We told you everything we know,' said Mr Smith, sagging into a battered armchair by the unlit fire. 'We've told you over and over. I thought Kain's mate Lucas had explained where they'd been planning to go.'

'Yes, he did,' said Steve. 'My colleague has driven the route and interviewed a number of businesses along the way to see if they saw Kain. It seems he *was* seen at Waxham Barns, and he *may* have been seen at Hickling Broad. But we haven't found any sign of him anywhere on that route. So, I was hoping you might know where else he might have gone. Did he, for example, have any friends who lived near that route that he might have gone to visit? Or any favourite spots he might have deviated from the route to call on?'

'No and no,' said Mr Smith. Mrs Smith just gulped, shook her head and buried her face in the little dog.

Steve tried asking what, he had to concede, were broadly the same questions in several different ways. Unfortunately, as he said to Bill on the phone, when he left the Smiths' small bungalow in Hemsby, all he got was the same answer.

Bill had been in touch with the dog team and obtained the promise of Meg and Pat, plus handlers, later that day.

'The sooner the better,' he stressed. 'It's only a few days since the lad went missing. There's still a faint chance...'

'Sorry,' said the coordinator. 'But they had a late one yesterday, searching for a missing child near Barton Broad. The dogs aren't machines, you know. They need downtime too. I'll get them to you within a couple of hours.'

'If that's the best you can do,' grumbled Bill, but kept it under his breath, in the interests of diplomacy. Then he reported to Greg, before heading to Hickling to see if he could narrow down the search area.

Greg was having a frustrating morning too. First, he couldn't get hold of his usual contact at the Mental Health Trust. *On leave*, he was told. *And no, I can't give you his mobile number.* The person he was directed to as an alternative, was *in a meeting* and *not available until lunchtime. If then.* After a lot of expostulation and complaint, Greg extracted a promise that he would be able to see the man at 12.30, if he kept it short. With a mental proviso that once he got the chap nailed down, he wasn't going to slide off until he gave him some useful answers, Greg agreed to this.

Unfortunately, answers of any kind, useful or otherwise, were in short supply.

'Sorry,' he kept saying, with little evidence of contrition to support his repeated assertion. 'I can't give you that information.'

'Can't or won't?' asked an exasperated Greg at last.

'I'm not permitted,' replied Dr Lancaster, leaning back in his substantial leather office chair and steepling his fingers. The woman sitting to his left and behind him made a note on her pad and then looked across at Greg, awaiting his reaction.

'The patient confidentiality rules are quite clear, and as the Trust's Caldicott Guardian it is incumbent on me to set a high standard. I simply can't give you what you're asking. The Caldicott Guardian, by the way, is the director—'

'I know what a Caldicott Guardian is,' interrupted Greg. 'The director with responsibility for patient confidentiality across the Trust. But you must understand that I am talking about an active police enquiry into what we suspect to be a serial killer. Considering recent failings across various mental health services that have led to well-publicised deaths, I would have thought you would want to cooperate.'

'My hands are tied,' responded Dr Lancaster, spreading the hands in question on the desk in front of him. 'At least as far as individual cases are concerned. But if you were to ask me what sort of disturbed mind might perpetrate the acts you have described, then I could advise that you should be looking for a sociopath with anger management issues and psychopathic tendencies. In other words, someone who believes that their wishes and preferences trump everyone else's, has little or no empathy, and reacts with extreme anger when they perceive themselves as thwarted.'

'But you can't point me towards someone, or several someones, with that type of diagnosis.'

'No.'

'Then I think we're done,' said Greg, rising from his seat. 'I hope you will be able to face the families of the victims when we eventually catch your psychopath and explain to them that the perpetrator's rights to confidentiality were more important that their son's or daughter's right to live.' He left abruptly, marching from the room with a heavy tread.

Back in his car, he got straight on the phone to Margaret.

'You surely can't have expected anything different,' she said in a severe tone, after he explained the outcome of his meeting. 'And I hope I'm not going to get a complaint from our NHS colleagues, about heavy-handed tactics. From the sound of it, he was doing a good job of covering his back, if he had a note-taker present.'

'I don't think so,' responded Greg, closing the car windows notwithstanding the heat of the day, and cranking the aircon up to maximum. He didn't want passers-by overhearing his conversation. 'And no, I got more or less what I expected, although not what I hoped. But it was a faint hope. However, I do now have more clarity on what we're looking for.'

'You have an idea?' asked Margaret, detecting a level of excitement in Greg's voice.

'Two, actually. But I'm not sure whether you'll like them.'

'Try me,' she offered.

'First, I thought of a press conference, explaining the personality type we're looking for, and asking for responses from the public.'

'No,' said Margaret without hesitation. 'We'll start a panic at best, and at worst a pogrom against anyone perceived to be even a little bit odd or weird. Next?'

'OK,' said Greg. 'My second idea concerns *our* intelligence. Who is most often called out to mental health crises; at least as often, maybe even more often, than the NHS? Who ends up picking up the pieces in more incidents than not?'

'We do,' said Margaret, light dawning. 'At least, the uniform branch does. And your idea...?'

'Is to trawl our reports from those incidents and pick up, from our own data, details of anyone who fits the profile we've been given. And check them out.'

There was a short pause while Margaret considered the implications.

'Do it,' she said. 'I don't see we have much choice. Obviously, you continue to explore all the other, more traditional channels of detection, but check this data as well. I'm not sure you'll find it easy though. I don't think it's recorded centrally in the manner that you need.'

'No. But I do have someone who's proved good at spotting patterns and knows, or is known by, nearly every police officer in Norfolk.'

'Quite right. Set Chris on it and let's see what she can turn up. In the meantime, those traditional approaches...'

'I'm on it, Boss,' he confirmed.

Over in Hickling, Bill had organised a house-to-house in the immediate area around the pub, but with his limited resources (two constables) he was getting nowhere fast. His on-foot sweep around the accessible bits of the Broad hadn't turned up anything of interest either. When the dog team arrived, more or less simultaneously with Steve, Bill was already hot and bothered. Swatting midges away with one hand, he explained the situation to Philips and Scouller, neither of whom looked impressed.

'So, you've no real evidence that Kain Smith is likely to be found in this area,' said Philips, with a sweeping gesture that took in the wide expanse of water, tangled undergrowth and bobbing boats. 'If there weren't already a lot of wild geese visible from where I'm standing, I'd say this is a wild goose chase. All you have is a probable sighting at the pub, and that's it?' If he sounded incredulous, it was a good reflection of how he was feeling.

'We could do a quick sweep and see if the dogs find any traces,' offered Scouller, trying to pour oil on the troubled water.

Philips took a long breath, but whatever he was about to say was interrupted by Bill's phone ringing. Bill glanced down, about to hit the reject button, then stopped. 'Sorry, I do need to take this. Yes, Boss,' he said into the phone. 'Where exactly? Got it, Boss. Meet you there.

'Change of plan,' he said to Steve, Philips and Scouller. 'That was DI Henning. Martham Boatyard have reported finding a bike. Apparently, it's the same model as that Kain Smith was riding. They texted a photo and the office sent it on to the Smiths' FLO. They think it could be Kain's. The DI says to meet him at the boatyard and start the search from there.'

24

Alpacas and neighbours

Tristan was in her weaving shed when she heard a car pull up. It wasn't a good moment to stop, so she continued passing the shuttle across the loom until the hank of raw alpaca fleece in her hand was exhausted. She paused to admire the colour contrast of the black with the grey fleece, frowned a little as she realised the texture was a little flat for her liking, then realised that no one had come into the shed to find her. She put the shuttle down and got up from her chair, stretching her stiff back as she did so, and headed out to the drive.

A single car was parked in front of the barn, and the driver was visible, poking about near her Land Rover. She recognised the detective sergeant she had met a few days before.

'Can I help you?' she asked in a voice that had distinct overtones of sarcasm.

Jill looked up from where she was bent over a pink ladies bike lying against a straw bale.

'Have you had this bike long?' she asked.

'Ever since I came to Norfolk,' replied Tristan. 'There wasn't much call for a bike in North Yorkshire. At least, not for someone like me, who doesn't like pedalling up steep hills and isn't much keener on shooting down them. But Norfolk's the perfect place for a bike. Very flat, as Noël Coward famously observed. I have the receipt somewhere, if it's an issue.'

'Unusual colour,' said Jill, stepping back to 'admire' the baby pink and chrome frame.

'Ah, well that's my precaution against theft,' said Tristan. 'Given it's usually some toerag with macho tendencies and very little brain that nicks bikes, I thought the chances of them nicking one that looks as though it belongs to Barbie were much slimmer. So far, I've been proved right.'

'And the damage to your Land Rover,' said Jill, moving to the vehicle to run a finger over the dents. 'Do you have any evidence of when this occurred?'

'You'd better come into the house,' said Tristan with a sigh. 'As I seem to be suspect number one. I'll look out the receipt for the bike, and see what else I've got.'

Half an hour later, Jill was on the phone to Jim. 'I think we can exclude the alpaca lady,' she said. 'I did find a bike, but it's a vile shade of pink and she has the receipt. As for the Land Rover damage, she has a good photo of the damage to the bumper, dated last year, and an exchange of emails with a garage about sorting it all out from earlier this year. She says she didn't get the job done because Covid intervened, and she hasn't got round to it since. It all sounds OK to me.'

There was a pause while she listened to Jim, then she said, 'OK. I'll have a look around more of the neighbours while I'm out here, then head back. Good luck at Martham Boats.'

Inside the cottage, Tristan was also on the phone. 'Ben,' she said. 'I think I might need your help.'

Jill stopped her car just down the road to consult her notes. As far as she could see, there were at least two neighbours with four-by-fours and one with a van. She decided to take a second look round each in turn.

The van-owning off-gridder was the nearest, so she called there first. She was unsurprised to find that the van was a dilapidated-to-the-point-of-illegality small model of the type she mentally described as 'Noddy-van'. It had once been white, with a logo of some kind affixed to the side panels, but the paintwork was both rusty and grubby, while the old decal on one side read just 'ape services'. The other side had lost its decal altogether, assuming it had once had one. Amid all the rust damage, it could be seen that there were several dents, but none that looked like front runners for a recent contretemps with a bike. She was interrupted in her perusal of the sorry sight by the owner, who turned very defensive indeed when he was shown her warrant card.

'Don't panic,' she said, a tad wearily. 'I'm not a traffic cop, although I do have a nasty feeling that if I asked to see your MOT certificate it wouldn't be forthcoming.' She arched an eyebrow, and he shuffled his feet a little, then held out a bunch of greenery he had in his hands.

'Do you like fresh veg?' he asked. 'I pulled these only this morning.' 'These' turned out to be a bunch of skinny carrots.

'No, you're OK,' said Jill, reflecting that as a bribe they weren't very tempting. 'I'm just following up on our visit a couple of days ago, about the death of your neighbour Ann Cooper. You're Mr...' She looked at her notes again. 'Mr River?'

'Yes. Moon River,' said the man with a straight face. 'Terrible thing,' he said earnestly. 'Mrs Cooper's death, I mean. She was a nice lady. Used to get herbs and stuff from me.'

'Did she get on well with all her neighbours?' asked Jill.

'As far as I know,' said Mr River. 'All of the reasonable ones anyway.'

Thinking that if the, presumably self-styled, Moon River was classifying himself as one of the reasonable ones, it didn't say much for the others, Jill asked, 'Were there some she didn't get on with?'

'Only the ones nobody gets on with,' said Moon River. 'That bitch at the chicken farm and the nutter of a woodsman down the road from here. But they're not murderers,' he added hurriedly. 'Just nasty and weird. But don't tell 'em I said so. I don't want 'er dancing round dead 'ens at the full moon, and I don't want trouble from 'im eether.'

Noting that stress seemed to remove his aspirates, Jill put her notebook away. 'I won't say anything,' she promised. And got back in her car.

Esther Meadowcroft of Meadowcroft Eggs did not, at first glance, seem a prime candidate for dancing sky-clad at full moon, with or without dead-hen accessories. She was sensibly clad for the weather in light blue t-shirt and jeans, with sturdy walking shoes on her feet.

'If you're looking for eggs, I've got hen and duck eggs,' she said. 'I'm out of goose eggs for the moment.'

Jill held out her warrant card and succumbed to curiosity. 'Do you sell many goose eggs?' she asked, which she hadn't intended as her opening question by a country mile. Her mind was boggling at the thought of a giant egg occupying an entire plate.

'As many as I have,' said Esther. 'They're great for scrambled eggs and omelettes. Really tasty. But I assume you're not here about eggs,' she added, nodding to the warrant card which Jill was replacing in her pocket. 'Is this about Ann?'

'Yes,' said Jill. 'Did you know her well?'

'Fairly well,' responded Esther. 'But would you like to come in and have a cuppa?'

'Maybe in a moment,' replied Jill. 'Could I have a look round first?' There was a grubby Land Rover Discovery in the yard, and she was hoping for a crafty squint at the front of it, without having to go into details about why.

'Of course,' said Esther.

Jill set off across the yard without waiting for any further invite and her hostess trailed after her, talking about hen breeds and runner ducks. Luckily the gate from the yard into the adjacent paddock was close to the target vehicle, so Jill got a good view of its pristine bumper as she walked past. Some fifteen minutes of bird talk later, she managed to hint that the promised cup of tea would be welcome. They both returned to the yard and the shabby bungalow beyond.

In the space that seemed to combine the attributes of both living room and office, Jill took out her notebook and settled in one of the two armchairs by the fireplace. It seemed the fire was not currently in use, since the space was occupied by a display of feathers from a range of species. Esther was soon back with two mugs, a jug of milk and a plate of biscuits on a tray.

'What were you wanting to know?' she asked as she put the tray down on the coffee table, cavalierly pushing a pile of spreadsheets onto the floor as she did so. Jill took a mug, and blinked as the biggest black cat she'd ever seen came through the door and rubbed itself on Esther's ankles. 'Meet Mordred, my familiar,' said Esther, then laughed at Jill's expression. 'You've been talking to Moon,' she said. 'I bet he's got you looking for pentacles, runes and sigils.'

'If I even knew what to look for in the last two,' agreed Jill.

'I do it to wind him up,' said Esther. 'He's so gullible. I bumped into him once in the woods when I was picking herbs for my hens. I do believe in herbal medicines, and I was picking dandelion greens. It makes the yolks lovely and yellow. Moon seems to think the woods belong to him and no one else is allowed to forage, so he took exception to me picking stuff. I told him some rubbish about it being dangerous to cross me, just to get my own back.'

'How did Mr River get on with Ann Cooper?' asked Jill, trying to get back to the subject in hand.

'I doubt they saw much of each other,' said Esther. 'Ann's interests, the ones I knew about anyway, were more in things like knitting and crafting. I used to see her at knit and natter in the village periodically, and we'd often sit next to each other. But that's what I mean about knowing her fairly well. We'd often sit and chat together at village events, but I don't think I ever visited her in her home, and she only came here if she wanted eggs. Moon rarely leaves his smallholding, and when he does, as far as I know it's to trade work for food at places like the farm shop. I assume he draws his pension but, apart from that, he's more or less self-sufficient. You have to admire him for that,' she added. 'It's a lot of hard work living off the grid.'

'To sum up, you had a sort of friendly acquaintance with Ann Cooper, and Mr River saw little of her as far as you are aware. Can you think of anyone who might have been an enemy?'

'No,' replied Esther. 'I didn't know her well enough to know if there was anyone in her past. But around here, we all just sort of live and let live. Even Warren, and he's a bit odd, if you like.'

'Warren?' asked Jill.

'The tree surgeon and firewood man,' said Esther.

'Odd in what way?'

'Very changeable,' replied Esther. 'He can be all charm one minute, and then he's taken offence and gone off on one. You never know quite where you are with him.'

'He's my next stop,' said Jill. 'Thanks for the heads-up.'

She heard Warren Thorne before she saw him. Or at least, she heard the evidence of his activities. A circular saw was whining in the background, and the sound of splitting timber was interspersed by the bang of logs falling on a wooden floor. She got out of her car and followed the sounds round the corner of a long low shed. In the open space beneath a lean-to was a short but muscular man, stripped to the waist, pushing logs onto the saw to be cut into lengths suitable for a domestic fire. The pile below the saw was growing fast and a pickup stood alongside, the cargo bed already half full of firewood. As she approached, the man flipped a switch, and the whine of the saw wound down the scale into silence. In the sudden stillness her footsteps rang loud, and the man turned round sharply, startled.

'Hi,' he said, recovering his self-possession. 'What can I do you for?'

Jill held out her warrant card and, for the fourth time that morning, explained why she was there and what she wanted. As she spoke, she was taking a crafty look at the front of the pickup. The radiator and headlights were covered by a protective grill, which did show signs of hard wear.

'Call me Warren,' he said, wiping his sweaty hands down the sides of his jeans and holding one out for her to shake. 'I'll help all I can, but I don't think I know anything useful. I only knew Mrs Cooper as someone who bought firewood occasionally.'

'How did you get on with her?' asked Jill.

Warren perched himself on the edge of the saw bench and reached out for the t-shirt lying discarded on a pile of wood. 'Fine,' he said. 'She was a nice lady. Paid promptly. I had no issues with her.'

'Did you know of anyone who didn't get on with her? Anyone who might have had...' Jill was about to say *an axe to grind*, but felt it inappropriate in the circumstances and amended it to, '...a problem with her?'

'No,' he said.

'How well do you know your other neighbours?' she asked.

'Esther the Hens is OK. Bit of an organic nut – you know, all herbs and health – but OK really. River is just a plain nutter. I mean, really out there. Talk about conspiracy theories – I reckon he wrote the book on 'em. Wouldn't put it past him to have a nuclear bunker and an arsenal hidden away on his place, ready for Armageddon. Know what I mean.' Warren put his finger alongside his nose and winked at Jill. 'If you were looking for someone who'd shot up a town, I'd be pointing you at River. No doubt about it. But I can't see any reason why he'd have it in for Ann Cooper.'

'What about your new neighbour, Tristan Smith?' asked Jill.

'Well that's just it. She's new. I don't know her really,' said Warren.

'And that's all I got,' said Jill, reporting back to Chris. 'Not much for your spreadsheets, I'm afraid. The only one with a damaged Land Rover had a good alibi for the damage having happened long before the incidents we're investigating, and no one knows of any reason why anyone would have it in for Ann Cooper.'

'OK,' said Chris. 'Thanks for the update. I'll pass it to Greg when he gets back in touch. Where are you going next?'

'Wroxham, to see if I can find anything on Ben Lyell, the chef,' replied Jill. 'I know Greg said to prioritise Kain Smith, but it seems Jim and Bill have everything concerning him in hand.'

25

The search

When Greg arrived at Martham Boatyard he found Jim standing in a swirl of police officers, dogs, boaters and a throng of volunteers whose numbers were increasing by the moment. Crime scene tape was fluttering merrily in the stiff breeze off the river and preventing access to a stretch of bank roughly one hundred metres long. At least two of the public bending Bill's ear at the margin of the disputed zone were boat owners who could not access their vessels moored on that stretch of the river. A couple of boats were lingering near the boatyard slipway and two more were turning circles in the river nearby, apparently waiting for a chance to moor up.

Jim hailed Greg's approach with relief. 'Am I glad to see you,' he said in an undertone. 'Kain's family hit the social media as soon as they heard about the bike, and it's turning into a bit of a circus down here. They appealed for help to mount a search, and this is the result.'

'I heard,' said Greg briefly. 'That's why I'm here. I thought you could do with some assistance. Is that Ned I see over there?' He nodded in the direction of the taped area.

'Yes. The bike had been handled by Uncle Tom Cobley and all by the time we arrived. SOCO are checking out the area around. The bike was found by the chap talking to Bill. His yacht grounded on it when he tried to sail off this morning. He went off to have a moan at the boatyard staff, and between them they hauled the bike out of the water. It was the same boatyard expert who showed us where to find the Saunders body, and, remembering the bike clips, he thought it might be Saunders's bike. They called it in, and as soon as I saw the photos, I realised it was much more likely to be Kain's. I got the local team to seal off the bank, had Kain's family identify the bike and asked Bill to bring the dog team down here. That's when all hell broke loose with this lot.' He gestured at the increasing crowd of volunteers.

'OK. Thanks, Jim. You concentrate on SOCO and retrieving what we can from the bike and the place it was dumped. I'll sort this little lot out. Jill is on her way here.'

Greg walked over to where Bill was talking to the man who'd found the bike: a weathered, lean man in his fifties clad in long shorts and sweatshirt topped by a lifejacket. The two dog handlers were hovering at Bill's elbow, trying to get his attention. Greg turned to them first.

'What do you need?' he asked.

'A clear space, more dogs and, if possible, something of Kain Smith's,' responded Scouller succinctly.

'Right, let's get this sorted.' Greg glanced round and spotted a pile of pallets on the bank near the slipway. 'Bill, take the gentleman's details and tell him we'll get back to him shortly. Scouller, get on to your despatcher and see what you can do about more dogs. Steve, come with me.'

He walked briskly to the pallets and, with Steve's help, stacked four to form a rickety pile and two more to give him a step up. Then he mounted his improvised platform and surveyed the car park. There were knots of people talking and waving phones all over the space, with two big groups by the tape preventing access to the riverbank and more arriving all the time from the road. Uniformed police were turning cars away but struggling to contain those arriving on foot.

'Right,' bellowed Greg. And when that went unheeded, he put two fingers in his mouth and blew a long, penetrating whistle. A silence fell, broken only by the honking of a pair of geese flying slowly upriver, their wings beating strongly.

'I am Detective Chief Inspector Geldard, and I am in charge here.' Now that the crowd was still, his voice carried clearly over the wind and the geese. 'We are grateful for your offers of help, but we need to get this search organised. Everyone who is not a police officer, kindly leave the car park area now and gather at the end of the road there.' He pointed. 'You will be organised into search teams and we will get the job underway as soon as we can. Thank you for your cooperation.'

With a few, relatively quiet, murmurs, the crowd gradually moved off the car park and gathered where Greg had indicated.

'Steve, take Bill and any uniformed officer not defending the barricades, and start sorting them into search teams. But make them understand the dogs need space to work. Keep them clear of the car park and the immediate riverside for now. Ensure every team has either a police officer or trained search and rescue volunteer, and make sure they understand their role is to look, not to meddle, and definitely *not* to film for social media. Anyone gets caught doing that, and they're out.'

Jumping down from his mini stage, Greg looked round for his search experts. 'Scouller, where would they provide most help and least hindrance?' he asked.

'At home,' she muttered. 'But I don't suppose that's an option!' More loudly she said, 'There are six more dogs and handlers on their way. Two of them are nearby and should be with us very shortly. The others are around half an hour away. We and the other two dogs will start from the car park and search the riverbank and fields alongside. The others will relieve us, and then we'll leapfrog first along the river and then up Cess Road. Looking at the map, I think this crowd are probably best employed checking round the gardens and sheds behind the river properties, and the two big industrial yards up Cess Road. Hopefully, quite a few will soon get tired and go home. Have we got that item from Kain's home yet? We can manage without, if it's not possible. The dogs will track where someone has disturbed undergrowth.'

'I've got some of his clothing from his parents,' said Steve. 'I'll get it for you.'

'You heard the expert,' said Greg to Bill and Steve. 'Get the crowd organised.'

A quick chat with Ned sufficed to confirm what Greg had guessed. That the multiple hands which had been all over the bike as it was pulled from the river and carried to the car park had done a good job of removing or obscuring any evidence that might have survived immersion. Ned was also particularly disgruntled about the crowd in the car park.

'That's removed any chance we had of finding how the bike got into the river,' he grumbled.

'Speaking of which,' said Greg, 'that's the other specialist team we may need. I'll give the dogs a chance, but if they don't find anything, or if they find traces of Kain near the river, we're going to need the divers.'

The next couple of hours were a vivid reminder, to Greg at least, of the last time he'd participated in a mass search. That had been near Loe Pool in Cornwall and had not resulted in a find of any body, dead or alive. As he struggled through long grass and over deep ditches, pulling his legs free of snagging thorns and always an unobtrusive distance behind the dogs, he clung to a hope that this time might be different. At intervals Bill and Steve, joined by Jill after a short delay, reported on the progress made by the volunteer teams. As they too failed to turn up anything of interest and teatime approached, the numbers began to fall away significantly. By 5pm the dog teams reported that they had been unable to find any traces on the riverbanks: neither a body nor any trace of Kain Smith's scent.

'We're going to move to the woods, further up Cess Road,' said Philips. 'We can backtrack if you want and repeat the searches of the boatyards and so on, but according to the reports, those have had a pretty thorough going over from the foot patrols, so I'd say they were lower priority than the woods.'

'Thanks,' said Greg. 'Let's make the most of what's left of the light. If we find nothing, then I'm asking for the divers in the morning, just in case he ended up in the river like Phil Saunders.'

The woods were a whole other environment. The trees were not growing very closely together, but the space between them was boggy and strewn with fallen branches, while any break in the canopy overhead was celebrated at ground level by mounds of brambles and thickets of nettles. Despite their long search, the dogs, mainly springer spaniels with a couple of Labradors for variety, seemed to welcome the change in terrain and renewed their search with undiminished enthusiasm. Greg, following on tired legs, wished he had their energy. He sniffed to see whether he could sense what they were so clearly enjoying, but all he could pick up was wet ground and the earthy smell of fungi.

'If he's dead,' he said to Jim at his elbow, 'wouldn't even humans be able to smell him by now?'

'After three days?' replied Jim. 'Maybe. Given the warm weather and the damp environment. Perhaps that means either the body's not here, or he's still alive.'

'Let's hope the latter,' said Greg. 'But finding his bike isn't encouraging.'

'True,' said Jim. 'I wasn't thinking clearly. I suppose I've always hoped he wasn't one of our series.'

They both froze at a shout from the dog team ahead of them. It was one of the handlers they hadn't met before, with a big, sturdy, golden Labrador named, appropriately, Goldie. Looking towards the handler, they saw Goldie sitting amid a bed of nettles, still as a statue, her nose pointing at a large bramble bush in front of her.

'Oh no,' said Greg as, at a word from her handler, she broke her pose, bounded towards him and claimed her reward: the tennis ball from his pocket. The handler's radio crackled just as Greg and Jim caught up with him, and he indicated with his hand the location of Goldie's find as he used the radio to stand down the rest of the dog team.

From a discreet distance, Greg and Jim viewed the crumpled remains of what had been a young man, full of future promise. 'Damn,' said Greg bleakly. 'Get the SOCOs in. And the doc. I'll get over to Hemsby and tell his parents.'

He rang Jill on the way. 'We found his body,' he explained. 'Can you halt the volunteer search, those who're still out there, and thank them for me. Tell them we found a body, but no details about who, how or where. I'm on my way to speak to his parents. And I'll get a statement out to the media, saying the search for Kain Smith has found a body which has yet to be formally identified.'

It was Greg's least favourite job. And it was no comfort that, as so often in these circumstances, he hardly needed to say anything. His mere presence and solemn expression were sufficient for the parents to reach a conclusion. Kain's father gave a low moan and turned to hold his wife, as she sagged against him, too distressed to cry.

The tears will come later, Greg thought, and realised that the imminent arrival of his first child had made him more sensitive to the grief of a parent.

'I'm so sorry for your loss,' he said quietly. 'Clearly there has been no formal identification of Kain yet, but there can be little doubt that the body is his.'

His mother stood up. 'I want to go to him,' she said. 'Now.'

'I'm sorry, but that wouldn't be wise,' said Greg. 'The body we've found is in woodland, and not easy to access in the dark. Tomorrow morning it will be taken to the mortuary, and you can see him then if you wish. In fact, we'll need one of you, or another close family member, to identify the body formally.'

'So it may not be him then?' cried Mrs Smith, clutching at straws.

'I'm afraid there can be little doubt that it is,' said Greg gently. 'The clothes, the photo, the bike found a little way off in the river, they all match.'

'But why can't I go to him? I can't leave him all alone out there all night,' she wailed.

'I'm sorry,' repeated Greg. 'The location is a crime scene. But I can promise you that he won't be left alone. And as soon as it's possible, I will take you to see him.' He stood to go, and Mr Smith stood with him.

'I'll see you out,' he said. At the door he put a hand on Greg's arm. 'Was it murder?' he asked, in a quiet voice not designed to carry to the sitting room. 'Was my boy murdered?'

'I think so,' said Greg.

'Get him,' said the father. 'Get him and put him away for good. Because if I get to him first, he won't survive to stand trial.'

Greg opened his mouth to respond, then realised both that nothing he could say would make anything better, and that trying to speak past the lump in his throat was next to impossible. He shook his head mutely and left in silence.

Heading for home and Chris, on impulse Greg turned his car back towards Martham. Cess Lane was closed off by a manned police barrier. They let him through, and he pulled up beside the wood, now lit with an unearthly glow from the floodlight inside the blue tent. Outlined against the glow, Greg saw a shape walking towards him, stumbling slightly on the uneven ground. He reached into his car for his powerful torch and shone it on the ground in front of the doctor, to light her path to the road.

'Thank you,' she said as she reached Greg. 'I always forget my torch, and my phone is nowhere near as good as that.' She indicated Greg's police issue torch.

'Not much good as a makeshift weapon either,' agreed Greg. 'You've been taking a look at the body?'

'As much as I can in the circumstances,' she replied. 'I'll know better after the postmortem, but it certainly looks like another in the series. Hit by a car, I'd say, and died subsequently of his injuries after being dragged into the wood.'

'Died instantly, or later?' asked Greg. 'I'm sorry, I know you may not be able to give me a time of death yet, but the condition of the body puzzled me. No smell to speak of. Little decomposition.'

'You noticed that,' said the doctor. 'He went missing when?'

'On the eleventh,' said Greg. 'After four days, I'd have thought...'

'Yes,' said the doctor. 'And you're right. I'm pretty sure he didn't die straightaway. Probably only a couple of days ago. But as I said, I'll be able to tell you more after the postmortem. I'll do it as soon as I can tomorrow.'

26

Research and leads

Chris was torn between relief that she wasn't yomping through boggy woodland, and frustration that she was missing out on the excitement. She sighed for the old days, and turned back to her draft shortlist of the attributes she was seeking in a potential suspect. So far, her list ran:

Hallucinations leading to violence
Delusions ditto
Narcissism ditto
Paranoia / anxiety ditto

She ran her pen down the list, hesitated and deleted the third item, on the grounds that the average police officer was unlikely to make a note to that effect; then added:

Reported failure to take medications

to her red flags. Then she picked up the phone and embarked on the first of a series of calls to colleagues around the county.

By late afternoon she had a depressingly, but unsurprisingly, long list of incidents involving mental health cases to which police officers had been called. She was able to discount more than a few as not triggering her red flags, and after much debate with herself, she removed another batch which involved people threatening or committing violence against themselves, rather than other people.

After a brief interruption to feed cat, parrot and self, she laid out the results of her morning's research all over the kitchen table and took a step back, both physically and mentally, in order to assess what she had learned. One individual stood out as triggering two of the red flags as well as fitting other criteria, and she picked up the phone to Greg.

Unfortunately, he was in mid-search at the time, and her call went to voicemail. So did the calls to Jim and Jill. Chris left *Ring me!* messages in various digital locations, then turned back to her laptop with more duty than enthusiasm. There was a long tail of neglected emails sitting in her inbox to which she directed her reluctant attention. The first four or five were dismissed with alacrity and an invitation to an assertiveness training course was trashed even quicker, on the grounds that Greg had long ago offered her hard cash not to get any more assertive than she already was.

About halfway down the list of emails was one that immediately stopped her scrolling. She read it twice, then made a note and switched screens to the Word document that summarised Jill's report on her visits to Ann Cooper's neighbours.

'Bingo,' she said aloud. 'I thought I was remembering correctly.' Then she rang Greg again. This time the message was a little longer.

'I've just seen the report from Bill about the incident at Waxham Barns between Kain Smith and a Land Rover driver,' she said. 'The number plate caught on CCTV is a match for Tristan Smith's. I think someone needs to have another chat with her. Oh, and if you picked up my earlier message, it was about the research into mental health cases involving the police. There was one that triggered two of my red flags – delusions with threats of violence and failure to take medication. It was one Mr Moon River, also a Cooper neighbour. However, you might feel the number plate evidence trumps that.'

Greg didn't pick up the messages until after his encounter with the doctor. He was about to head home when his phone informed him that Chris had rung him several times during the afternoon. He'd just finished listening to the second of Chris's voicemails when Jim rang.

'I've had a call...'

'Yes, from Chris, I imagine,' said Greg.

'Well, yes. But also from Ben Asheton,' said Jim. 'You might think of him as our neighbourhood first responder, but it seems he's also an old mate of Tristan Smith's from way back. He's had her on the phone, complaining we've been pestering her and seem to have her in the lineup for multiple deaths.'

'Oh Lord,' said Greg. 'I'd forgotten she was a friend of Ben's. What's he saying?'

'Well, you know Ben,' said Jim. 'Not one to step over a line. He's asking, as carefully as is humanly possible, whether we've lost our senses. Or at least, words to that effect. He says he realises we need to investigate any leads, but that he's known Smith for decades and any suggestion she could be involved is nonsensical. That she was very upset by what went on in North Yorkshire, and we need to cut her some slack. If possible.'

'Which, in light of Chris's latest, is a little awkward,' said Greg. 'Jim, can you go and see Smith in the morning, and take Jill with you? You see, I got to know her a little during the Yorkshire case, so I think I'm compromised. I'll cover the Kain postmortem first thing, then go and reinterview the other possible lead that Chris has turned up. Our Mr Moon River.'

By the time Greg got home, the evening was well advanced. Bobby had already gone out for her evening's hunt along the riverbank, while Chris and Tally had settled down for a cosy curl up on the sofa.

'Good day?' asked Greg as he dropped a kiss on Chris's head.

'Not bad,' she said, craning her neck to see him properly. 'But I gather you had a pretty grim afternoon. Bad news about that poor lad?'

'Yes,' said Greg, helping himself to a wedge of bread and a hunk of cheese.

'Sorry,' said Chris. 'I didn't cook because I didn't know when you'd be back.'

'It's fine,' said Greg indistinctly, through the huge mouthful of crust and Camembert. 'I couldn't be bothered with anything fancy anyway. And yes, it wasn't a good afternoon, and it means another postmortem in the morning. We have to stop this nutter before they do it again, Chris. Thanks, by the way, for all that work on mental health call-outs and such. We'll be following it up in the morning.'

'And the alpaca breeder?' asked Chris. 'The friend of Ben's?'

'Ah, you heard that, did you? Yes, her too. I've asked Jim to deal, as I knew her in North Yorkshire. Between you and me,

Chris, I think Ben's right. I think she's an unlikely candidate for serial killer. So, I'm compromised. Let's see what Jim and Jill turn up.'

***

'Oh no, not again!' was Tristan Smith's greeting when Jim and Jill arrived the following morning. 'Look,' she said, 'I have an alpaca on the verge of giving birth and I'm behind on two weaving orders, so unless this is important, I'd rather you came back another day.'

'DI Henning. Pleased to meet you too,' said Jim. 'And it is both important and urgent, so no we won't be coming back another day. But if it's inconvenient for you to see us here, we could always take this over to the station in Great Yarmouth.'

'We most certainly cannot,' responded Tristan. 'I told you. I have an alpaca about to give birth. If you want to ask me questions, yet again, you'll have to do it out in the barn.' She led the way to the largest of the farm buildings, through the half-open double doors and into an open space surrounded by smaller pens. 'And keep the noise down,' she said. 'I don't want her disturbed.'

All the pens were empty save one. In that, a grey alpaca with a white, grey and black topknot was moving gently round a well-strawed pen, picking occasionally at the hay in one corner. She came over to take a closer look at the strangers in her midst, making a strange crooning noise, then leaned her nose in the direction of Tristan, who scratched it.

'What a pretty animal,' said Jill, trying out her good-cop routine. 'With that topknot, she looks as though she's wearing a Philip Treacy hat!'

'Exactly what I thought,' said Tristan, smiling for the first time. 'Which is why her stable name is Hatty.'

'Not what we came to talk to you about however,' said Jim in a deliberately harsh tone. 'Why didn't you tell us you knew Kain Smith? Was he a relation by any chance?'

'I didn't know I did,' said Tristan, turning to look at Jim. 'And no, I have no relation with that name. Smith's a pretty common surname, as you must know.

'What do you mean? *Was* he a relation? Has something happened to him?'

'Didn't you see the local news last night?' asked Jill. 'About the body found near Martham?'

'I saw something,' said Tristan, distracted by Hatty moving around restlessly. 'But I don't see why it has anything to do with me.'

'Where were you on the eleventh of September?' asked Jim.

'What? The eleventh? Here I suppose,' said Tristan, watching Hatty lie down, stand up and lie down again.

'Not at Waxham Barns?' asked Jim.

'Waxham Barns? Oh, don't tell me this is about the ridiculous fracas in the car park!' exclaimed Tristan. 'Was that on the eleventh? Oh, for goodness sake! Haven't you anything better to do? Here, get out of my way.'

She abruptly pushed past Jim, who was on the verge of arresting her until he realised that the cause of her move was the second head that had suddenly sprouted from Hatty's rear end. Jill and Jim watched, fascinated, as Tristan pulled gently on a couple of tiny hooves, until feet and head were joined by a body and hind legs. The whole lot fell to the floor and lay in the straw, being nosed and hummed at by the triumphant mother. Tristan picked up an aerosol can from the corner of the pen, and briskly sprayed the youngster's navel with purple disinfectant, then put the can down and rubbed the wet, black body with a handful of straw.

'Doesn't the mother lick it dry?' asked Jill, with memories of lambs and calves.

'No. Alpacas don't do that,' said Tristan, standing up. 'Come on, we'll go into the house now, and leave these two to get acquainted.'

'I thought the baby would be grey like its mother,' said Jill as they walked across the yard.

'Cria,' said Tristan. 'A baby alpaca is called a cria. The father was black, so the cria was most likely to be grey or black, depending on how much of the colour-diluter gene she inherited.'

They went into the cottage, where Tristan led them into the kitchen and sat them down at the kitchen table.

'So all this is about the idiot in the Waxham Barns car park,' said Tristan. 'It's quite simple, and I think the man at the coffee bar would support my version of events. The lad on the bike pulled out in front of me without looking. I stopped just in time, stuck my head out of the window, and if I remember correctly, I shouted something like "Who knitted you, you great wazzock?" He called me a clumsy bitch and few other, ruder, epithets, probably because he'd spilled his coffee, and then we both continued on our way. End of, as far as I'm concerned.'

'Did you follow him out of the car park?'

'No. Why would I? I was headed back here. I had jobs to do. I'd only called at the Barns to see if they'd like to sell some of my rugs. Why all the questions?'

'We think it was his body we found last night,' said Jim. 'So naturally we were interested in an altercation that took place earlier on the day he went missing.' The words fell into the silence like lead bricks.

'I think I need a solicitor, before I answer any more questions,' said Tristan at last.

'Which is, of course, your right,' agreed Jim. 'But that will be enough questions for now. Please don't leave the county without notifying us.'

27

More digging

Chris waved Greg off for his morning of postmortem followed by conversation with a potential homicidal maniac, and decided she'd got the mucky end of the stick. Yesterday's glow, arising from identifying possible leads, had subsided, leaving cold ashes and the realisation she faced another day in front of the laptop scrutinising databases. Repeating the sigh, she fetched some biscuits from the cupboard as reward and encouragement for dealing with the boring stuff, then put it away again after removing only two from the packet.

'You've got a lot to answer for.' She addressed her little stranger. 'Boring job and no biscuits. You'd better be worth it.'

With the comfortable realisation that he or she probably was, she addressed the long list of registration plates identified as both belonging to four-by-fours or small vans *and* moving along the A149 in the vicinity of the cyclist deaths on the days in question. Even with all those provisos, it was a long list. Just as she was about to settle down to a morning of eyestrain as well as tedium, she had a brainwave. Whipping out her iPad she had recourse to Google with some pertinent questions about

AI. Then she rang the Chief Super's office and checked what was available on police systems. Her final move was to list the registration plates of all the vehicles that had come to their attention as belonging to the victims, their neighbours, friends and relatives. Finally, she loaded both lists into the relevant AI facility and pressed go. In less than a minute she had a new list – all the numbers that appeared on both datasets. Better still, the associated information about ownership, status, etc, had been preserved as well.

'Bingo,' she whispered. 'All I have to do now is see what makes sense.'

Running her eye down the much-shortened list was a matter of moments. Aware that most of the key team were already tied up, this time instead of making phone calls she wrote a short email summarising her findings. She checked it twice against the AI report, then clicked send.

Checking the findings of the ANPR team against our other data has produced a priority list of two. In the cases of Phil Saunders, Ann Cooper and Kain Smith, vehicles belonging to Tristan Smith and Moon River were recorded in the vicinity and on the relevant days. Specifically, TS number plate turns up near Ann Cooper on 1/9 and Kain Smith on 11/9. For MR, on the other hand, it's Phil Saunders and also Kain Smith. So the data doesn't explicitly tie any one person to all the cases, but I do think these two are worth another look. As previously advised, MR has also been the subject of a mental health intervention by the Great Yarmouth police, including suspicion that he had not been taking his prescribed antipsychotic medication. I would suggest that these two are priority for closer scrutiny and potentially a search warrant for their properties.

Over to you!

Over in Norwich, Greg arrived at the mortuary to find that Dr Paisley had already completed the postmortem – somewhat to his relief, as the sound of a saw grinding through skull bones was not his favourite start to the day.

'This was an easy one,' was her greeting. 'Come in, Greg, and I'll walk you through my findings.'

Greg hastily donned a white coat and followed the doctor into the cold room with the steel tables and bright lights. Today, he was pleased to note, the smell was bearable.

'First,' she said, leading him up to the nearest table and pointing at the young man's right leg. 'His knee joint was shattered by the impact from what I'm guessing was a vehicle, like the others. But it could, of course, have been a blow from a weapon with a very large blunt head, like a mallet. The associated bruising on that side of the body, however, supports the RTA theory.

'There are signs that the body was moved prior to death, as there are both scratches and bruises on the back and left side. He was then left in the supine position in which he was found, but I don't think he died immediately.'

Walking to the head of the table, she removed a cloth from Kain Smith's head to expose the open skull and brain beneath. 'I left this for you to see,' she said. 'It's pretty clear to me that when he was knocked from his bike, he hit his head on something when he landed. Most likely a tree trunk. Ned will probably be able to find evidence on site. The blow both stunned him and caused a slow bleed on the brain, from which he eventually died.'

'How long would that have taken?' asked Greg.

'Given that I estimate his time of death as around forty-eight to fifty-six hours ago, a day or maybe two. He would almost certainly have been unconscious the whole time.'

'But would his injuries have been survivable if treated?'

'Possibly, possibly not,' said Dr Paisley, making a rocking movement with one hand to indicate the conclusion was in the balance.

'Another case where the victim might have survived if they had not been concealed,' concluded Greg. 'The case for these being murder rather than accident or negligence is getting stronger all the time.'

'Was there ever any doubt?' asked Dr Paisley, surprised.

'Not in my mind,' said Greg. 'But every little helps when a case comes to court.'

Back in his car he read Chris's latest email on his phone, then rang her.

'Smith and River,' he said. 'OK. I've seen Jim and Jill's reports on Tristan Smith. Not enough to rule her out, but not enough to rule her in either. I'll send them back to question her on the specific ANPR results you've turned up. I'm on my way to Mr River now.'

'Not on your own, I hope,' said Chris.

'No. I've asked Bill to meet me there. Don't worry,' he added.

By the time Greg had extracted himself from the Norwich traffic, now picking up as Covid restrictions were eased, Bill had already reported arriving in the vicinity of Moon River's off-grid establishment.

'Wait down the road,' instructed Greg. 'Don't go in without me. I'll only be around ten minutes.'

It was, in fact, well within that time that Greg drove past Bill parked in a lay-by, flashed his lights and continued down the narrow drive that led to Moon River's yard and shack. The dilapidated van mentioned by Jill in her report was in evidence, which Greg took as confirmation that Mr River was on the premises. Bill pulled up behind him, and both men swivelled round to survey their surroundings.

'Scruffy set-up, isn't it?' said Bill, not troubling to mute his tone.

'I've seen tidier,' agreed Greg, noting the random piles of scrap iron, torn black plastic and broken concrete. 'Tristan Smith's place for one. But while tidiness may be next to godliness, it doesn't necessarily mean innocence.

'Mr River,' he shouted. 'We'd like a few words. Mr River!'

Bill added his voice to the calls, but no one responded.

'Perhaps he's out and about foraging whatever it is he does forage from the wood,' said Greg. 'Let's have a look round.'

A detailed scrutiny of the yard didn't reveal anything of interest, other than a broken bike frame among the other rubbish. Bill's initial excitement at the discovery was, however, swiftly quelled when it became clear that it had probably been in situ for at least a year, as evidenced by the brambles growing through it. After a bit more shouting, Greg went over to the shack which constituted Mr River's home. Part of it was a sturdy construction of brick and tile that appeared to be an old garage or shed. It had been extended by the addition of a lean-to porch and two wings, one to either side, which owed a lot to scrap timber and corrugated iron. Water from the roof was ingeniously channelled into a couple of storage tanks, and each wing bore a rudimentary chimney. Greg knocked on the door, waited a moment, then pushed it open and went in, followed by Bill.

It seemed the brick-built centre of the shack was Mr River's living quarters. There was an old kitchen table and chair, plus a sagging sofa and cupboard that Greg suspected had been rescued from a skip. A fireplace on the right seemed to enjoy the benefits of one of the chimneys, but not very efficiently, judging by the soot deposits on everything. One of the wings was a combined bathroom and toilet, with an old stove providing a crude means of heating water. The opposite extension was clearly the bedroom. All the spaces were empty of occupier.

'Where does he cook?' asked Bill.

'On the fire in the living room or outside, probably,' responded Greg. 'Clearly he's not here at the moment. Let's have another look outside, and if we can't find him, we'll have to come back later. Perhaps with dogs.'

Wandering around behind the shack, Bill found a pile of non-recyclable rubbish (small) and a compost bin (impressively large). As he turned to look at the vegetable beds behind the shack, a flicker of movement caught his eye.

'Hi, Mr River,' he called.

Greg looked over in the same direction, quickly enough to see a small shabby man heading back into the wood. 'Don't make us chase you,' he shouted, taking a few steps in pursuit nonetheless. 'We just have a few questions. Bill,' he said in a hurried aside, 'go that way and cut him off if he makes a run for it.'

Their quarry, clearly in two minds about his best course of action, hesitated, and was lost. The two burly policemen trapped him between them on the narrow woodland path, and he held his hands up in surrender.

'What d'you want?' he asked. 'I answered all the questions that nice lady copper had.'

'We've got a few more,' said Greg. 'I'm DCI Geldard and this is DC Street. Come back to the house with us,' he added, upgrading *shack* to something more tactful, 'I'm sure we can soon sort this.'

Back in the shack, Greg and Bill took the sofa, leaving the unstable kitchen chair to their host.

'Nettle tea?' he offered.

'We're good, thanks,' said Greg, correctly interpreting Bill's look of horror, although whether that was at the nettles or the likelihood of food poisoning from the cooking arrangements, he didn't know. 'That your van out there?' He nodded towards the off-white vehicle currently gracing the yard.

'Yes,' said Mr River, apparently pleased to get a question he could answer.

'We have some questions about where you and the van were on…' Greg referred to his notes and listed the relevant dates. Mr River looked blank.

'No idea,' he said. 'I drive most days, but I couldn't tell you precisely where I was on specific dates. I don't have a calendar. All the days are pretty much the same to me.'

Repeated and assiduous questioning elicited nothing more helpful, and after an hour Greg was forced to the conclusion that Mr River was genuinely unable to help, whether or not that failure was a convenient smokescreen for something more sinister. At last, he changed tack.

'Can I ask you about something a little different,' he said. 'You have had some contact with us in the past. We have a record of you calling the local police out in June. Do you remember that?'

Mr River looked down at the floor and muttered something.

'Sorry, can you say that again,' said Greg.

'I said, I wasn't well,' said Mr River. 'I rang 999 and asked for some help, but I didn't get an ambulance. Not at first anyway. It was your lot that came.'

'Why did you need help?' asked Greg.

'I was afraid I was going to hurt someone. Or me,' admitted Mr River. 'I was really, really stressed and I just needed someone to help.' He looked over at Greg, seemed to come to a decision, and pulled up one of his sleeves. His arm was criss-crossed with thin scars that Greg recognised as evidence of self-harming. 'It's horrible, feeling like that,' Mr River muttered. 'Horrible.' He shuddered at the recollection.

'Have you ever hurt anyone?' asked Greg.

'No. I never. But I was afraid I might. When it gets really bad, I can't see a way out. I feel trapped.'

'According to our records, you told our chaps that you hadn't been taking your medications,' said Greg. 'Was that true?'

'Yes. Then,' he said. 'I am now though,' he was quick to reassure them. 'Honest.' He crossed his heart. 'They changed the prescription, and I'm taking them now. Look.'

He got up and went over to the old cupboard, opened the door and reached inside. 'Look,' he said again, holding out a packet, showing Greg and Bill the half-empty blister pack. 'I take them every day now. Honest.'

Over by the cars, Greg and Bill looked each other. 'That's not evidence he's taking the pills,' remarked Bill.

'No, it's not,' said Greg. 'And we're none the wiser about his movements on the key dates.'

'I suppose we could try talking to his mental health team, now we're asking about a specific person. And if we got a blood test, we could see if he's taking the meds,' said Bill. 'He might consent to that.'

'Worth a try,' replied Greg. 'I could also try for a warrant to search his property, but the grounds are shaky. Let's see what Jim and Jill get out of Tristan Smith, but I still can't see her as a prime suspect.'

He got into his car and looked up at Bill. 'I think my next conversation needs to be with the boss,' he said. 'I'm petrified there's going to be another case. I think we need to increase patrols in this area.'

'Won't have much impact,' said Bill sceptically, poised to get into his own car. 'There's a lot of back roads to cover.'

'I know,' said Greg. 'But I'm getting desperate.'

28

Taking stock

Jim was on the phone before Greg got to Wymondham.

'Tristan Smith's in the clear,' he reported. 'She has an alibi for three of the occasions when her registration plate was caught on ANPR. One of them involves Ben Asheton. She was having supper with Ben and his wife. So, either the ANPR data is wrong, or someone cloned her plate.'

'That's progress of a kind,' said Greg, navigating the Thickthorn roundabout with some care as he spoke on his hands-free. 'At least it rules her out, even if it opens up another can of worms. If someone's cloned number plates, it could be anyone.

'And we're no further forward with our Mr River. He doesn't know one day from the next, so we need to do some further checking. I'm on my way to have a chat with the boss about precautionary patrols and maybe a press conference.'

'Did I hear you say press conference?' asked Jim in mock astonishment.

'You did. I'm getting desperate, Jim. We don't seem to be any closer to an arrest and in my estimation, the risk of another incident is high.'

'The boss isn't going to like the patrols suggestion,' predicted Jim. 'Too resource-expensive.'

***

'Greg, excellent – that was quick,' was Margaret's greeting when Greg entered her outer office. 'Come through. I thought you would be ages yet.'

Frank Parker from the CPS was already sitting in front of Margaret's desk when Greg entered. He took the other seat and nodded a hello.

'I didn't know I was expected,' he said. 'I just popped up on the off chance you might be able to see me, so I could update you on where we are with the cyclists case.'

'You didn't see my message asking you to call in?' said Margaret. 'No matter. You're here now. We want to talk to you about Irwin Lloyd.'

Greg blinked. His focus on Kain Smith and his fellow victims had been so complete he struggled to switch gears. 'Irwin Lloyd,' he said. 'Yes. I thought he'd been committed for trial, and we were waiting on court availability. What's to discuss?'

'The charge,' said Frank flatly. 'You charged him with murder. We're considering downgrading it to manslaughter.'

'Ah.' Greg took a drink of the coffee Margaret had, with typical generosity, just poured. Then another as he waited for his brain to catch up with developments. 'Why?' he said at last.

'Because the delays in getting cases heard are getting worse,' said Margaret. 'The backlogs are ever longer, and a murder trial will wait over a year. Possibly more than two.

'Lloyd's solicitor has indicated that he'd be willing to plead guilty to manslaughter, but not to murder. A sentencing hearing could be dealt with much quicker, and we're struggling to see the public benefit in pursuing a murder trial in this case. He could still get a long prison term. Lloyd is not a young man and he's no threat to wider society.'

'And he could get community service or a suspended sentence, depending on the whim of the judge,' objected Greg. 'Look, we only have his word for it that Fred Hamilton was threatening or assaulting his wife when he was stabbed. The evidence tells us he was stabbed in the back, that the knife was handled by Irwin Lloyd and Hamilton's blood was on Lloyd's clothes. On top of that, Lloyd has confessed to the stabbing. Everything else is an unsupported statement from one man.'

'On the other hand,' countered Frank, 'we have a case involving a man who presents no risk to the public, who is willing to plead guilty to manslaughter, thus getting him off the court lists and freeing time to deal with genuinely dangerous criminals. I can see no public good in pursuing a murder charge—'

'Save justice for Fred Hamilton,' interrupted Greg.

'Who on all accounts, even that of his daughter, was a nasty piece of work who bullied her mother,' countered Frank. 'Thus supporting the version of events put forward by Lloyd.'

'The decision's been made,' said Margaret, intervening before the argument became still more heated. 'Justice will be seen to be done with a conviction for manslaughter. That is sufficient in the circumstances. Thank you, Frank.'

After the CPS lawyer had left the room, feathers somewhat ruffled, Margaret turned again to Greg. 'I gather you wanted to see me,' she said. 'What progress finding the cyclist killer?'

'Not enough,' said Greg bluntly. 'The data suggested two suspects, one of whom has been ruled out, the other requires more investigation, but I don't have enough yet to go for an arrest. I think we should commission additional patrols in the area around Ormesby, Rollesby and Martham, and I also think we should put people on their guard.'

'Are you suggesting a press conference?' asked Margaret, with a level of incredulity that almost matched Jim's.

'Yes,' said Greg.

'We'll start a panic,' said Margaret. 'And what do we have to reassure people that we have the case in hand.'

'Not enough. And maybe we need to start a panic,' said Greg. 'If it keeps cyclists off the roads for a bit, while we catch this chap.'

'No,' said Margaret. 'I'll consult, but my reaction is no, and I think the Chief will say the same. We could put out a warning about increasing cyclist fatalities. We could even point to the roads that are a particular risk. But I'm not prepared to go public with any suggestion that these accidents are deliberate. Not until you have something more to say than *We are investigating*.' As Greg opened his mouth, she added, 'That's final, Greg. And don't even consider going behind my back on this. I'll get the warnings out, leave that with me. And

I'll see about additional patrols, although we do have resource problems, as you know. And that's it. You can get back to work.'

29

Checking up

The following morning, back at HQ, Bill was being given the runaround. He'd spoken to multiple gatekeepers in multiple NHS mental health teams. A proportion had eventually passed him on to a team leader, but none had provided anything useful. Some said they'd get back to him, others referred to data protection and flatly refused to tell him anything.

At long last, he had recourse to the safeguarding team at the county council and struck lucky; the woman who answered the phone turned out to be someone he'd spoken to before.

'You rang me when you were investigating the case of modern slavery,' she said. 'How can I help this time?' Bill outlined his problem, and there was a long silence. 'I'm not sure I can help,' she said, 'but let me have a look at the records and I'll see if there's anything I can do. I'll get back to you...'

Reluctant to lose his one friendly contact, Bill asked, 'How about I hang on for a bit, while you take a look?'

A clear hesitation came down the line, then she replied. 'OK. I'll put you on hold while I review our files.'

Wishing he could see what was on her screen, Bill sat listening to a rather scratchy version of 'Spring' from *The Four Seasons*, idly doodling faces on his scrap paper. He'd just added a cartoon cat to a barely recognisable sketch of his wife, one which he felt sure she would not regard as flattering, when 'Spring' came to a sudden stop and was replaced by a voice.

'I may have something for you,' she said guardedly. 'Can you run those key dates past me again?'

Bill did so, hope mounting that he might, at last, be getting somewhere.

'OK,' she said at last. 'I'm going to be careful what I tell you because of our policies on safeguarding and data protection. But I think I'm OK with the following.

'First, Moon River, aka Ted Fisher, is on our list of vulnerable adults. Second, on one of the dates you've listed, the third of September, he was staying overnight in a secure unit, while they worked on stabilising his medications. You told me you already knew he wasn't very compliant, so that's not news to you. Does that help?'

'I don't know,' said Bill honestly. 'No, of course it helps. It's always helpful to get new, accurate data, but I'm not sure where it leaves us. We thought we had him on camera as driving in a key location that evening. If he was in hospital, then that begs the question of who was driving his van! I need to report up the line asap.'

When Bill shared the intelligence with Greg, Jim and Chris, he got an instant reaction.

'That's the second possible suspect who has an alibi for a time when their registration number was caught on ANPR.

We need to run a check to see if the vehicle carrying the plate was the one it's registered to,' remarked Greg.

'You mean, you think the plates may have been cloned?' said Jim.

'It's the obvious explanation,' said Greg. 'Bill, have a word with the surveillance team and see what they can turn up.'

'There's an obvious problem, though,' said Chris from the speakerphone. 'Since ANPR doesn't automatically record anything other than the plate unless there is some other breach of regulations going on, like speeding, we may not find anything. They may need to cross-check with CCTV on other roads nearby in order to turn up any useful footage. That will take time.'

'Fair enough,' said Greg. 'Soonest started, soonest finished. Get on to it, Bill.' As Bill nodded and shot off to pass on the new instructions, Greg went on. 'There's something else we can be getting on with, meantime. And that's our other potential victim, Ben Lyell. Any joy with the bike-parking idea, Jim?'

'Not yet, no. I was planning on having a catch-up with the surveillance team too.'

'We're leaning on them too much', remarked Greg. 'If we're not careful, they'll have too many competing priorities. Still, it can't do too much harm to ask a quick question about progress before they get stuck into the next task. I'll come with you. Best I keep out of Margaret's way for the time being. She's not too happy with me at present.' Jim raised an eyebrow, and Greg explained. 'I'm using too much resource and making too little progress. Don't worry, Jim. It's something and nothing.'

In the incident room, Steve was perched on a desk with his usual mug in hand and his feet on a chair, chatting to the girl who should have been buried in CCTV tapes. He sat up so suddenly he spilled his coffee and got up from the desk.

'Morning, Boss,' he said cheerily. 'I gather from Bill you've something new for us.'

'Quite,' said Greg drily. 'I'm a bit surprised you've time to chat! Have you turned up anything on those two registration plates?' he asked the girl. She looked confused.

'Just getting down to it,' she said, and turned to her screens.

'Steve, a word,' said Greg, and walked away into the middle of the room. Steve put his mug down and followed hesitantly.

Greg waited a moment until the silence became uncomfortable, reviewing Steve's appearance. He realised he hadn't been paying the officer much attention recently as he took in the hair, which, although thinner than he remembered, was also longer, and the indefinably scruffy attire.

Then he asked bluntly, 'What's the problem, Steve? You've been under par for a week or so now, and I don't understand it. You've been a valuable member of this team for longer than I have. Yet now, you can't be trusted to keep focussed and you've made silly mistakes. What's going on?'

Steve flushed, and looked down at his fidgeting feet.

'I'm waiting,' said Greg. 'I want to understand, and I want the Steve that I knew back. Otherwise, you'd be better off back in uniform.'

'It's complicated,' muttered Steve under his breath.

'So explain it to me,' said Greg. 'What's complicated?'

'Nothing's the same any more,' said Steve. 'Not since Covid. I spend most of my time staring at a computer. That wasn't what I signed up for. And it seems that those who like computers are the ones who get promoted, so maybe I *would* be better off in uniform. Or just out of it. Maybe it's time I did something else.'

'Do you really mean that?' asked Greg, hooking a chair from under the nearest desk and sitting down. He indicated a second chair nearby and added, 'Sit down, Steve.' Behind Steve he saw Jim give a wave, indicating that he understood what was going on, and leave the room. 'Seriously, do you really want to leave? I thought you were one of the ones who enjoyed feeling they were making a difference. That what they did mattered. Isn't that true?'

Steve sat, sighed, and said, 'Partly. But all this' – he gestured round the room – 'it's not me. I know we have to do it some of the time, but not all of the time. I like to be out and about, getting some of the action.'

'I know the pandemic has changed the way we work, for the time being,' said Greg. 'But that's the point. It won't last forever. Soon, by all accounts, we'll have a vaccine and then the world will start to get back to normal. Would you really want to find, at that point, that you've burned your boats and lost the job you loved? Having said that,' he added, 'some desk work is always going to be necessary; you know that too.'

Steve nodded. 'Yes, I suppose so,' he allowed grudgingly. 'But not quite so much, maybe?'

'For now, it is what it is,' said Greg. 'Seriously, Steve, do you want in or want out? If the former, then I need you to buckle down and focus. I want the old Steve back. If you want out, then I won't stand in your way, even if I do think you're being rash.'

'I'll give it a go,' said Steve. 'Honest, Boss. I'll give it my best.'

'OK,' said Greg. 'Can't say fairer than that. You get stuck into the camera work for now, because that's the most urgent task we have on hand. And I promise that when we're ready to mount a raid or execute a search warrant, you'll be on the team.'

'Thanks, Boss,' said Steve. He leaned over to pick up his, now cold, mug of coffee and went over to the surveillance team. But this time, after a swift review of what everyone was up to, he sat down at his own desk and got stuck in. The concentration was palpable.

Greg smiled to himself with relief and returned to his office. *Although,* he said to himself, *that's only part of the issue. Where is Jill, and why didn't she deal with Steve?*

By lunchtime, Steve wasn't the only one sick of his desk. Greg was starting to pace, eager to get on with the next phase of the investigation but frustrated by the lack of leads. He went through all the reports he had so far, trying to see what he'd missed. *Nothing, so far as I can see.* He was standing in front of the whiteboards in the incident room, lost in unconstructive thought, when Jim appeared at his elbow.

'Do you want the good news, or the bad news?' he asked. Greg turned to look at Jim, and noted Steve was lurking in the background, looking shifty again.

'At the moment, almost any news would be welcome,' replied Greg. 'Go on. Hit me with it.'

'In that case, first the bad news, although it's kind of good as well. Steve has gone over the footage again, that he looked at earlier when he was trying to see whether Lyell's bike had been dumped at a railway station. And he found what looked like Lyell going into Norwich station. Steve, you tell him.'

'I just checked the footage inside the station for the day he went missing. He got on a train to London later in the morning, the day he was sacked from his job. I'm sorry, Boss,' said Steve. 'I missed seeing him on the car park footage first time around, so it never occurred to me to check the camera footage inside the station. It was my fault. But I'm sure this time. He definitely got on a train.'

Greg took a moment to assimilate the intelligence. 'So, the likelihood is that he buggered off to London when he got sacked and isn't one of our victims. Get on to the Met, report him as a misper, and report the latest to his family. Another check on his credit cards would be useful too, but if he's chosen to do a runner, that's a job for child support rather than us.

'Steve, you know what you did wrong. No need to labour the point. What was the other news?'

Steve looked relieved to have got off so lightly. 'Those cloned plates – one of the ANPR cameras picked up the vehicle as well as the registration,' he said. 'It was speeding. So we have an image of the vehicle and a blurry picture of the driver.'

'Wow!' Greg couldn't help the unseemly exclamation. 'Now that *is* good news. Show me.' The now grinning Jim led him over to the girl Steve had been chatting to (or up) earlier. She was ready and waiting, fully aware of the implications of her discovery, and flushed with excitement. She hit play, and they all watched the few seconds of darkish, blurred film. Then again. Then she looked up at Greg.

'That's all there is,' she said.

SPINNING INTO THE DARK

Greg stood up and led the way over to the whiteboard. He paused for a moment, reviewing all the summary data and photographs stuck to it. 'So, what we actually have, on that day at least, is a dark-coloured flatbed pickup with Tristan Smith's number plate, being driven by what appears to be a man with a beard, or at least a dark shadow. I think we need another chat with Mr Warren Thorne.'

30

Checking out

A brief conversation with Jim, joined remotely by Chris, then Greg was on his way to see Margaret.

'She in?' he demanded of her secretary, and was through the door to her office before the words, 'She's got the Chief Constable with her...' could make it past his ears to his brain. He stopped dead on the threshold, realising that he'd obviously interrupted a tense discussion.

'Greg,' said Margaret with what he would have thought was relief, if that hadn't seemed intrinsically unlikely. 'You clearly have something urgent on your mind. Can I get back to you on the other matter, sir,' she added.

The tall man in formal uniform stood, looking slightly disgruntled. 'Don't leave it too long,' he said over his shoulder as he left the room.

Margaret heaved a sigh and ran her hands though her hair as she sat back down behind her desk. 'That was particularly well-timed, Greg,' she said. 'Although probably best you don't do it too often. However, I gather you have something for me.'

Greg outlined the latest developments swiftly.

'Sounds promising,' Margaret agreed. 'What do you want from me?'

Greg sat down, belatedly realising that, in the excitement of the moment, he was still looming over her and giving her a crick in the neck. 'Sorry,' he said. 'Getting a bit carried away. This is the first time I've felt we've got a genuine lead. OK. What I have in mind is this: first, we redeploy the drive-by teams currently in the area, to create a cordon around Warren Thorne's establishment. And by that, I mean station them in these four locations to monitor movements in and out of this circle.' He unrolled the map in his hand, spread it out on the desk and pointed. 'If they spot Thorne driving out of the area, they follow him; but I don't want them spooking him prematurely and potentially giving him time to hide evidence. At the moment, he has no reason to think we're closing in, and the last intelligence we had was that his pickup was at the property.

'Second, I take a team of officers and SOCOs in with a search warrant and we turn the place over. And we bring him in for questioning, under arrest if need be.'

'Have you applied for the search warrant?' asked Margaret.

'Jim has it in hand.'

'OK. Get moving and keep me posted.'

It took only a few calls on the radio to redeploy the mobile teams in the vicinity of Ormesby Broad. One squad car, driven by the man Chris deemed to be the most discreet officer, was tasked with a drive-by.

'Pickup still in the yard,' he reported. 'Want us to check Thorne is there?'

'No. Keep going and park somewhere well out of sight,' responded Greg on the radio, mindful of the disaster caused by a clumsy officer with no discretion in the recent past. 'We'll be over in around half an hour. Just monitor the situation, and let me know instantly if he gets on the move.'

'Roger,' was the response and the radio fell silent.

Greg looked up as Jim came back into the incident room. 'Got it, said Jim, apropos the search warrant. 'And Ned's team are good to go.'

'Right. Let's get underway,' said Greg. 'Steve, you're with us. Bill follows with Ned. Where's Jill?'

'Morning off,' replied Jim. 'Something to do with those two kids they're adopting. She'll be pissed she missed this.'

With a beam of sheer delight, Steve leaped from his seat and headed for the door. 'Thanks, Boss,' he said as he passed Greg.

The drive to Ormesby passed swiftly – even the traffic on the single carriageway section of the A47 was less frustrating than normal – and Greg was feeling optimistic when they turned onto the A149. The journey had been punctuated by short updates from the teams monitoring the side roads which could be summed up as *No movement*.

As they got close to their destination, Greg instructed the teams to close in, two to follow directly behind their small convoy of cars and forensic van, the remaining two to block either end of the road past Thorne's place in the woods. He had one final instruction as they turned into the drive.

'Team A, follow Jim and me to the house. Team B, eyes on the yard and outbuildings. No one is to leave the property without my say-so.' Greg pulled up close to the house. Jim parked alongside and the forensic van behind. Teams A and B respectively, parked to block any movement of the pickup and at the end of the drive. Then deployed as instructed.

Greg went to the house, looking round him as he did so. As far as he could see, all was still. There were no sounds other than the wind in the trees and the flutterings of wood pigeons. He nodded and pointed to Bill to go round to the back door, then knocked once, twice, but got no response. He stepped back to survey the upper windows, but there was no movement evident.

Jim stepped forwards, hammered rather than knocked, and shouted, 'Police. Open up. We have a warrant to search this property.' Still no response from the house.

In the stillness after the hammering, Greg listened again, but heard nothing more than a startled pheasant leaving the vicinity in a hurry. 'We go in,' he decided. Jim tried the door, which was unlocked, and threw it open, just in case someone was standing behind it. Then Greg led the uniformed team in as Jim turned back to Ned in the van.

We'll just check it's clear first,' he said. 'Then you can go in.' Ned stuck a thumb up and turned to say something to the woman sitting beside him, but turned sharply back to Jim.

'I think I've just seen a movement. Over there.' He jerked his head and reinforced the signal by pointing, but carefully keeping his hand out of sight of anyone lurking over by the woodshed. Jim looked in the direction indicated. He couldn't see anything, but if Ned said he had, he was prepared to believe him.

He lifted his radio to his lips and said quietly, 'Possible sighting near woodshed. Team B, check it out, but keep your eyes peeled.'

Inside the house, Greg picked up the transmission just as Team A finished checking the upper floor.

'Nothing, sir,' they said.

'You,' he said, pointing at one, 'secure the front door and tell the SOCOs they can come in. You,' – indicating the second – 'come with me.' He headed for the back door and the backyard.

Over by the woodshed, Jim was approaching cautiously from the left while Steve headed for the central door, and Team B were clambering around the piles of wood that abutted the shed on the right. Steve pulled the door open with caution and swept his gaze swiftly round the building. The brightness from the door and a rooflight illuminated a workbench and circular saw. Everything was still, but the saw was humming slightly as though the electric motor was still live. The floor was littered with lengths of timber while longer branches were propped on the far wall, awaiting cutting.

'Clear,' he said, and came back out to follow Jim around the corner. The hardstanding behind the shed was stacked with logs on the left, while a rough pile of sawn timber lay askew the right corner. The yard backed onto open ground. Young trees, mainly ash, straggled towards a thicker growth of mature woodland beyond, undergrown by rough grass, bramble and gorse. Steve turned to Jim, just as a shout from one of the members of Team B, precariously perched on the woodpile, alerted them to a movement in the wood. Both Jim and Steve swung round in time to see a dim shape disappear into the distant trees.

Jim instinctively took a couple of steps after the runner, stopped and snapped into the radio 'Suspect running into the woodland, roughly south-east. In pursuit,' he added as Steve powered past him. The man on the woodpile also made a bold attempt to join the chase but rapidly discovered that galloping down a heap of loose logs was a quick way to A&E. He collapsed as he hit the yard, rolling over and clutching at his left ankle. That left Steve making up the ground steadily as he sprinted through the more open terrain scattered with the younger, thinner trees. He could see he was getting closer to an arrest and, flushed with the desire to show Greg he was worth the second chance he'd been given, speeded up a fraction more.

From where Jim was running, rather more sedately, Steve just seemed to disappear. Both he and the remaining member of Team B converged on the last sighting of their colleague and found him flat on his face on the woodland floor, badly scratched by brambles. The force of the fall had winded him, but after a moment, and much to Jim's relief, he sat up, gasping for air and furious with rage. Bill and Greg, catching up after a mad dash from the back of the house, were just in time to hear him snap, 'Tripwire,' as he indicated the cable that had caught him at shin height and precipitated him to the ground. 'He was ready for us.'

31

Checking around

'No. Hold it,' shouted Greg as several officers set off into the wood. 'Time to regroup. If we're going to mount a search in there, we need dogs for a start.' As everyone gathered round him, there was a shout from the man who'd slid down the woodpile. He was still clutching his ankle but staring at what he'd disturbed in his fall.

'Look,' he shouted again, reached forwards, then remembered procedure and snatched his hand back. Greg went over, waving the others back as he went.

'If he's uncovered something, best we don't all trample over here,' he said, then stopped. He turned back to Jim. 'Get Ned out here,' he said. 'It looks like one of the cloned plates.' He flipped the switch on his radio. 'Suspect fled into the wood,' he reported. 'We need a search team, helicopter and dogs. ASAP.'

'Armed police?' was the follow-up query.

'No evidence of guns so far,' he responded. 'But put them on standby in case we turn something up.' Leading his team over towards the cars, he looked round them. 'We need an ambulance for the chap with the ankle,' he said. 'Steve, we'd better get you checked out as well. Bill, can you see to that please?'

'I'm fine,' objected Steve. 'It's only a few scratches, honest, Boss.'

'We'll see, when the paramedics get here,' responded Greg, watching one of the other officers help their injured colleague hobble over to sit in a car. 'Meanwhile, we can best use the time until the dogs and helicopter get here to do a thorough search of the house and outbuildings. Under SOCO supervision, to make sure we don't compromise any of the evidence. Finding the registration plate was a good start. But there'll be more. Guaranteed. So, check in with Ned and get to it.'

Even as he spoke, one of the SOCO team emerged from the house, waving a small plastic evidence bag. 'Ned thought you'd like to see this,' he said.

Greg took the packet from him. 'Clozaril,' he read aloud. 'What is it?' he asked, suspecting he knew the answer but wanting confirmation.

'It's an antipsychotic,' said the man. 'The name on the pharmacy label is Warren Thorne. And the packet's full. Doesn't look like he's been taking them.'

'Well, well,' remarked Greg, and reached for his phone. 'Jim, keep an ear on the radio, will you. The helicopter should be here soon. I'll just update Chris on the latest.'

In the background of the phone call, Chris could be heard tapping on her laptop, getting on to her databases without delay. 'Funny that didn't come up before,' she said. 'Does the packet say who prescribed it?'

'Northgate Hospital,' replied Greg.

'OK. I'll get on to them as well.'

'Must go,' said Greg. 'Helicopter's here, and Ned's trying to get my attention too.'

'I'll get back to you,' Chris shouted. Greg heard the words just as he rang off.

This time, the find that Ned wanted him to see was somewhat larger. Uncovering the registration plates under the sawn timber – six so far – had revealed something else. An uncharacteristically excited Ned had seized Greg by the elbow and towed him over to where four officers and two SOCOs had been systematically removing cut logs from the untidy pile, checking them over and stacking them in the corner of the yard.

'Look,' he said, and pointed. All six searchers had paused their efforts and stood around in a circle, sweating slightly but looking very pleased with themselves, hands on hips, broad smiles on faces.

Greg stepped forwards cautiously and saw what was creating the excitement: a bike wheel, crushed and bent, was sticking out from the wood.

'Looks like the rest of the bike is there,' said Ned. 'And from what we can already see, ie part of the wheel and the fork, it could be the Phil Saunders bike.'

'The one that's missing,' said Greg.

'One of the ones that's missing,' corrected Ned. 'Kain Smith's bike was found in the river at Martham, and Ann Cooper's was with her body. Neither the Saunders nor the Hodds bike has been found so far.

'I'm afraid we're going to have to go slowly through the rest of this pile to make sure we don't miss anything. But why would anyone throw a bike under a woodpile unless they had something to hide?' He was interrupted by a clatter of rotors as the helicopter arrived overhead.

'Thanks, Ned,' said Greg. Then to the rest, 'Let's get this search organised. The dog teams should be here soon.'

The helicopter crew reported in, checked for updates, then started their grid search from the air. 'Problem is,' they told Greg, 'it's still a bit warm for us to pick up reliable infrared signals, and the tree canopy is too thick for us to see much at ground level. But we'll do our best.'

'Your presence might at least deter him from legging it away over open ground,' agreed Greg, accepting the limitations they were working under. 'We need the dogs,' he fretted to Jim. 'How far away are they now?'

'ETA five minutes,' said Jim. 'And the additional search teams are just behind them. We should be underway soon. As he spoke, an unmarked car, which he recognised as Jill's, drew up to the yard. 'About time too,' he said as Jill clambered out. 'I thought we were having to do this without you.'

'Not bloody likely,' she said. 'Me, miss all the fun? Where can I help most?'

'Liaise with the dog teams, will you?' said Jim. 'We need something off Ned, from the house, for them to use as scent, then we need someone to keep the rest of the searchers out of the dogs' way.'

'Can do,' she said, and headed for the house, pulling protective blue gloves on as she went.

The dogs did indeed arrive at more or less the same time as the van load of extra police officers from Yarmouth. For a moment, the yard was a cacophony of shouted orders, helicopter engine and a few barks, but order was quickly restored. The dogs took point and led off into the wood; the humans sternly ordered to bring up the rear and 'not get in the way'.

This time they had four dogs in two teams. Two were springers, and they took the lead. Without a clear idea of where precisely Thorne had left the yard, the dogs were offered some used clothes from his pile of dirty laundry, then they cast up and down the area of wasteland between the yard and the woodland proper. Greg watched their search pattern in fascination as they criss-crossed in front of him, occasionally one of the handlers sending one back to check an area he thought they'd missed, before they moved on. They weren't long in picking up the scent where Warren Thorne had run into the wood and, swiftly, they led the mixed group of officers and dogs into the wood – the general-purpose dogs, ie a German shepherd and a Belgian Malinois, now very much in evidence.

Greg's radio crackled as the helicopter reported in again. 'Sorry, but we need to go and refuel. Back shortly,' they said.

'Dogs are probably more use anyway,' Greg grunted to Jim as they too set off through the trees.

Over by the Bure, Chris was staring at her screen in mingled fury and frustration. 'I don't believe it! I just don't bloody believe it,' she was muttering over and over, channelling her inner Victor Meldrew. She reached for her phone and rang Greg.

'Warren Thorne. I've found him on the police database,' she said without prevarication. 'He's logged in connection with an incident back in 2018 to do with road rage, and there's a note about failure to take meds.'

'Why didn't he show up before?' queried Greg.

'Because I trusted this bloody stupid, moronic, congenitally thick, artificial, so-called intelligence,' she exploded. 'Someone had recorded the incident with the name reversed, as in Thorne, Warren, and this dozy system didn't recognise it.

'That's it. I'm back to old-fashioned eyes and doing it myself. I'll never trust another AI system ever again.'

'GIGO,' said Greg.

'You what?'

'Garbage in, garbage out,' he explained. 'It's what we were always told at uni if a computer turned up something that didn't make sense. It means—'

'I know what it means,' responded Chris grumpily. 'At least, I can work it out. Thank you very much!'

'Any luck with the Northgate?' he asked, changing the subject in a hurry.

'Yes, he had been a patient of theirs, but no, they haven't seen him recently and they discharged him because he wasn't attending any of his appointments. That was two years ago.'

'He wasn't taking his meds and wasn't attending his appointments, so they discharged him?' Words failed Greg. 'Did they say why they were treating him? When they were, that is.'

'Extreme narcissistic traits, paranoia and anger management.'

'Great! Thanks for the update, Chris. I'd better get back to finding him!'

The dogs led through the wood, out the other side and down the edge of an open field without hesitation or delay. As they reached a side road, they slowed as they crossed the tarmac, cast to either side then seemed to pick up the scent again and were off at speed. Greg realised they were entering the wood that surrounded Ormesby Broad. The ground beneath their feet rapidly became boggy, and shortly after that the previously purposeful advance through the wood faltered and the dogs were casting about again.

'Problem?' he asked the nearest dog handler.

'Lost the scent,' he said. 'They'll probably find it again in a moment.'

He was right. The on-duty springer kept returning to one particular tree in a close-knit copse and circling it. Then she stood on her hind legs, looking up and barking.

A thought struck Greg, and he craned his neck back to look up into the canopy. The light was fading fast, and he couldn't see much. He tapped the dog handler on the arm. 'Could the explanation be that he's gone up, into the trees?' he asked, pointing upwards as he did so. 'He's a tree surgeon after all. Aren't they trained to climb?'

'Some of them are,' said the dog handler. 'And yes, that's right. It would explain Susie's signals. I was just struggling to see how anyone would get up that smooth trunk. Was his climbing kit missing?'

'No idea,' said Greg. 'Hang on, I'll ask Ned.' After a moment on the phone, he went over to the dog handlers, currently huddled in close colloquy. 'He said there're a couple of empty hooks in the woodshed that could have held kit, and no long ropes. So yes, he could have taken stuff with him.'

'Or,' said Steve, who was hanging around just behind Greg, 'he had a tree pre-prepared with a rope for just this reason, like he had tripwires.' The latter was definitely an irritating memory.

The dog handlers looked round. 'We were just discussing how to proceed based on that assumption,' he said. 'Is the copter coming back?'

'Any time now,' said Greg, looking at his watch.

'They might have more luck, now it's cooling down,' said the man. 'In the meantime, we'll move the dogs out in concentric circles from that tree. He has to have come back to ground level pretty soon, and even if it is wet, we'll find his trail again. Or the copter infrared will locate him.'

'Get the word out,' warned Greg. 'If you come up with him, be cautious. We have reason to believe he's dangerously unpredictable.'

As darkness grew and the temperature fell, it was the return of the helicopter that did the trick.

For the best part of an hour, the dogs and men had crashed through the underbrush, collecting scratches and thorns – the wrong kind – en route. At least the men did. The dogs moved silently and uncomplainingly, also unlike the men, only visible when their high-vis coats caught the light from one of the heavy torches.

The night sounds of the wood also seemed to grow with the dark. Birds disturbed by all the human and canine bumbling about took off with a sudden clatter of wings. An owl, its hunting disrupted by all the lights, was seen and heard slipping away over the wood, and the bark of a vixen made everyone jump. When he seemed to pass the same tree for the second time, Greg seriously wondered if they were lost, the whole damn lot of them, and wondered if it was time to call off the search until morning. Then the helicopter was back, its searchlight clearly visible through the canopy and the clatter of its rotors shaking the air.

Suddenly it changed direction and swooped low over the wood in the direction of the Broad. The crewman's voice was audible on the radio.

'I think we've spotted him,' he said. A long pause, then he came back again. 'Definitely a heat signature in the trees near the Broad. I doubt he can retreat far in that direction. The water's edge is even wetter than where you are, and covered in tall reeds. He's nor'-nor'-east of your current location. But I'm sure he'll have to break east or west to get back to a road. Or retrace his steps of course, but as I said, you're all across his line of retreat.'

Greg waved to the dog handlers and to Jim. 'Hear that,' he said. 'I think we need to spread our line to cut off his retreat. But, everyone, take note: he's dangerous and unpredictable.'

'Noted,' said the senior dog handler, nodding. 'Which means, you all stay back. And that includes you, sir. Let the dogs do their job. They'll get to him much quicker, especially in this terrain. They'll take him down, and they'll scare the bejaysus out of him.'

The helicopter was still overhead, its searchlight now focussed on one particular patch. The pitch of excitement was rising in both men and dogs, especially the GP dogs, who seemed to sense that their time had come.

As they closed in on the patch of reeds highlighted by the copter floodlight, Steve pushed to the fore, suddenly convinced he could see the man they were seeking.

'He's there,' he said. 'Right there!' And he ran forwards just as the first of the GP dogs, the German shepherd, was released by her handler. The dog powered forwards far faster than Steve, or anyone else, could go.

'She'll have him in a second,' the handler nearest Greg stated confidently, and indeed at that moment the dog leaped for the dark shape that appeared briefly from cover, silhouetted against the lighter water of the Broad. The man went down, the dog on top. There were sounds of muffled shouts and a dog growling, then the dog fell back, coughing and sneezing. The man got up, and, in the light of the helicopter, could be seen to be wearing a mask.

'Shit! The bastard's pepper-sprayed her,' exclaimed the handler. Before he could do anything, Steve powered through the gap between the handler and Greg, gasping, 'He's not getting away now.'

'Steve!' snapped Greg, but he was too late. Steve outpaced the other officers. The second dog was yet to be released, and Steve was the man closest to the suspect as he fled along the edge of the lake. The two men were only yards apart when Thorne paused, turned, and flung something. Steve went down, and didn't get up.

32

Man down

There was a frozen moment when time seemed to run slow. Then the Belgian Malinois was off the lead. As he shouted, 'Man down,' and ran towards the point where he had last seen Steve, Greg saw the powerful arched back of the dog at flat gallop. He arrived next to Steve just as a scream rang out to his left and the dog handler shouted, 'Got him!' in triumph.

Greg dropped to his knees on the soggy ground and shone his torch on Steve's face. It was pale, but he realised with a gasp of relief that he was still breathing, although his eyes were closed. Then the torch beam drifted lower, and he saw the hatchet buried in the angle formed by his neck and shoulder. And the blood spurting.

'Shit. Shit,' he said. He dropped his torch to pull out his handkerchief and wad it against the wound. 'Man down! Get the paramedics,' he shouted. 'And the air ambulance. Tell them we have a serious injury.'

Using both hands to put pressure on the wound, he cursed the axe in his way but dared not remove it. Jim stumbled up behind him.

'They've got the bastard, Boss,' he wheezed, then focussed his torch on Greg's hands, now covered with a thick sheen of dark red.

'Shit,' he said. 'Can I help?'

'I don't think there's room for any more hands here,' said Greg. 'Give him your coat, can you? I think he's going into shock. Has someone called for the paramedics?'

'Yes. I heard it go out on the radio,' replied Jim.

Steve's eyelids fluttered in the light from Jim's torch. 'Steve,' said Greg urgently. 'Stick with us, lad. We need you. Stick with us. Look at me! The medics are on their way. You're going to be OK.'

The eyelids fluttered again, but didn't open. Then the body under Greg's hands shuddered, sighed and was still.

Greg still had his hands clenched on the wound, so hard they were starting to cramp. But the blood flow over his fingers was slowing.

Jim kneeled to put his hand on Steve's chest, then bent over and put his ear to it. When he looked up at Greg a sense of loss was reflected in his eyes. 'He's gone, Greg,' he said. 'There's nothing more we can do. He's gone.'

'We should try CPR.' Greg hadn't given up yet.

'All we'll do is pump what's left of his blood out faster. It must have hit an artery. He's gone.'

There was a stir behind them as more officers came over to see if they could help. Then a silence seemed to spread that encompassed even the dogs and the woodland creatures. The only voice to be heard was the swearing from their captive, complaining about dog bites, wrongful arrest, deep-state conspiracies and just about anything else that came to mind.

Greg peeled his painful hands from Steve's neck and rested them on the ground, where he kneeled next to the body. Without looking up, he said, 'Arrest the bastard, Jim. And charge him with the murder of DC Stephen Hall. Then get him out of here before I get my hands on him.'

Jim went away to do as he was bid, and the noise diminished towards the road. Dragging his eyes away from Steve's face, his pallor suddenly almost green and gaunt in death, Greg stood up stiffly and looked around him.

'Dogs alright?' he asked the nearest handler.

'One of them has sore eyes, and one got kicked, but I think they'll be OK.'

'Good,' said Greg tonelessly. 'They did a good job. There could have been a lot more casualties without them.'

Blue lights flashing through the trees indicated the arrival of an ambulance. Greg realised, with surprise, that their chase through the wood must have led them very close to a road.

Jim returned to Greg's side. 'The paramedics will be with us in a moment,' he said. 'Thorne's been taken into custody and he's on his way to Wymondham, complaining about dog bites and police brutality. I've stood the copter down.'

'Good. Thanks, Jim. I'll wait here until the ... until Steve is in the ambulance.'

'Jill's sending a squad car to pick us up at the junction with the road to the Broad,' said Jim, pointing. Whatever else he was going to say was interrupted by the arrival of the paramedics.

It didn't take them long to establish death, and Steve's body was swiftly on its way to the ambulance, on a stretcher, face covered.

'Anyone else hurt?' asked the lead paramedic before they turned to go.

'No, I don't think so,' said Greg. Seeing them look at him and the dark stains on his trousers and jacket, he added, 'This isn't my blood.'

'Come on,' said Jim, seeing more blue lights arriving at the edge of the wood. 'That'll be our lift back to where we left the cars. The inspector from Yarmouth is on his way to take control of things here.'

'No. I'm going nowhere just yet,' said Greg. 'I need to make sure we've secured this scene first and, indeed, most of this wood. We'll need to establish how he got here, and what he had with him in the way of weapons. Not to mention all the work we need to do back at his house and yard.'

'Someone else can deal with that,' urged Jim.

'Who?' demanded Greg. 'There isn't anyone else. Not here. Not yet. Send Bill home and you get off too. You've both had a long day, and I'll need you here in the morning, along with a forensic team. Send Jill to me and we can get things organised until the relief turn up.'

'You need—' started Jim.

But Greg said tiredly, 'Just do it, Jim. Believe me, I'll be out of here as soon as I can. But Steve and the other victims of this maniac need justice. So I need to know everything's done properly.'

Recognising an irresistible force when he saw one, Jim acquiesced. He left Jill and Greg to their task. Although not without major misgivings, which saw expression in his phone call to Chris.

***

Of the many long nights in her career, Chris was to conclude that was one of the longest. She curled up on the sofa while she waited for Greg to come home, but sleep eluded her. The hours dragged by until she could almost count the seconds, never mind the minutes, as she imagined every possible awful outcome of the scenes described by Jim.

Her first instinct had been to grab her car keys and race to the rescue, but she quickly realised that would just give Greg someone else to worry about. Moreover, she didn't know exactly where he was, and she was in no state to tramp through a tangled wood in the dark. So she stayed put, and worried herself sick instead. At least Jim had said Greg wasn't injured, and the nutter with the axe was under arrest. But even so, maybe Jim had been wrong. Maybe there were injuries he hadn't seen. Or more likely, knowing Greg as she did, injuries that *couldn't* be seen. All she'd had from him were two short texts, telling her that Steve was dead and his murderer under arrest. Then that he'd be late home after he'd sorted stuff out.

It was past two in the morning when, with an unutterable relief, she heard his car coming down the drive and pulling up in the usual scatter of gravel near the front door. She got up from the sofa, and he was suddenly there in front of her.

'Still up?' he said, attempting a normal voice and failing miserably. 'You should be in bed. I'm just going for a shower.' And he disappeared up the stairs.

She checked on Bobby and Tally, both put out by the disturbance to their routines, then followed him. She could hear the shower running in the bathroom. She picked up the heavily bloodstained clothing from the bedroom floor and dropped it over the banisters, to be dealt with in the morning. It lay in the hall, a mute memorial to duty.

She hesitated outside the bathroom door, then made her mind up and went in. Greg was in the shower, leaning on the tiled wall and facing the door. Through the misted glass screen, she could see traces of bloodstained water curling their way across the shower tray to the outlet. Jim had been right. There were no injuries on Greg's body. But one look at his face showed her where the pain lay. With an inarticulate murmur she pulled the shower door open and him into her arms. He buried his face in her shoulder and soaked her shirt with the tears coursing from his eyes.

33

The reckoning – part one

Sleep was slow to come to either of them. And then it was disturbed by nightmares. Greg woke several times, reliving the scene in the wood; except that each time he focussed his torch on the body at his feet, it bore Chris's face, not Steve's. Around seven-thirty, he gave up the unequal struggle and got back into the shower, this time brusquely turning the dial to cold and staying there with his teeth clenched until he felt he was approaching reality again.

When he got downstairs Chris was already there, a big mug of black coffee held out to greet him.

'How about I drive you this morning?' she asked as he sat down at the table.

'I don't think that would improve things much,' he said with a weak smile. 'You haven't had any more sleep than me. I'll be fine. Don't worry. You try and get some sleep while I'm gone.'

'Greg...' She put a hand on his arm to detain him for a moment, as he seemed about to depart with coffee unfinished. 'It wasn't your fault, you know.'

'It was my fault Steve was there,' he said without turning round. 'I knew he wasn't in a good place and I gave way to sentiment. I'd promised him he could come if we got any action, and it resulted in his death.'

'He'd have been gutted if you'd left him behind,' argued Chris. 'You gave him a second chance and he wanted to prove you were right. The only man guilty of Steve's death is the man who threw the hatchet. Not you. Never you.'

He turned back to her. 'But I was responsible. I was responsible for what happened last night, and I was responsible for Steve being there. You may be right about where the guilt lies. But there's no ducking the responsibility. That sits with me.' He came back and kissed her forehead. 'I'll be fine,' he said again. 'I always have been, haven't I? I'll let you know when I'm on my way home.'

Watching the car bump slowly down the drive, Chris pondered but rapidly dismissed the idea of a phone call to Margaret Tayler. She decided Greg really wouldn't like that. And on reflection, she was sure Margaret wouldn't need the prompt. She picked the phone up and rang Ben instead.

Greg stopped his car at the end of the drive. There was a phone call he needed to make, and he wasn't looking forward to it. He knew Steve's next of kin were his parents and that they lived somewhere in Cheshire. When he rang HQ the night before to report the death, he'd been told a local team would pay his parents a visit to break the news.

'Better that way than by phone,' the duty HR manager had said. When Greg had objected, she'd been quite firm. 'I understand you feel the need to talk to them, but you know I'm right,' she'd advised. 'Leave your call until tomorrow. I'll send you their contact details in the morning.' Clearly, she hadn't trusted him to take her advice. But the email with the telephone number had been sitting in his inbox when he'd looked just after seven.

He checked his watch, but it was still only just eight. A bit early perhaps. He decided to ring Jim first. Whether he turned left to the crime scene, or right towards police HQ depended on what was happening in the holding cells at Wymondham.

'Jim. Morning,' he said. 'Update me on Thorne.'

'He's demanded a solicitor. One of his own, not one from the pool. So, we can't interview him until he's solicitored up. In other words, not until later this morning.'

'Good,' replied Greg. 'In that case, I'll see you at Thorne's place for a briefing from Ned's team. Hopefully that will arm us with the info we need for our first interview. I should be there in fifteen minutes or so. After I've rung Steve's family.'

'Bugger. Not a nice job,' said Jim. 'I take it they already know.'

'Yes. Cheshire Police called on them last night.'

Greg rang off, checked his emails again, then rang the number supplied by HR. A female voice answered the phone.

'Yes?' it said, fairly curtly.

'I'm Detective Chief Inspector Geldard,' said Greg, introducing himself. 'Are you Mrs Hall?'

'No. I'm her next-door neighbour,' said the voice, losing the overlay of suspicion. 'I guess you know about—'

'About Steve. Yes,' said Greg. 'He worked with me, and I was with him when it happened. I just wanted to talk to Mr and Mrs Hall, if that's OK with them.'

'I think they'd be glad of that,' said the neighbour. 'Sorry if I was a bit abrupt. We've had the press on the phone already.' Greg suppressed what he wanted to say about the press. 'I'll get them to the phone,' she said.

There was a silence, broken by some clicking and wheezing, then a different voice said, 'I'm Sam Hall, Steve's father. Is that Chief Inspector Geldard?'

'Yes,' said Greg, clutching his phone so hard the case threatened to crack. 'I just wanted to say how very sorry I am for your loss. Steve was a valued member of my team and we're going to miss him a lot.' He paused, not knowing what else to say, but thankfully the father interrupted.

'His mother's in bed, asleep at last,' he said. 'The doctor's been and given her a sedative. I don't want to disturb her now, but maybe she could ring you when she's feeling a bit more herself.'

'Of course—' Greg started to say, but Mr Hall hadn't finished.

'Neighbour says you said you were there. When it happened, I mean. I know his mother will want to know if it was quick. If he suffered. You read such awful things...' His voice tailed off.

'It was very quick,' said Greg swiftly. 'So fast that we had no chance to save him, although we did our best. He can't have known anything about it,' he added.

'Thank you for that,' said Mr Hall. 'The officers who called here said that you chaps had done what you could to save him. Was that you?'

'I did what I could,' said Greg. 'I'm only sorry it wasn't more.'

'I hope you get the man who did it.'

'We've got him in custody,' Greg assured him. 'And if I've anything to do with it, he'll never see the free light of day ever again!'

***

By the time he arrived at Thorne's place in the wood, it was a heaving mass of uniformed police and forensic scientists. Jim and Jill were already in evidence, getting out of their cars by the barrier of crime scene tape.

'Morning,' he said, joining them. 'Seen Ned yet?'

'He's in the house, putting together a report on what they've got so far,' said Jim. 'We opted to stay out of the way.'

'Quite right,' responded Greg.

'You OK, Boss?' asked Jill.

'I'm fine,' said Greg. 'What about you? You had a late night too. Are you sure you're OK to be here?'

'I feel I owe it to Steve,' she said. 'There'll be plenty of time to sleep later.'

As they spoke, Ned emerged from the front door of the cottage, clutching a notebook. He waved them over and met them in the centre of the yard. 'I'm putting the final touches to my interim report. I assume you're in a hurry to get the interviews started, so it'll be on your desktop by the time you get to HQ. Meantime, these are the highlights.

'First, you already know we found antipsychotics in the house. We found more when we searched the bathroom. At least three months' worth. All with Warren Thorne's name on them. All untouched.

'Second, we found three different sets of registration plates tucked under the edge of the woodpile in the yard. Two sets were registered to Tristan Smith and Moon River, as we expected. The third set rightly belong to Esther Meadowcroft.'

'The egg lady?' said Jill.

'Correct,' said Ned. 'We've gone over all of them for prints and DNA. Nothing so far.

'Third, the bikes.'

'Bikes plural?' asked Greg. Then added, 'Sorry, Ned. I'll shut up and let you get on.'

'Two bikes,' said Ned. 'One is almost certainly Phil Saunders's bike and the other is a match for the description of Carol Hodds's machine. Again, we've gone over both for fingerprints and DNA. Saunders's bike is clean, except for a fragment of fabric caught on a broken spoke. It looks like shorts or trouser material. That's gone off for analysis too. I think there's a good chance of DNA on that.

'The other bike – I think that's been wiped down, but, if so, the wiper missed part of the underside of the frame. We've got a couple of good prints off that.

'Finally, my theories, for what they're worth. I think the Hodds's bike was picked up by bare hands early in our man's career of terror. He wiped it down but missed a bit. By the time of the second bike, Phil Saunders's machine, he was taking more precautions. He wore gloves, and it's sheer luck that he snagged his trousers on the broken spoke, probably when he lifted it into his pickup.

'So, that's where we're at. I just wanted to show you where we found the bikes.'

He led them round the woodshed, and as they turned the corner, Greg had a flashback so vivid he almost called out. For a split second he could see Steve setting off at a run through the trees. He dragged his attention back to Ned, suddenly aware of the birdsong and the movement of the breeze on his face. The call of a blackbird grounded him in the present, and he was able to focus on where Ned was pointing.

'The registration plates were found here, at the edge of the woodpile,' he said, pointing. 'Invisible to a casual passer-by but easy to recover if wanted. Which is why they popped into view when that lad slid down the heap.

'But the bikes were different. They were well hidden. I'd guess the first was laid on the ground before the wood was tipped on top. Then the second bike laid alongside, and more wood tipped. They were both invisible *and* inaccessible, until we started moving all the timber.'

'But the plates, they could be got at fairly easily,' said Greg. 'Meaning that he didn't want the bikes to be found anytime soon, but he wanted to be able to use the plates.'

'That's my assumption too,' responded Ned.

'Anything else we need to see?' asked Greg. 'What about his climbing stuff and other kit?'

'In here,' said Ned, leading the way again, this time into the woodshed.

The rotary saw lay silent now and the workbench was empty save for a couple of handsaws and a pair of pruning shears. 'The rest of his kit seems to have hung here,' said Ned, pointing at a half-empty wall of hooks and brackets. 'I reckon there's a couple of ropes missing as well as the hatchet he threw at Steve.' He glanced apologetically at Greg, regretting his choice of words, and moved on. 'I don't know what else hung here,' he said. 'We're still searching the woodland nearer the Broad. But there's one more thing I did want you to see.'

Yet again they all followed Ned, this time into the thin belt of trees nearest the yard. 'It was lucky no one ran into this.' Ned indicated something lying half concealed in the long grass. Greg moved forwards cautiously, stopped dead and turned to Ned.

'Is that what I think it is?' he asked.

'Yup. Illegal outside a museum since 1827 – I looked it up. It's OK. It's been made safe, but it was armed and ready when we found it. One of the PCs searching triggered it with her staff, thank God. And we're bloody lucky one of the dogs didn't find it!'

They stood round in a circle, surveying the powerful spring and lethal teeth of the nineteenth century answer to poachers.

'Where on earth would he get a mantrap?' asked Jim.

'And what sort of nutter leaves one armed, out in the open?' asked Jill.

'This sort, obviously,' said Greg. 'At least, I take it it's been checked for prints and DNA.'

Ned nodded. 'The prints we found are smudged, but despite being out in the open I think there's a good chance of DNA,' he said. 'The weather's been kind and I think it was set, or reset, relatively recently.'

'Oh boy, I'm really looking forward to interviewing this chap,' said Greg, and there was an ugly glint in his eye. 'How long before we have the results from the DNA analyses?'

'In the circumstances, they've been expedited. But low count DNA takes some time, as you know. I'll get them to you asap. Piecemeal, if need be.'

'Good. Thank you. I expected no less. Jim, let's get over to HQ. Jill, can you keep an eye on things here while Ned is still working? I'll send Bill to relieve you later.'

***

Back at Norfolk Police HQ and looking into the interview room through the two-way mirror, Greg noted that Thorne's solicitor was an old acquaintance.

'That's Ken Wood, isn't it?' he said. 'I thought Thorne had said he didn't want a duty solicitor.'

'He did, and he hired Wood directly from his firm in Norwich, not off our list,' replied the duty sergeant. 'I get the feeling Mr Wood would rather that bit of information wasn't mentioned in front of his client.'

'He's got a good one, anyway,' remarked Jim. 'Experienced and pragmatic is our Mr Wood. At least there shouldn't be any grounds for complaints if he's looking after things.'

'Ready?' asked Greg. 'I'll kick off. Keep a sharp eye on our man. I think his reactions might be interesting. I plan to charge him with Steve's murder at the very least. The others might need to wait until the results are through from Forensics.'

'A tenner he goes no comment,' predicted Jim pessimistically. 'That's what Wood will have told him to do.'

'You're on,' said Greg. 'I think Mr Wood might find his client rather unpredictable.'

Thorne looked up briefly as the two detectives entered the room. His left arm was heavily bandaged. *Because of dog bites*, Greg assumed, and hoped Thor, the Belgian Malinois, had got a good one in for Steve. *Pity they are trained to go for the arms*, he thought, as one or two other bits of Thorne's anatomy struck him as better targets for large teeth.

'DCI Geldard and DI Henning entering the room,' said Greg as he took his seat. 'Please introduce yourselves for the tape,' he said to the other two men.

'Kenneth Wood, solicitor,' said Mr Wood. The burly man with the reading glasses nudged his client, who remained silent.

'Also present is Mr Warren Thorne,' remarked Greg, undisturbed by this show of non-cooperation. 'Mr Thorne, you are charged with the murder of Detective Constable Stephen Hall, last night at around 10.20pm in the woods near Ormesby Broad. You are further charged with causing unnecessary suffering to two police dogs under the Animal Welfare Act of 2006, and with setting a mantrap with the intention of causing death or grievous bodily harm under the Offences Against the Person Act 1861.' (Greg had needed to look that one up, and even Mr Wood blinked.) 'Other charges may follow. You do not have to say anything. But it may harm your defence if you do not mention when questioned something you later rely on in court. Anything you do say may be given in evidence.'

'I have not been warned about the mantrap charge,' objected Mr Wood.

'I'm happy to share the evidence with you,' said Greg. He pushed a batch of photos across the table. 'These clearly show both the mantrap and its location. I also have a witness statement from the officer who set it off.' Thorne grinned nastily, and Greg added, 'With her staff. No harm was done, but it was an undoubted offence under the Act.'

'Do you have any evidence it was my client who set it?' asked Wood.

'In his field? Just yards from his backyard? The mantrap he bought from the Museum of Country Life in Northamptonshire when it closed last year?' asked Greg. The last piece of information had been the result of some strenuous telephoning round by a couple of bright civilian staff who had been as shocked by Steve's loss as anyone. *Perhaps more shocked, in the case of the girl he was chatting to the day before*, reflected Greg. And made a mental note to have a word with her when he had a moment.

'That's still only evidence he may have owned it, not that he set it,' argued Wood, fighting a determined rearguard action.

'I'm sure the DNA evidence will remove any ambiguity,' answered Greg, fingers metaphorically crossed. 'But to be blunt, that's not the charge at the top of my list. First, I'd like to know why he threw a hatchet at my officer.'

'No comment,' said Thorne, almost before Greg finished speaking.

'Let's go back a stage then,' said Greg. 'Why did you run when my officers and I entered the yard?'

'No comment.'

After an hour or so of questions and no comments, Kenneth Wood was starting to fidget.

'I think it's time we took a break,' he said at last. 'Both my client and I could do with a visit to the washroom, and some coffee would be welcome, after I've had a chance for another chat with him.'

'OK,' agreed Greg. 'No problem. We'll take a half hour break. That enough for you?' When Wood nodded his assent, Greg recorded the change on the tape and the two detectives left the room.

'I think the tenner's mine,' said Jim once they were back in Greg's office. 'And I take no pleasure in saying it.'

'Not yet,' said Greg, his expression grim. 'I've barely got started yet. We'll grab a coffee, and I'll check in with Ned. Then we're back. You OK to carry on?'

'Yes. What about you?' asked Jim, noting the bags under Greg's eyes.

'I'll be fine,' he said again. 'I'm not stopping until I've got the bastard where I want him.'

34

The reckoning – part two

On their return, Greg paused by the interview room door. 'I'm going to change tack,' he said to Jim. 'I'm going to switch to the cyclist deaths for a bit. I think, if I can unsettle him on those, we might be able to break the no comment barrier.

'DCI Geldard and DI Henning entering the room,' he said for the tape. 'I hope you're both ready to recommence?' He looked at Mr Wood and his client in turn, but didn't wait for a response. 'I'm going to turn to another incident,' he continued. 'Mr Thorne, where were you on the eighteenth of August?'

'No comment.'

'Or the early evening of the first of September?'

'No comment.'

'The night of the third of September?'

'No comment.'

'Or, and this is very recent, so I'm sure you know the answer to this one, the afternoon of the eleventh of September?'

A silence this time.

'Come, Mr Thorne, I'm struggling to believe your memory is so bad you can't remember what you were doing four days ago. Even if you haven't been taking your medication.'

Still a silence, but Greg was pleased to notice a slight flush on the face of the man opposite him. Maybe needling him was the way to go.

'Why was that?' he went on in a deliberately conversational tone. 'Not taking your meds, I mean? We have it on record that you can be a little, shall we say, unpredictable, if you don't take your medication. And judging by what we found in your house, you haven't taken them for quite a while. Three months at least. Perhaps we should have a mental health specialist on standby. Setting mantraps and tripwires, hurling hatchets and gassing dogs are not exactly the considered actions of a man in full control of himself.'

'No comment,' shouted Thorne. 'No comment. No comment. Got that into your thick skulls yet?' Kenneth Woods frowned at him, but he took no notice, leaning back in his chair with the flush on his face a little more pronounced. 'When are we getting out of here?' he demanded of his solicitor. 'I've had enough.'

'Oh, dear me,' responded Greg. 'Did you think this was voluntary? I'm so sorry if your solicitor didn't make the position clear to you. You are being interviewed under caution. You are under arrest. You have been charged with serious offences. You're going nowhere, Mr Thorne. So I suggest you start cooperating. Let's go back to square one.'

A tap on the door interrupted him, and Jill came in with a sheaf of notes in her hand. She handed them to Greg, smiled with an expression of triumph which pre-warned her two colleagues of what they might find, and left the room again.

'Excuse us for a moment,' Greg said to Woods and Thorne, then bent his head to the notes before him, Jim reading along with him. It was a series of bullet points from Ned.

- *Bike 1 identified as belonging to Phil Saunders. DNA on cloth fragment is Thorne's.*

- *Prints on the underside of the frame of Bike 2 are also Thorne's. Assumed to be Carol Hodds's bike but no prints from her found so far, so ID still awaiting confirmation.*

- *DNA on mantrap is Thorne's.*

'OK,' said Greg. 'Back to the start, as I said. The eighteenth of August ... have you remembered where you were yet?'

'No comment.'

'If it's going to be like that,' said Greg, coming to a sudden decision, 'then perhaps I should tell you where you were, and you can tell me if we've got it wrong. Since you seem to be struggling. Perhaps it's the lack of the meds,' he added as an aside to Jim. Thorne flushed some more, opened his mouth, then seemed to think the better of it and shut it again.

'Eighteenth of August, you were driving your pickup from Rollesby to Fleggburgh,' said Greg. 'Somewhere between Narrow Corner and Dyke Farm you saw Carol Hodds pedalling her bicycle, also towards Fleggburgh. You drove into her so hard you knocked her flying into the verge and broke her neck. Then, instead of reporting the incident, like any normal man, you picked her up, carried her to Town Dyke and dropped her in. You threw her bike into your pickup and took it home with you, wiped it down with a cloth of some sort and buried it under a pile of wood. Where we found it.' He paused. 'And found your fingerprints on it.'

'And how did you do that if I had, as you say, wiped it?' sneered Thorne. Kenneth Wood shook his head at him, and he subsided slightly.

'Because you failed to wipe under the frame,' said Greg equably. 'I'll go on, shall I?' He didn't wait for agreement. 'Exactly two weeks later, you were driving down Snare Road, not far from your home, when you came across Ann Cooper, also cycling peacefully along. You did to her much the same as you'd done to Carol Hodds, only this time you dumped her in a ditch not far from the road and dropped her bike on top of her. She was still alive at this point,' he added. 'You left her to die and drove off.'

'And you've got my prints on that bike too, I don't think,' said Thorne.

'No. No prints this time,' admitted Greg. 'I think you realised your mistake and wore gloves this time. But we have got you on CCTV.'

'There're no cameras on Snare Road,' snapped Thorne, then shut up at another glare from Kenneth Wood.

'Quite right,' agreed Greg. 'I'm interested that you know exactly where the cameras are. You'll be aware then, that there *are* cameras on the A149. Quite a few actually. One of them captured an image of you in your pickup, turning into Snare Road shortly after a lady on a bike.' He put a photo on the table in front of them.

'That's not my number plate,' snapped Thorne, almost before he looked at the image.

'No, it's not,' agreed Greg. 'It's the cloned number plate of one of your neighbours. Tristan Smith to be precise. And it's the plate we found under the wood in your yard.'

'Anyone could have dumped a plate there,' said Thorne.

'Possibly true,' responded Greg. 'But why would they? And there are a limited number of places people can obtain duplicate plates. It won't take us long to find where you got them from.' There was a silence.

'I'll go on,' he said. 'Just two days later, on the side road that leads to the old bridge at Potter Heigham, you drove into a semi-retired carpenter named Phil Saunders. This time you dumped his body over the parapet of the bridge and into the river, where the tide carried it down to Hickling. The bike went into your pickup again. No prints because you were wearing gloves, but you broke a lot of the spokes when you drove over it, and one of them snagged on your trousers. You might not have known this, but fabric that comes into contact with your body picks up DNA. We have your DNA on that bike, Mr Thorne. We recovered that from the woodpile too.

'We also have an interesting registration plate caught on camera just before the turn-off to the bridge. It's interesting because it belongs to another neighbour of yours, Moon River. Mr River—'

'Mr River,' scoffed Thorne. 'Mr Nutter. He's quite mad, you know. And that's not his real name. If you're looking for a nutter knocking folk off their bikes, perhaps you should be talking to him.'

'We did,' Greg assured him. 'The interesting thing is that on the third of September he was in hospital, getting his medications reviewed. And his number plate was also one of the sets we recovered from your woodpile.' He paused to take a sip of his cold coffee. All this talking was making him thirsty.

'I think we should take a break,' attempted the solicitor with fading hope.

'In a moment,' said Greg. 'Nearly finished, thank God. We've now reached the eleventh of September. This time it was a young lad, out for a day's cycling, just enjoying himself, minding his own business and harming no one. As luck would have it, he had a slight altercation with Tristan Smith in the car park at Waxham Barns. On this occasion, her plates were on *her* vehicle, being driven *by* her, and apart from an exchange of insults, no one came to any harm.

'That didn't happen until you came across Kain in Cess Road, on his way to the riverside at Martham. You drove into him too. And again, you left an injured person to die alone. You took the bike, in your pickup, down to the riverbank and dumped it between a yacht and a private cruiser. Then you drove home. The CCTV at the car park has your pickup entering and leaving, again wearing Moon River's plates. He was still in hospital, by the way, so don't try suggesting it was him.' There was a pause while Greg took another sip of cold coffee.

'This is all circumstantial,' tried Kenneth Wood. 'Do you have a shred of real evidence to tie my client to any of these incidents? Any witnesses, for example?'

'We have around fifteen witnesses to his murder of our colleague DC Hall,' snapped Greg. 'How many more do you want?'

'He felt pressured. Was being chased and panicked,' argued Wood. 'I have no doubt he deeply regrets what happened…'

'He does, does he? I bet he does. He thought he was getting away with it until then, no doubt. But what I *really* don't understand, is why he did what he did to all those cyclists. What the…' Greg thought the better of the word he was about to use, bearing in mind the tape. 'And he thinks Moon River's a nutter,' he muttered.

Jim gave him a sharp dig in the ribs and stepped hastily into the fray. 'That doesn't explain the mantrap and the tripwires,' he said. 'They were already in place. They weren't the result of panic.'

'Possibly,' said Wood, but his client burst in.

'I can speak for myself,' he said. 'If we're not keeping quiet' – he glared at his solicitor – 'I can speak for myself. Anyway, the fact you lot came after me, armed, with dogs, and hunted me down like an animal, isn't that proof enough I needed to take precautions?'

'There were no armed police that night,' said Greg, having got hold of his temper again. 'No one was armed with anything other than a baton or maybe a taser, except you.'

'And you think that's OK? You think you can put me down with a taser? Me?'

Under the table, Greg's foot nudged Jim's. It was the pre-arranged signal. Thorne was losing control. Wood realised it too and tried to intervene, but by doing so he just enraged his client further.

'Shut up!' he snapped. 'I've had enough of your advice and your pussyfooting around. It's time I had some respect around here. Don't you know who I am?'

'Oh, I think so,' said Greg. 'I think we know very well. You're the paranoid, unstable man, without even the sense to take his medications, who for no reason that any sane person could understand has slaughtered four innocent cyclists. And a policeman.

'But why?' he demanded. 'I can imagine the first was an accident, but why the others? Or was it just that having got away with it once, you thought you could do it again. No,' he mused, 'that doesn't really make sense, does it. You must have got some sort of satisfaction out of it. That must be the answer. You're not just...' He considered *nutter* and *mad*, then opted for: '...unstable. You're a pervert too.'

'I'm not a pervert. I'm not unstable. I'm not mad,' Thorne shouted. 'You've set me up. You've had it in for me all along. You planted those plates. You—'

'And the bikes with your DNA and fingerprints on them?' asked Greg softly.

'The bikes? The bikes! Sod the bikes and sod the cyclists. What the hell did they think they were doing, anyway? Pootling along in the middle of the road. Nothing better to do. No reason to be there. Holding me up. Me. Getting in my way.'

'So that was why they had to die,' said Greg into the sudden silence. 'Because they were getting in your way.' The silence stretched out as Greg regarded the flushed and angry man in front of him. Ken Wood fiddled with his notebook, looked at Greg then looked down again.

'Interview terminated at 16.30. We'll be back,' Greg said to Wood.

As his client kicked off again, Kenneth Wood regarded him uneasily. 'Are you leaving a constable in here?' he asked.

'Not if you want to be alone with your client,' replied Greg, noting with interest the solicitor's lack of enthusiasm for the suggestion.

'Perhaps if he stayed for a while. Just until he calms down again,' responded Wood.

Greg decided to stop winding him up. 'He'll stay until you ask him to go,' he said. Nodding at the constable, he and Jim left the room.

35

Following up

Out in the corridor, the door safely closed behind them, Greg turned to Jim.

'Get someone to monitor the interview room unless, or until, Wood asks to be alone with his client. On the one hand, he might say something interesting. On the other, if his behaviour escalates, we may need to send in a rescue squad. It would be embarrassing to have Ken Wood assaulted by his own client on our watch. I'm going to see the CPS about the charges.'

'Should I get the doc on standby?' suggested Jim.

'Yes. Better had. He might need tranks. Although I wouldn't want to be the one wielding a needle anywhere near him. He's a powerful man.'

Greg didn't bother with phoning ahead. He shot straight across the building to the CPS offices and caught Frank Parker on the point of a dash down the corridor to the gents.

'Sorry, can't put it off again,' he said to Greg. 'Gippy tummy and I've been on the phone for the last half an hour.' And off he sped.

When he came back, there was an expression of relief all over his face. 'Sorry,' he apologised. 'Had some mussels last night and it wasn't a good idea.'

Greg screwed up his face. 'If I suggest you may be oversharing, would that be OK?' he asked.

'Sorry! Yes,' replied Frank, sitting down at his desk a touch gingerly. 'Just that, if I dash off again...'

'OK, I've got the picture,' said Greg hastily.

'Is this about Warren Thorne?' asked Frank, turning to business, much to Greg's relief.

'Yes. I used the time of your, ahem, temporary absence,' – Greg coughed – 'to make a list of the potential charges. I need to know what you're comfortable with, before we go ahead. It's a long list.'

'Carry on,' invited Frank. 'Let's see if it matches my tentative list.'

'OK,' said Greg. 'Let's start with the offences connected with Constable Hall's death. These are: murder of a policeman, causing unnecessary suffering to two police dogs and setting a mantrap with the intention of causing death or grievous bodily harm.

'Then with regard to the four cyclists, four more charges of murder, ie, of Carol Hodds, Ann Cooper, Phil Saunders and Kain Smith. All the dates and locations are here.' He pushed a scribbled list across the table to Frank.

Frank looked at the list, then across the desk to Greg. 'I agree the first three charges,' he said. 'You have enough witnesses, in all conscience. I'm sure his defence team will come up with a raft of explanations, but I'm not too concerned about that. However, when it comes to the four cyclists, I have some concerns about the circumstantial nature of the evidence. There are no witnesses, and as I understand it, the forensic evidence can be challenged.'

'We have a confession now,' said Greg. 'Or near as dammit.' He tapped at the iPad in front of him on the desk and played a snippet of the recorded interview.

'Helpful, but not a confession, as you well know,' was Frank's considered response. 'What else do you have?'

'Nothing you haven't seen already,' admitted Greg. 'Ned is waiting for some more results, but I don't expect much more from that quarter. We're checking on where he got the cloned number plates from...'

'Why not go with what you have?' asked Frank. 'The murder of Steve Hall is more than enough to hold him securely, and the other charges can be added later.'

'I'd rather hit him with the lot now,' persisted Greg. 'I know we've got the right man, and I'm sure we can prove it. It feels like a betrayal of these four people if we don't proceed. And it's going to look like we care more about the death of a policeman than we do about a carpenter, a care worker, a retired lady and young man with his whole life in front of him. And that couldn't be further from the truth.'

There was a silence while Frank thought, obsessively turning a pen end-for-end in his hands. Then he put it down on the table with a decisive click and stood up. 'Sorry. Got to dash again,' he said. 'OK, charge him with the lot. But if you haven't got more by the time he sees the magistrates, I might pull the additional murders for the time being.' He paused by the door, and added, 'You do realise his defence will probably run a "not of sound mind" argument and ask for the charges to be reduced to manslaughter?'

'They can try,' said Greg grimly. 'But with all the evidence of premeditation – the plates, the tripwires, the mantrap – I'll be waiting for them.'

36

Winding up

When Greg went into the incident room to communicate the charging decision, and his congratulations, he was surprised to find a ferment of activity surrounding the girl who'd been getting on very well with Steve, and a lad Greg mentally described as *one of Ned's computer nerds*. He knew this one, he realised. It was the lad who'd so successfully mined a car database for evidence in his first big case in Norfolk.

'What's going on?' he asked.

Both the girl and the lad started to speak at once, stopped, then went through a 'you first, no, after you' routine, until Greg interrupted with the closest thing to a smile on his face since Steve had died under his hands. Their enthusiasm and excitement were infectious.

'Has to be you,' the girl said firmly, and the lad – seeming quite smitten, Greg noted – spoke up at last.

'We found an old laptop at Thorne's place,' he said. 'Dead as a dodo. Looks as though someone put a hammer through it. But I got the hard drive out and I've been checking it ever since. Lots of stuff that might be of interest when this case goes to court. Relevant to state of mind, I mean,' he added. 'But the best bit was his search history. He hadn't done a very good job of deleting it, and I found where he went online to buy registration plates. Unfortunately, I couldn't find what was on the plates he bought, but that's where Kay comes in.' He pointed at the girl. 'Your turn,' he said.

'I'd been ringing round the most obvious local places to get duplicate registration plates, and I'd tried a couple of the online options, but without any luck until Gee came up with his evidence,' she said. 'That told me who to ring and gave me some leverage. In short, I've got a contact at Plates4U who's confirmed that a Mr W Thorne from Snare Rd, Ormesby, bought plates on three separate occasions. He's sending me the summary of what was ordered and when. Should be through by now,' she said, turning back to her desktop.

'And,' added Gee, 'I forgot to say that I found photos of the vehicles belonging to Smith, River and Meadowcroft also on Thorne's hard drive. I'd guess he took the photos so he got the numbers right when he was placing the orders.'

'Well done, both of you,' said Greg, as heartily as he was able. A sudden weariness was sweeping over him, even as he spoke. 'That should clinch things for the charge sheet. Brilliant.'

***

Not for the first time, Greg pulled into his drive with a profound sense of thankfulness for the safety features on his BMW, without which he would probably have run off the road or into someone on the way home. He parked by his cottage, noting without a great deal of surprise that there was a second car alongside Chris's little runabout. He wasn't sure whether to be pleased or disappointed that they had a visitor. He had been hoping for a quiet time with Chris, but Ben's arrival was, he supposed, predictable.

He dropped his car keys into the fruit bowl on his way in, patted Bobby as she twined around his ankles, noting that there was half a dead mouse on the doormat, which he couldn't be bothered to pick up, then pushed the kitchen door open on a scene of warmth and good smells.

'Hi, sweetheart,' he said, kissing Chris. 'Hi, Ben.'

'I gather congratulations are in order,' replied Ben, putting down the bottle of zero-alcohol Ghost Ship he'd been about to swig down. 'Chris says you've got the murderer in custody and charged him with all five murders.'

'That's right,' replied Greg, sinking into the sofa, and accepting a bottle himself. The 'full fat' version he noted with pleasure, although he wasn't planning on crawling into a bottle. He'd tried that when his former wife left, and it hadn't worked.

'Supper'll be ready in about half an hour,' said Chris. 'It's a beef casserole, since I didn't know what time you'd get home and I thought that would be best. I'll just...' She made a vague gesture without completing her sentence and left the room.

'That's Chris being tactful,' Greg remarked to Ben. 'So we can talk man to man.'

'I thought so,' responded Ben. 'Would it help if we did?'

'No idea.' Greg took another swig of his beer. 'But women always reckon it will, don't they?'

'Margaret referred you to the counselling team yet?' asked Ben, correctly guessing where Greg's thoughts were heading.

'Not yet. But it's only a matter of time.'

A silence fell, companionable but not entirely relaxed. Both men drank more beer, then Greg stood up. 'Peanuts?' he asked. 'Just don't give any to Tally; she's not supposed to have them.' He got a packet out of the cupboard, then while he had his back to Ben he added, 'Did Chris tell you about the nightmares?'

'She said you woke with one this morning,' said Ben. 'Reliving the night before?'

'Yes.' Greg sat down again. 'Only the victim had Chris's face.'

'Nasty,' Ben agreed. 'It happened to me too. Once. When I pulled a teenager out of the sea at Caister. Silly sod had tried to get to the wind farm in an inflatable canoe. Didn't realise it was two miles off, and when he started drifting out to sea, he tried to swim for it. I saw his body for nights after that. And it wasn't always *his* face. Had any flashbacks?'

'One,' replied Greg. 'When I got to the Thorne place today, I thought I saw Steve running across the yard. Did it take long to wear off?' he asked.

'The shock?' asked Ben. 'We're all different, Greg. It takes as long as it takes, but it does wear off in time. Rest, positive experiences, family support, a healthy lifestyle – they all help. Being willing to talk about it is a good sign too. I realise why you went into work today,' he went on, 'but I seriously think you should take some leave now. Take time for yourself. And for Chris.'

'In an ideal world, yes,' said Greg. 'But we're short-handed and others had the same experience too. I can't take time off and leave Jim holding the baby, for example.'

'You're underestimating the impact of responsibility.' Ben looked him in the eye. 'You were the one in charge. You were the one who agreed Steve should be there. Don't think I don't know how that makes you feel. Jim, no matter how good he is, and how experienced, Jim was sheltered by you and your authority. So don't worry about him too much. The best thing you can do for him and your whole team is get yourself fit again. And back to your normal, relaxed self.'

'You've been talking to Jim as well,' said Greg with resignation. 'Is this a conspiracy?'

'If it is, it's one of goodwill,' replied Ben. 'He did happen to mention he thought you might punch your suspect in the middle of a formal interview.' He cocked an interrogative eyebrow at Greg, who smiled then picked up another handful of peanuts.

'I was tempted to knee him in the balls,' he admitted. 'But I stopped myself when I thought about what Chris would say. Come on, let's tell her she can come back in and let's eat this delicious-smelling casserole.'

'And you will book some leave?'

'Tomorrow morning,' Greg promised.

***

He kept his promise, although it was afternoon before he managed to get hold of Margaret. The morning was taken up by Warren Thorne's appearance at the magistrates' court for the plea hearing.

As indictable only offences, it was a foregone conclusion that the case would be referred to the Crown Court. Greg was hoping that refusal of bail would also be a given, but having experienced too many slips between cup and lip, he was present to do his damnedest to make sure. The case had been scheduled to be heard by a district judge at Great Yarmouth magistrates' court. For a miracle, he'd actually been able to park in the court car park, which made a pleasant change from trawling the narrow back streets for a space. Unfortunately, things went downhill from there. First, some of the paperwork was missing, and for a long half hour Greg was left wondering if the hearing would be postponed to another day. Then Thorne's transport from the nick was delayed by an accident on the Acle Straight, a notorious black spot on the county's roads.

When they did, at last, get into court, Greg recognised the district judge as one of his least favourite. A fussy woman with an overdeveloped sense of her own importance.

Confined in the glass-walled dock, Thorne looked rather calmer than the day before and someone, possibly his solicitor, had provided him with a change of clothes. The pale grey tracksuit top and bottoms were not a great improvement and seemed a little over-sized. Greg realised, with surprise, that he hadn't given any thought to the possibility of Thorne mustering a cohort of supporters, whether family or friends. He needn't have bothered. Apart from Kenneth Wood, Thorne was alone in the courtroom.

The clerk to the court read out the charges, and Thorne, as expected, pleaded not guilty to all of them.

'I turn to the matter of bail,' said the district judge, surveying them all over her reading glasses. 'I'll hear your representations, Mr Wood.'

Kenneth Wood stood, cleared his throat, and picked up the paperwork in front of him. 'My client is seeking bail,' he began, 'not least because the current delays to court proceedings mean that refusal is likely to result in a long spell in prison, on charges for which there is only controversial and circumstantial evidence. Moreover, my client cannot be deemed a flight risk, as all his business and social links are local.'

'And the view from the prosecution?' asked the judge.

'We oppose bail your honour,' said Frank Parker. 'The first indictment on the charge sheet relates to the murder of a serving police officer, in the course of his duties, and in front of multiple witnesses. The other murder charges relate to no fewer than four victims, killed within less than two weeks. The accused may or may not be considered a flight risk, but it is our contention that he is a risk to the community. DCI Geldard, the SIO on the case, is present in court if your honour requires more detail with regard to the evidence.'

There was a long pause. Greg held his breath. Ken Wood looked down at his papers, and Warren Thorne smirked in the dock.

'Bail denied,' said the judge. There was a frozen pause, then Thorne erupted into action, clouting the dock officer for six and scaling the glass walls, assisted by a leap from the desk in front of him. He got his fingers on the top of the glass screen and, for a moment, looked as though he would be successful in pulling himself up to the top. As he heaved himself up, the loose trackie bottoms slid downhill, leaving Thorne's personal equipment appliqued to the glass screen. Ken Wood blinked at the unfortunate sight. Greg leaped to his feet, ready to grab the prisoner when, or if, he descended into the courtroom, while the judge abandoned her papers and headed for the door at the back of the court. Then an additional police officer rushed into the dock and, seizing Thorne by the ankles, heaved him back to ground level and an approximation of decency with rough efficiency. Everyone in the courtroom heaved a sigh of relief, and the last thing Greg heard, as he left, were complaints of police brutality and harassment.

Back in his car, Greg rang Margaret Tayler to update her on developments.

'Very satisfactory,' she said approvingly. 'What date's been set for the trial?'

'Over a year hence,' said Greg. 'That's the bad news. But at least he'll be in prison while we all wait.

'While we're speaking, I wanted to ask you something else,' he said. 'Would it be possible for me to have a week's leave...?'

'Take two,' she said. 'I thought you'd never ask. Take at least two. I'd recommend three, but I know you. Either way, make sure you and Chris get some you time and do some winding down. You need it.'

37

Five months later

Chris felt fidgety, restless and generally disgusted with the state of their home. 'Needs a right good spring clean,' she muttered. 'Even if it is a bit early.' She looked through the window at the cold, grey February morning, and noted that although the river was bare of ducks, snowdrops had bravely pushed their way through the iron-hard earth of their garden.

By the time Greg came downstairs, whistling, she had got the new mop out of the utility room and was studying the instructions for filling its reservoir.

'I thought that was for Mel to use, not you,' he exclaimed, regarding the heavily pregnant shape of his wife-to-be with some alarm.

'Mel doesn't like it,' replied Chris, still studying the instructions. 'I can't see the problem myself. You just put the detergent in here' – she tapped a finger on the reservoir – 'then press the trigger here while you're mopping. But she says she prefers the old-style string mop and a bucket.'

'Each to their own,' said Greg, not inclined to participate in a detailed discussion of their cleaning lady's preferences.

'Either way, for goodness sake sit down before you go pop. Put your feet up.'

'Wish I could go pop,' grumbled Chris, regarding her significantly expanded torso. 'If I get any bigger I'll be a match for that blue whale hanging in the Natural History Museum.' She fidgeted on the sofa, rubbing her back.

'Problem?' asked Greg. 'Are you sure you're OK with me going in to work this week?'

'Of course I am. Bit of backache, that's all. I'm not due until the end of next week, and that's when I'll need you on hand. To do all the messy bits like changing nappies,' she clarified. 'If I've got to do the actual pushing out, you can jolly well do the catching.'

'OK,' said Greg, kissing her. 'It's a deal, provided you take it easy now. No mopping!'

When he turned the car out of his bumpy drive towards Wymondham, he was still whistling, and realised with a start that he felt happier than he had since… For a second his mind shied away from the recollection, then he took a grip of his thoughts. *No use pretending it didn't happen*, he thought. *Steve died and there was nothing I could do about it, but we got his killer, and he'll be in court later this year. Meanwhile, I'm going to be a father any day now, the Covid vaccine's being rolled out, so things should get back to normal soon, and I've got our wedding to look forward to as well.*

His good mood lasted all the way to the office, through picking up his customary strong black coffee and all the way to his scheduled meeting with Margaret Tayler. Then a bit of the glow went off the day.

'Greg, how's Chris? Must be getting close now.'

'Yes,' he said. 'Next week in theory, so I will be needing that paternity leave soon.'

'Shouldn't be a problem,' she replied, shuffling through paper on her desk. The paperless office seemed to have passed her by, Greg noted, as he had before. He took the seat she indicated across the desk from her. Margaret sat down too and ran her hand through her fluffy brown hair in her signature gesture. Greg noticed, with surprise, that there was more than a little grey in it and wondered when that had happened. Perhaps he hadn't been paying attention.

'But it's why I wanted this chat with you now,' she went on. It was a second or two before Greg connected the two phrases across his own thoughts about hair, and then wondered, with a stir of foreboding, what had to be said before he went on leave.

'When you burst into my office a few months ago and interrupted the Chief Constable,' she went on, 'we were discussing my retirement.' She paused a split second to let that sink in. 'And my replacement. How do you fancy sitting this side of the desk?' she asked.

There was a pregnant pause while Greg tried to think of an emollient way of saying not at all. Then he gave up. 'Not at all,' he replied.

'That's what I thought you'd say, but hear me out,' she said. For a moment she sat in silence, marshalling her arguments, then looked at the man opposite. In the years she'd known him, he'd aged a little but, she had to admit, he was aging well. His regular features and muscular frame meant she'd always had a secret soft spot for him, while his good humour and incisive intelligence made him a near ideal colleague. His hair was now beginning to grey a little at the temples. *He's going to be a silver fox*, she thought, *lucky sod*, and unconsciously she tweaked at her own greying locks.

'There are two reasons why I think you should give this careful thought,' she said. 'First, you, above all the other possible candidates, have a unique attribute. There are quite a few chief inspectors who are good at their job, by which I mean solving cases and catching criminals. There are several who are better than you, much better than you, actually, when I come to think about it, at dealing with senior management, budgets and politics with a small 'p'. But there is no one who can touch you, nor even get near to you, when it comes to building and leading a team. I've been watching you closely these last few years, and I've seen you do it time and again. You create a team culture that's inclusive, committed and driven by serving the public, and what's more you do it because of something inside you, some innate integrity that sets the standards and sets the example too. I watched you deal with that egregious idiot Fellowes and his malicious, misogynistic attitudes. And I watched your empathy for Sarah in the aftermath of her kidnap.'

Greg could feel himself reddening.

'I want that leadership for this wider team when I move on,' she said. 'I want to know that the commitment to service that you have embodied will be spread across the whole team. Then I know standards will be safe at Norfolk Police. The Chief Constable agrees with me,' she added.

'You said there were two reasons,' prompted Greg, hanging on to his caution.

She laughed. 'The other one?' she asked. 'Quite simply that you'll hate anyone else doing it.'

There was a long silence, which Greg filled with thought and Margaret with filling her coffee mug.

'You've been very flattering,' he began.

'I don't flatter,' she interrupted.

He waved a hand dismissively. 'Whatever,' he said. 'And you may be right about the second point. But the problem is, I don't like being stuck behind a desk. When I joined the police, I had big ambitions to make it to the top. But the more I've seen of the top jobs, the more I think I don't want one. I'm good at what I do, and I get a big kick out of doing it. I'd hate to be stranded in an ivory tower, miles from the frontline.'

'I thought you'd say that,' she responded with a touch of complacency. 'In fact, I told the Chief that when we discussed my successor. But the truth is, the job you'll be doing isn't the one I've been doing. In the first place, as I'm sure you appreciate, the proposal is promotion to detective superintendent, not chief super, although no doubt that will come in time. There's going to be a bit of restructuring around here, and I'm not going be replaced at the same grade. Second, we are different people, and these are different times. We can't resource ivory towers, and we can't afford pen-pushers. The person who takes over as detective superintendent needs to be willing to get their hands dirty just as much as they need to have a broader vision across the whole of the serious crime scene in Norfolk and how it relates to the adjacent counties.

'What you have here, Greg Geldard, is the chance to build *your* sort of team right across serious crime. And to tackle the big cases, hands-on. Give it some thought, and talk to Chris about it,' she recommended.

Greg would have responded, but the door to the office flew open without warning, with Jim and the duty secretary side by side in the doorway.

'Excuse me, ma'am,' said the secretary, 'but we've had notice that Warren Thorne is to be released from the Bure prison and sent to a secure mental health unit on a Section 48 notice.'

'Just what I was about to say,' added Jim. 'And I think we need to intervene.'

Once in his own office, Greg decided to push Margaret's bombshell to the back of his mind and focus on what Jim and Frank Parker were telling him. They'd scooped the CPS man up on their way across the building and now the three of them were having a council of war.

'Tell us exactly what this means for our case,' requested Greg.

'Essentially, that because of his recent behaviour in prison, two doctors have advised that he needs to be in hospital for treatment of a serious mental health problem, specifically paranoid schizophrenia complicated by extreme narcissism. Because he's only on remand, not yet sentenced, their advice goes to the Secretary of State to make the decision. If they take the advice, then he is, in effect, committed under Section 48.'

'For how long? And what happens to the court case?' demanded Greg.

'He's kept in hospital until either his responsible clinician thinks he no longer requires treatment in hospital or until his case has been decided by the court. So, the court case goes ahead, although obviously the fact that he has been sectioned will impact any assessment of his capacity to understand the proceedings. If or when he returns to court for final sentencing, the direction ceases to have effect and he'd be sentenced either to prison or possibly detention under Section 37.'

'Can we contest it?' asked Jim.

'Why would we want to? countered Frank. 'Either way, he's held in secure accommodation until the trial, and after it too, if he's found guilty.'

'There's no question of him being released into the community?' asked Greg. 'If, for example, he cons a doctor into thinking he's safe to be released.'

'Not unless he sought bail again,' said Frank. 'He'd go back to prison.'

'There're two things worrying me,' said Greg. 'First, that he's putting it on or, at least, exaggerating his symptoms, and once in hospital there'll be a miraculous recovery which can only be sustained by releasing him into the community rather than back to that "nasty prison". Or, the hospital is not as secure as the prison, and he gets out. How do we get these concerns across before the decision is made?'

Frank was reaching for his phone. 'I think we need to talk to the official who will be advising the Secretary of State,' he said. 'Ideally by Zoom, so we can set up a meeting quickly. Back to my office. Come on.'

Greg and Jim followed Frank out the door as he gabbled down his phone to his assistant. Even before the three men reached his office, the Zoom was set up.

'Come on,' said Frank again. 'We can all sit in front of my desktop. Phones off now, chaps, so we don't create a feedback loop.' He sat in the centre chair, breathing heavily, and tapped on the keyboard. 'Connecting,' he said as the screen flickered and lit up to reveal a domestic kitchen. Greg looked at Frank, surprised. 'She's working from home,' he hissed, and tapped the microphone symbol on the screen before him.

***

At their home near the Bure, Chris had finished mopping the kitchen floor, in direct contravention of her promise, and was now cleaning down worktops. Her backache was worse, and she had to pause a couple of times to breathe hard and press a hand to her spine. She was in that position when her mother arrived, unannounced. She took in the scene before her in a flicker and put her shopping bag down on the kitchen table.

'I brought you some food shopping,' she said. 'But by the look of you, you may not be wanting it today.'

'Why not?' asked Chris, catching her breath at a particularly sharp spasm in her back that seemed to run round to her groin.

'How long have you been having labour pains?' asked her mother calmly.

'I'm not. Don't be ridiculous. I'm not due for another week,' replied Chris. But a seed of doubt had been sown. 'Am I?' she asked.

'You've scrubbed your nest and now you have contractions,' said her mother. 'You're just like me. I did the same. I'd say you're having this baby now. Where's Greg?'

'Work,' wailed Chris. 'I told him to go. I didn't think anything would happen until next week.'

Her mother was already on the phone. 'I'm ringing the hospital,' she said, then after a pause while watching Chris, she said, 'Around ten to fifteen minutes. I've been here that long.' Another silence, then she said, 'Not yet,' listened for a moment longer then rang off.

'You're to go in ASAP. I'll drive you,' she said. 'Where's your case? You have packed one, as I told you?'

'Yes. It's in the bedroom,' said Chris. 'It's really happening, isn't it? Can you ring Greg?'

'I'm trying. He's not answering,' replied her mother. 'Don't worry, I'll keep trying. I'll just fetch your bag, then we'll be off.' She looked across at Chris, still standing near the kitchen table. 'You might want to get off that rug,' she recommended. 'I can tell you from experience, it's a lot easier to clean amniotic fluid off tiles.'

38

Action here

The senior official from the Ministry of Justice turned out to be a dark-haired woman in her early forties, sporting elegant, smart-casual sportswear and a large badge pinned to her jacket that read 'Top Mum' in sprawling multi-coloured capitals. She grabbed for the badge and removed it hurriedly as she caught sight of her own image on screen.

'My turn to child-sit,' she said briefly. 'How can I help you?'

'It's more, how can we help you?' replied Frank. 'You have an application before you for a Section 48 removal of Warren Thorne from the Bure prison to a secure hospital. DCI Geldard and DI Henning, sitting either side of me, are the officers who arrested Thorne and investigated his case. As you know, he is charged with five murders, one of them being of a serving police officer. DCI Geldard was a witness to that murder.

'As, I'm sure, *you* know,' said Ms Forrester as a toddler staggered past behind her flourishing a saucepan lid, 'it is rare for the Secretary of State to refuse a properly completed

Section 48 application. We have to rely on the expertise of the doctors involved.'

'Yes, we understand that,' said Frank. There was a loud bang and clatter from the loudspeaker as the toddler obviously found another lid and started to play their cymbals with enthusiasm. Then silence fell as Ms Forrester muted her mike and, judging from her mouth movements, instructed someone off screen to remove the improvised musical instruments and the energetic performer.

'Sorry about that,' she said. 'Where were we?'

Greg decided to step in. 'We are not competent to comment on the doctors' recommendations, but we are in a position to advise on public safety,' he said. 'My main concern is, where will Warren Thorne be housed? He is a highly dangerous and devious man. If his mental state has indeed deteriorated since his arrest, that's likely to increase his risk, not lessen it.'

'I believe you have a number of secure hospitals in Norfolk,' said Ms Forrester. 'I assume he'll be sent to one of those.'

'None of them are high-security,' said Greg. 'I would be seriously concerned if he were sent to *any* of the Norfolk establishments. I would also point out that the Norfolk and Suffolk Mental Health Trust has been deemed inadequate and placed in special measures. One of the issues was inadequate staffing. I'm sure you understand my worry.'

There was a pause while Ms Forrester considered. 'Where would you advise?' she asked.

'One of the three top-security hospitals,' said Greg at once. 'Broadmoor, Ashworth or Rampton. Rampton would be the obvious choice. And his transfer there should also be subject to top security.'

'You really think he's that dangerous?'

'I do.'

The call ended; Frank looked at Greg. 'Well done,' he said. 'I thought we would be wasting our time, but you did it.'

Greg looked at him, phone in hand. 'There's something else bugging me, Frank,' he said. 'Usually, violent offenders start small, and their behaviour escalates. Thorne seems to have gone from nought to ninety instantaneously. Which makes me think…'

'There may have been other victims in his past. Cases we've missed.' Frank finished his sentence for him. 'Not a nice thought,' he added.

But Greg wasn't listening. He'd switched his phone back on, and paled when he saw the raft of calls and messages from his soon-to-be mother-in-law.

'Chris has gone into labour,' he said. 'Must dash.'

***

By the time Greg arrived at the James Paget, Chris was in the delivery room. Once masked, gowned and gloved, he was ushered in to find Chris already with her feet in stirrups. He took his place at her head, and her mother stepped back. 'I'll let you take over now,' she said to Greg.

Chris gasped. 'About bloody time too. I thought you'd deserted me.'

'Sorry,' he said. 'I had my phone off at just the wrong time.'

'You had your phone—' Whatever she was saying was interrupted by a contraction.

'Just breathe through it,' instructed the midwife. 'Use the gas and air.' She handed the mask on the end of a tube to Greg. 'Here, make yourself useful,' she said with a smile. 'Everything's proceeding well.'

'Hear that, darling,' said Greg to Chris. 'Everything's going well.'

'Depends on your point of view,' she snapped, and grabbed for the gas and air.

'Should you take so much?' asked Greg, worried, but shut up when he intercepted a fierce glare.

As another contraction hit, and remembering the books they'd both read, he added helpfully, 'Just pant, sweetheart.'

'You bloody pant,' she snarled.

More contractions and a flurry of activity at the other end of the table seemed to herald an imminent end to his ordeal. Greg decided, if he got out of there in one piece, that he'd be having words with Ben about his failure to warn him of the risks of maternal aggression. Then a wail from a new arrival wiped everything else from his mind.

THE END – FOR NOW

Someone is reported missing every 90 seconds in the UK. Most, thankfully, are found within days.

There is help out there for the families and friends of those who may be missing. The obvious first port of call is the police. In the UK, ring 101, or if there are immediate welfare concerns, 999.

Missing People is a UK charity devoted to helping anyone affected by someone going missing.
Ring 116 000 or contact www.missingpeople.org.uk

Hungry for more?

follow Greg into Norfolk Mystery Book 9 – to be published Autumn 2025

LAST ACT

Life begins to flourish again, but so does something darker...
With the Covid vaccination programme in full swing, England is stirring into life. Nightclubs reopen, streets buzz with renewed energy and a sense of normality begins to return. But as the crowds grow, so does trouble. Greg thought adjusting to fatherhood and a new job would be his greatest challenges. Instead he finds a disturbing spike in murders across the county – senseless, brutal and seemingly unconnected. But are they?
Is this deadly surge just coincidence? Or the sign of something more sinister?

CHAPTER ONE: 19 July 2021: The curtain rises on The Garage, Norwich

Chalk lines on the rehearsal room floor marked the entrances and exits. A row of chairs indicated where unpainted scenery flats would be propped, and more chalk announced the edge of the stage. The first rehearsal of *Kiss me Kate*, as interpreted by the Northfolk Players, was underway.

Most of the cast, jubilant about rehearsing after the long period of lockdowns, were celebrating their reunions and the return of drama to their lives. Sitting in the centre of a row of chairs, as far away from the chalk stage as possible, Aubrey Sinclair was clutching his head in his hands.

'No, no. Nooo,' he howled at the lady, very much of a 'certain age', holding centre stage. 'OK, I said come down to centre stage, but I also said, keep all gestures light and airy. Which bit of *light and airy* didn't you understand? I said keep all gestures at shoulder level, so they're dramatic and flamboyant. And what do I get? Someone who looks more as though they're shovelling coal! I really don't feel you're channelling this part dear. Come on darling. This is the opening scene. It sets the, the...'

'Scene,' suggested Hattie helpfully.

'All right, yes, it sets the scene for the drama to come; and for an evening of hilarious entertainment for the audience. At the moment, the audience will be anticipating either hemlock shots all round or leaving in droves.'

Hattie marched to the chalk line with determined steps. Given that she weighed north of 900 kilos, the sound on the echoing wooden floor was impressive.

'Look here Barry,' she said. 'Just give it to me straight. If you want louder or softer, say so. If you want me to come forward or move back, say that. I just don't get all this high falutin' poncing about. Tell me what you want in words of one syllable and I'll deliver it'.

'Aubrey,' corrected Barry/Aubrey. 'I don't use Barry now.'

'Humph,' said Hattie and retired to the back of the stage before her impulse to bluntness overcame her again.

'Let's leave the opening scene for now,' said Aubrey, knowing when he was beaten. 'Where're Lois and Bill? Let's go through *Why can't you behave*, and make sure Fred and Lilli are ready to block *Wunderbar*.

'Ok Maggi,' he said to the long-suffering pianist, who had seized the opportunity to open a packet of wine gums and shovel a few in. She could see this was going to be one of those evenings when a high blood sugar level would be a prerequisite. 'From the top, and speed it up a bit.'

'Ok Aubrey,' she muttered through the sweets, and set off at a merry gallop. But at the end of the introduction, there was a marked lack of Lois.

'Cut,' shouted Aubrey, forgetting for a moment that he was producing an amateur theatrical company not a film. 'Where the hell's Lois?'

There was a scuffle, then a teenager dressed all in black emerged with some difficulty at the back of the stage. 'Sorry Aubrey,' she gasped. 'I parked my bike in the alley, and then I couldn't get up the back passage.'

There was a snort from Hattie, still hanging around stage left, and an outright guffaw from Bill, waiting his turn for some dialogue. Aubrey decided to rise above it.

Printed in Dunstable, United Kingdom